PRAISE FOR FOOL ME TWICE

"A **spell-binding thriller** that hooks the reader in the very beginning, building tension and suspense on every page."
— Long and Short of it Reviews

"This was an **amazing suspenseful thriller**. A word of warning: this is the type of **book that you cannot start when you have other things to do. Absolutely brilliant.**"
— Goodreads Reviewer

"I'm an avid reader of **Patterson, Baldacci, Clancy, Sheldon, Koontz** ... well, this rated up there."
— Goodreads Reviewer

"The **writing is absolutely phenomenal**. The **twists and turns just keep coming** throughout the book and kept me on my toes with each passing chapter."
— Angie Martin, Award-Winning and Bestselling Author of *Conduit* and *The Boys Club*

"If you haven't read any of Glede Browne Kabongo's thrillers before, DON'T wait to get your hands on this read! I personally love a book that will grab my attention and **throw my mind for a proverbial loop** and this woman **does it to me every single time. She has quickly become one of my favorites when it comes to thriller crime novels. I just can't get enough.**"
— Goodreads Reviewer

"A **truly diabolical psychological thriller**. If at any point you think you have this one all figured out, you probably don't."
— LaDonna's Book Nook

ALSO BY GLEDÉ BROWNE KABONGO

Our Wicked Lies

Conspiracy of Silence

Reign of Fear

Winds of Fear

Autumn of Fear

Game of Fear

Available in Audio

Conspiracy of Silence

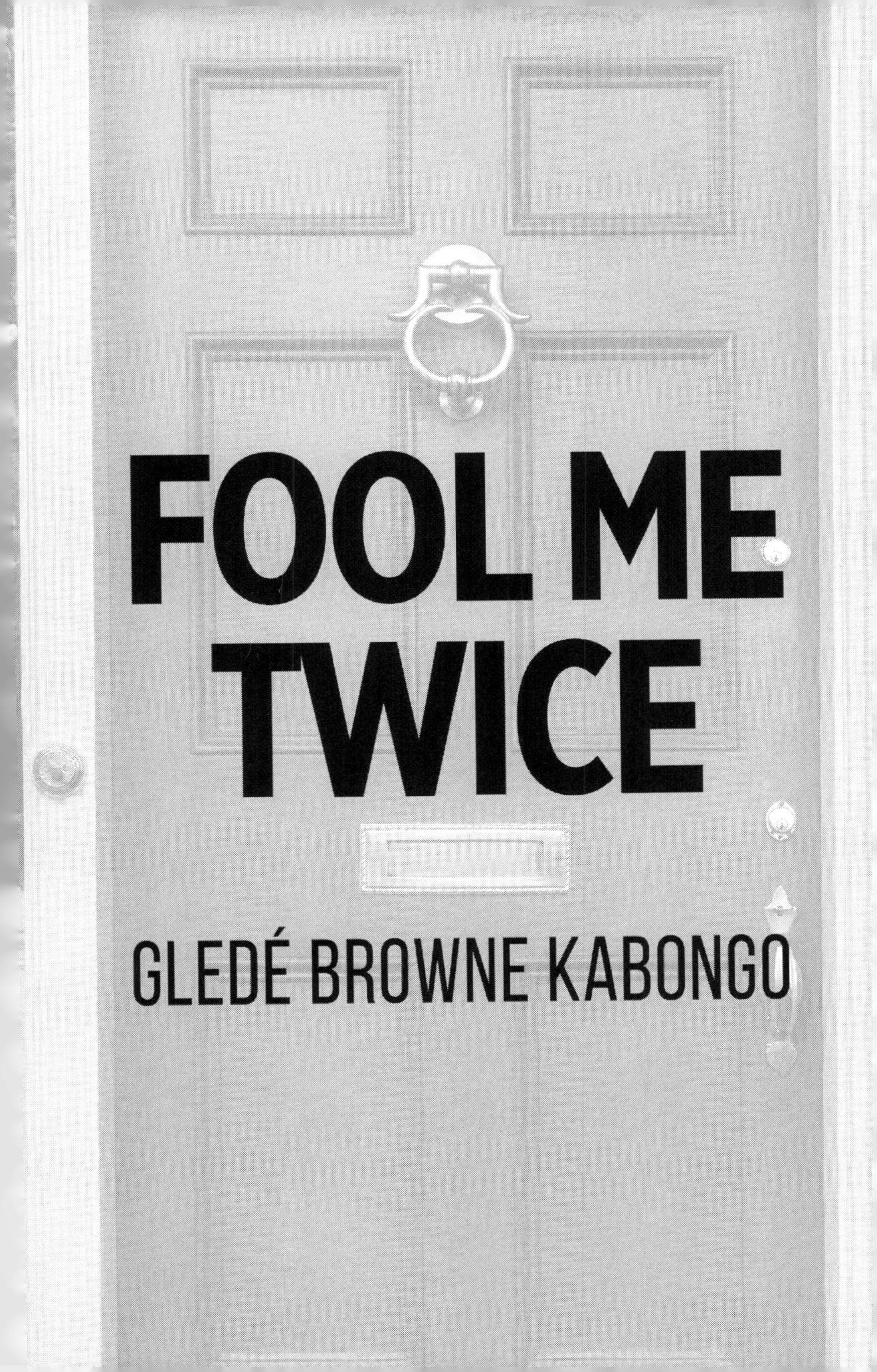
FOOL ME TWICE
GLEDÉ BROWNE KABONGO

BrowneStar
Media
www.brownestarmedia.com

FOOL ME TWICE

Cover Design by Qamber Designs & Media

ISBN: 978-1-7333-253-5-6

"Oh what a tangled web we weave,
when first we practice to deceive."
— Sir Walter Scott, Marmion

1

A SUDDEN JOLT OF panic hits me when they arrive at the trendiest restaurant and café in town—the handsome, successful husband, his beautiful wife, and their two adorable daughters, the perfect family. Except they're not.

I quickly shift my gaze back to our table when the husband turns around and looks directly at me. My fingers tighten around the steaming cup of green tea as I force my brain to focus on the ambience surrounding me—the chatter and laughter of patrons out for an evening of dining, the accompanying background music, and busy servers tending to their enthusiastic and upscale clientele.

"What's wrong? You look like you just saw a ghost," my husband Jason quips.

I knock over the cup, spilling my tea. I grab napkins from the dispenser and spring into action before the drink finds its way all over the table and causes a huge mess. Or worse, burns the children.

"Aliens hijacked my brain to perform scientific experiments. I don't know when they'll give it back." I laugh weakly at my lame joke.

"I don't think so. What spooked you, Shelby?"

Jason sits across from me at our booth near the window, eyeing me through ridiculously long lashes, the kind women envy on a man. The tube-shaped lantern dangling over our table illuminates his deep bronze complexion and Blair Underwood-like features that appear as though a makeup artist gave him a velvet matte finish. Our daughter, Abigail, is texting friends. Her stylish bob covers most of her acne-free face and large, expressive doe eyes—so like mine. Miles, a mini version of his father and quite tall for his eleven years, gripes about his food, his peevish behavior grating on my already frayed nerves.

"I'm fine," I assure Jason. "Just had a sudden flash of all the work piling up. I'm drowning, frankly. I missed another deadline to turn in my research manuscript. Dr. Nouri has already cursed me out in three languages."

Jason reaches over and gently runs a finger down my cheek. "Then consider cutting back on your workload. You're overextended as it is."

I'm a research scientist in the field of bioinformatics, which combines biology, computer science, and mathematics to develop tools that can analyze complex biological data and genetic codes. There is also a huge gender gap and even fewer women of color working in this specialty. Publishing my research is one way I get ahead, but work is the furthest thing from my mind tonight.

"I don't see any reason to slow down. Besides, why does the woman always have to be the one to make career sacrifices?"

Abbie pays attention, sensing an argument is about to begin. Miles makes obnoxious slurping sounds with his hot chocolate.

Jason narrows his eyes at me. "You're not yourself tonight," he says finally.

I place my small hands over his enormous brown ones. "I'm sorry. I shouldn't have snapped at you. I'll get a full eight hours of sleep tonight. That should take care of my attitude."

"Are you sure that's all it is, work?" Jason asks.

I must tread carefully. It's not a good idea to get defensive, especially since I'm keeping secrets that could destroy my family. When my cell phone rings, I'm grateful for the distraction that saves me from having to tell more lies. I reach for my phone in the side pocket of my bag and glance at the screen. I recognize the incoming number and return the phone right away. The caller won't give up, though. The phone keeps ringing.

"Aren't you going to get that?" Jason asks.

"It's Vivian. I'll call her later."

"Who knows what part of the world she's calling from? Pick up."

I have no choice but to answer the call. "Hey, Vivian, what's up?"

"I need to see you. It's urgent," says the anxious caller.

"I'm at Pennybaker's with Jason and the kids."

"Meet me out back." Then the caller hangs up.

I keep the phone pressed to my ear despite the silence on the other end of the line.

"Can I talk to Aunt Vivian?" Abbie asks.

"Not right now, honey," I say, pressing my hand over the phone. "Your aunt just met a new man, and she's eager to give me the details. Knowing her, it's probably X-rated."

I tell the family I need a quick bathroom break. I wade through the noisy crowd, then exit the restaurant. It's the end of October, with temperatures dropping by the hour. I adjust my scarf and tighten the belt of my Burberry coat as I arrive at the parking lot located behind the restaurant.

The man who made eye contact with me inside the restaurant leans against my car, his figure highlighted by the splash of light from the lamppost. He sports a brown leather jacket with a double collar and dark jeans. His thick, dark hair is an unruly mess. His usually vibrant blue eyes are clouded over by something I can't quite identify.

"Are you nuts?" I whisper. "We can't be seen out here. Do you want to get caught?"

My eyes dart all over the parking lot, looking for nosy neighbors or acquaintances who might spot me.

Alessandro Rossi, my former physical therapist, to whom I owe a massive debt of gratitude, pats the front bumper of the Mercedes AMG S65 sedan. "I like the new toy. I wonder if Jason would be so generous if he knew you've been a bad girl."

"Is that supposed to be funny?" I ask.

"Relax, Shelby," he says. "If anyone sees us, we have nothing to hide. It's over, and besides, we're friends, aren't we?"

"Alessandro, both of our spouses are here. I told Jason I was going to the bathroom. I have to get back. What is so urgent that you hauled me out here?"

His next words have me feeling flabbergasted. "I'm leaving. For good."

I jam my hands into the pockets of my coat to ward off the chilly New England night. I stay silent for a beat, unsure of what to say.

Then I ask, "When?"

"Soon," he says.

"Why?"

"You know why. It's not safe for my girls. Or me."

"Did something happen?"

"Isabella slapped Morgana across the face, after I warned her not to," he says, clenching his jaw.

"I'm so sorry, Alessandro. How are the girls?"

"They're terrified of their own mother. That's why I need your help."

"I don't see what I can do."

"Help the girls and me leave the country, undetected. We're going back to Brazil. If we stay here, I don't know what Isabella will do next, and I'm not sticking around to find out. In exchange for your help, I'll sign over half ownership of the business to you.

All the centers are profitable. It will be a good investment."

"You don't ask for much," I say, mustering a half-grin. "But you don't need to compensate me. You built that business from nothing, and you should continue to be the sole owner, no matter where you end up."

"So you'll help us?" he asks eagerly.

"Of course I will. You're doing the right thing, protecting your children." I lightly stroke his forearm and then pull back.

"Time is of the essence," he says and then scans the area as if looking for someone.

"Well, I need time to pull some resources together, and you haven't told me the plan yet," I remind him.

"We don't have much time because something bizarre is going on, and I want the girls and me gone as soon as possible."

"What do you mean by *bizarre*?"

"Strange phone calls. The person hangs up whenever I answer. I also think someone is following me. Mostly on my way to or from work. That's why I wanted to meet out here. When I saw you inside the restaurant, I thought I should take advantage of the opportunity to talk."

"Do you think Isabella could be behind this?" I shudder, and the tiny hairs at the back of my neck stand at attention.

"I don't know anything for sure," he says. "I'm sorry I called you out here like this, but you're the only person I trust."

"Okay. Then we should avoid contact. I'll do what I can on my end and then hand things over to you."

Alessandro lets out a deep breath as if he's been holding it since the conversation began. "Thank you. And you'll let me know if you run into any trouble? I would never forgive myself if something happened to you."

"Chill out, Alessandro. Nothing is going to happen to either one of us."

2

AS I PULL down the visor to shield my eyes from the sun's glare, a black SUV cuts in front of me. I slam on the brakes, hard. The driver behind me aggressively beeps his car horn. He misses rear-ending me by a split second. The stench of burned rubber floats in the air, triggering bad memories. *I can't get into another accident. The last one nearly killed me.* Then, just like that, the SUV switches lanes. I breathe in and out to collect my bearings, then accelerate before the driver behind me honks again.

When I check my rearview mirror, I can't believe my eyes. The SUV is on my tail and gaining speed. My gut tells me the earlier run-in was no accident. I rev the v12 engine of the Mercedes to put some distance between us, then switch to the opposite lane. I'm on the Framingham stretch of Route 9, a major east-west highway in Massachusetts, only twenty minutes from my hometown of Castleview.

My pursuer also switches to the opposite lane as I do. I'm nervous now. This isn't some kid out joyriding. I'm being chased on purpose. *Stay calm*, I tell myself. Take deep breaths. The SUV remains on my tail, and I can't shake it. The driver must have a sixth sense. He anticipates all my moves.

The Wellesley police station is only minutes away, and I contemplate exiting to the side street that would lead me there.

I switch lanes again to take the exit, and to my surprise, the car speeds past me and disappears around the bend in the road. I exhale and loosen my hands on the wheel. My heart pounds louder than Miles whaling on his drum set.

My cell phone rings. I fumble for it on the passenger seat and swipe to answer without taking my eyes off the road.

"Hello."

There's no answer.

"Is anyone there?" I ask.

Silence.

I hang up.

I'm speeding now, eager to make the appointment I can't miss. I turn over the strange encounter in my head. Why did the SUV suddenly back off? Why do I have the strong feeling that the driver was a man? And why was he tailing me?

I FEED THE parking meter with coins and take in the quaint village feel of the area, with its boutiques, restaurants, businesses, and parked cars lining the street. I stand at the entrance of Citibank in the town of Wellesley—home to the distinguished Wellesley College. Nervous energy overtakes me as I contemplate whether I'm doing the right thing, considering what Alessandro told me a few days ago, and now my recent run-in with an unknown driver.

I'm only a few minutes late for my appointment with Andrew Clarke. Andrew is built like a tank, his massive chest tugging at the buttons of his expensive dress shirt. The volunteer firefighter and my personal banker came into my life five years ago and has been my go-to guy for many financial matters, both simple and complex.

Andrew ushers me into his third-floor office with dark-red and gold oriental carpeting and a giant oak desk at its center. I decline his offer of Fiji water as he takes a seat behind the desk and repositions a wedding photo. I remove my gloves, undo the top two buttons of my coat, and take the seat across from him.

"It's always a pleasure to see you, Shelby. How is the family?"

"Abbie has a major crush on Ty, although she won't admit it to me. I think she's falling for him. Miles wants to play football. I'm glad the boy is fearless and willing to try anything, but I wish he would pick something and stick to it."

"They grow up fast," Andrew says. "Before you know it, Abbie will be off to college. Are you still pushing her to pick Duke?"

"You bet. I have to save her from her father's influence, though. He keeps telling her she can go to any college she wants, and I agree—as long as it's my alma mater."

We both chuckle, but it's time to shift my attention to more serious matters.

"Do you have what I asked for?"

"Yes. The funds came from your individual account, not the joint one, as you requested. And as I mentioned over the phone, I'll take care of any paperwork without inconveniencing you. But if you don't mind me asking, are you sure you want to walk out of here with that much cash?"

"I don't have a choice," I say.

"That's okay. My job is to make sure you have what you need when you need it."

I sense a *but* coming. The normally straightforward Andrew is hesitant, hedging his bets as to whether or not he should speak his mind.

"Shelby, you're more than a client. I consider you a friend—"

"Is there a problem, Andrew?"

"Just making sure you're not in trouble of any kind. I know it's none of my business why you need that kind of cash, but I had to put it out there."

"A friend needs help," I explain. "She's starting over, coming out of an abusive relationship."

I don't know why I'm explaining this to Andrew, but I feel compelled to, as if I need him on my side.

"That's awful. I'm sorry to hear that."

His reaction spurs me on. "There are children involved. I want to help her get as far away as possible and stay safe. What's the point of having money if you can't use it to help others?"

"Your friend is lucky to have you in her corner," Andrew says, completely buying into my explanation.

"She certainly thinks so, but I'm lucky, too."

I bid Andrew goodbye and walk out of the bank with more cash than the average American makes in a year, all carefully hidden in what looks like a conventional ladies' tote bag. I toss the bag on the front passenger seat and walk around to the driver's side of the car. A white piece of paper trapped beneath the windshield wiper catches my attention. I snatch the paper and read the message.

Have you forgotten what you've done? I haven't. Game on.

My eyes case the area like I'm a nervous thief. I expect the black SUV to come barreling down the street any minute. It takes great effort to hold on to the note as I unlock the driver's side door and drag myself inside. Fear pools in the pit of my stomach. Someone is watching me.

3

I'VE BEEN STARING at a 3D model of the same gene cluster on my computer screen for a while. My mission is to identify which genes in the cluster need to be shut off. If we can design a drug based on my findings, it will effectively prevent an individual with a genetic predisposition, to diabetes in this case, from ever developing the disease. I'm determined to keep up my work routine, despite the paranoia that creeps up on me from time to time.

Someone taps me on the shoulder, and I spin around in the swivel chair with such force I almost injure myself.

"Are you all right?" Emma Chan, my postdoctoral fellow, frowns at me, concerned.

"I'm fine. What's going on?" I ask.

"Inez wants to see you. She says it's important. Something about a group of kids visiting the lab."

Crap! I forgot! "Thanks for letting me know, Emma."

I bump into a few colleagues as I make my way through the narrow aisle of the lab, apologizing on the way out. My assistant, Inez Diaz, meets me at the door.

Inez says, "You've been looking forward to this for weeks. It's not like you to forget."

"Sorry. Time got away from me. Where are they?"

"Milan Conference Room. I have refreshments ready for after the tour."

"Thanks, Inez. You're a lifesaver."

Half a dozen high school girls are visiting as part of GeneMedicine's STEM (science, technology, engineering, math) program, implemented when I came on board. The STEM fields are in dire need of more female representation, and I do my part to further that agenda. Twice a year, I host students from various parts of the state, explaining what we do and what's possible for them in the STEM fields.

The lab tour is over, and we sit around the conference room table. It's time for Q&A, my favorite.

"What made you decide to become a scientist?" The question comes from Anita, a junior from Everett High School.

"I liked science classes in high school, and in college, I discovered there are many ways to use science to change the world."

"Did your parents encourage you?" Anita probes. "They must be so proud."

My mouth clamps shut. The innocent question shouldn't have distressed me, but it did. *What is wrong with you? You're over this. Aren't you?*

I pin a smile on my face. "Parental support is important. If your parents aren't available, don't let that stop you. Stay focused. Hang out with people who have the same ambition you do. Take advantage of all opportunities. Never give up."

I PACE BACK and forth in my office after my near meltdown in the conference room. A knock on the door startles me. "Come in," I say.

Inez walks in, waving a padded manila envelope. "This just came for you by messenger."

I don't know what I would do without my administrative

assistant of three years. Inez was fresh out of community college and didn't have as much experience as the other candidates who interviewed for the position, but something in my gut told me she was the right person for the job. I'm glad I took that chance. Inez is efficient, highly capable, and we've developed somewhat of a friendship.

I take the envelope from her and head back to my desk. She asks, "Can I get you anything?"

"What's on your mind, Inez?" She knows when something is bothering me.

"Nothing. Just making sure you're okay."

"I'm fine." If I keep repeating that phrase, it's bound to come true.

After Inez leaves, I inspect the envelope. There's no return address, and my name is typewritten on a white label. Alarm bells ring in the back of my head. I reach for a letter opener on my desk and rip the envelope open. I pull out an eight-by-ten glossy photograph of Abbie on her way to class.

My breath hitches. My skin tingles, as if some invisible, slimy creature is crawling all over the surface. The time stamp shows that the photo was taken yesterday, two days after the incident with the SUV. I look closer to make sure my eyes aren't playing tricks on me. They're not.

Abbie prefers the preppy chic look and has on a flouncy, navy-blue skirt that stops above the knees, a white open collar blouse, and a gray cardigan sweater. Her footwear is a pair of knee-high Prada boots I bought her last year for doing well on her report card. Someone got a full-length shot of her at close range, inside the school. Game on, indeed.

I'm barely able to digest this latest development when my cell phone rings. I reach for it in the pocket of my lab coat. The screen says it's a blocked number.

"Hello."

"Now, do I have your attention, Dr. Cooper?" It's a man. He speaks with the slightest hint of an accent.

"Who are you? You tried to run me off the road the other day. What are you after?"

"You already know the answer," he says.

Keep him talking.

"I don't ask questions I already know the answers to."

"It's time you paid for your sins, Dr. Cooper."

"What about yours? You're targeting my underage daughter. That will not go unpunished."

He cooks up a hearty, deep-throated laugh, as if my anger is purely for his amusement.

"Don't be so dramatic, Shelby. I was just having a little fun."

He calls me by my first name in a tone that implies he knows me well. He has my personal cell phone number and gained access to my daughter's school. That makes him a dangerous adversary, one who could do irreparable damage if provoked.

"What do you want?" I ask, hoping to extract some scrap of information about his identity.

"Patience, my dear. Answers will come, although you're not very good at practicing restraint, are you?"

"I don't know what you mean."

"You disappoint me, Dr. Cooper, with the phony innocence. I expected better from you."

"You're a very sick man. I'm done playing your games."

"We're just getting started, Shelby. There's so much to discuss: The rules of the game, the consequences of breaking the rules, and how and when you will pay for your sins."

"How about I get you acquainted with the police? Perhaps they already know you and would welcome a reunion."

"Rule number one: do not repeat a word of this to Jason or

the police. Consequence of breaking rule number one will be your children in matching coffins. I will not be kind in my methods."

My heart beats at the speed of a runaway freight train. He found my weak spot and knows how to exploit it. This was meticulously planned. The chase, the note, the prank calls, the photo of Abbie. He wants me scared, isolated, and vulnerable. Miles and Abbie are his weapons of choice.

"Stay away from my family and me," I say. "That's my rule number one. Consequence for breaking rule number one: I will put my considerable resources into hunting you down and eliminating you. I will not be kind in my methods."

I hang up. Tremors take over my hands and fingers. I place them in the pockets of my lab coat. How do I protect my kids without their father finding out there's a problem? Will the stalker really carry out his threat, or is he just a wannabe tough guy getting his kicks?

I pick up the photo of Abbie from the desk. I turn it over and shiver. Abbie's class schedule is written in heavy black ink. The stalker most likely used a Sharpie. The letters are neat and deliberate in all caps, almost impossible to analyze.

Tears of frustration sting my eyes. I need to think, strategize, decide how best to protect my family. Our IT department is as good a place as any to start. I can ask one of the guys to see if they can track the blocked number. I suspect Mr. Stalker uses a burner phone, as do I when I communicate with Alessandro.

I instruct Inez to cancel my remaining meetings for the day. I have much to do. First, I need to call Alessandro. I didn't mention the incident with the SUV when I called to tell him where he could pick up the bag of cash. Now that I've discovered that the SUV driver and stalker are one and the same, I want to find out if there are similarities in the MO. Alessandro received strange phone calls where the caller hung up without speaking, and he mentioned being followed.

"It's me," I say, when he picks up. "Any strange calls in the past few days? It's happening to me too."

I explain the SUV chase; the note trapped underneath the windshield wiper, the anonymous call only minutes ago, and the photo of Abbie. He listens attentively and then says there have been no calls, but he noticed a suspicious-looking vehicle parked across the street from the gym where he works out. When Alessandro tried to leave, the suspicious car pretended to be heading in the same direction but then backed off.

"You'll be out of here soon with your daughters," I say. "Just be careful in the meantime and make sure your wife doesn't suspect a thing."

He assures me Isabella is clueless about his plans and he's been careful, despite the suspicious car and calls. He hasn't changed his routine in any way that would raise red flags.

After I hang up, I research private security firms and narrow down my choices to two possibilities, just in case. I resent that I can't share this burden with Jason. But I can't gamble that the psychopath who's stalking me won't carry out his threat if I breathe a word to anyone.

4

ABBIE COOPER'S ELEGANT fingers flew over the letters on her smart phone as she composed an urgent text message.

Meet me in the chapel!

Abbie walked briskly down the main hallway of St. Matthew's Academy, administrative offices and student paintings on the walls a blur in her haste. Abbie was a sophomore day student at the elite boarding school. The school sat on two hundred and fifty acres of pristine property, with a series of interconnected, Tudor-style buildings in her hometown of Castleview.

She arrived at Westford Chapel, eager to unburden the secret she'd been keeping from her parents. The sanctuary, endowed with rich architectural detailing and beautiful stained-glass windows, created an atmosphere of serenity.

Ty was already seated in the first row. Butterflies roiled in Abbie's stomach. She plopped down next to him, dropping her backpack at her feet.

"This had better be good, Cooper," he said. "I almost had a date with Kerri Wheeler before your text threw me off my game."

Abbie snickered. "You have no game. As for Kerri, no comment."

"Thanks for supporting a brother," he said, grinning. "I thought we were friends."

"We are. But if I don't give it to you straight, who will?"

He winked at her. "You know I love it when you boss me around. So, what's up?"

Ty Whistler Rambally adored Abbie, and she knew it. They instantly formed a bond when they met at a school function her freshman year at St. Matthew's. But things had been awkward lately. When Ty returned to school in September for the beginning of his senior year, he wasn't the boyishly cute, goofy kid Abbie remembered. He went on summer vacation and came back a major hottie.

He ditched the chin-length curly hair that always hung in his face for a short, tapered haircut. Abbie could see Ty's face more clearly now. His hazel eyes sparkled, as if they had a hidden electric charge. The warm, medium brown complexion had deepened under the summer sun.

And suddenly he had muscles—or maybe Abbie didn't care to notice before. The worst thing about this new physical transformation was that her stomach turned to knots whenever Ty was around. She should just walk around with a swooning couch, if that was even a thing. But Abbie would rather rip her fingernails out one by one with a rusty old pair of pliers than admit her growing attraction to Ty.

Abbie reached for her backpack and removed an envelope from the side pocket. She handed it to Ty. He removed the thick cream-colored paper inside and read aloud.

Dear Abigail:

Sometimes, our loved ones deceive us. Don't be alarmed when the universe attempts to correct this injustice. The storm is gathering speed and will explode with a bang. Remain calm, and all will be well.

Ty said, "What does that mean?"

"I'm not sure. It sounds like a warning or something."

He handed the note back to Abbie, his expression solemn.

"When did you get the note?"

"Yesterday."

"Were there other notes before this one?" Worry crept into his voice.

"No. Why?"

"Cooper, someone sent you a strange note in the mail, someone who could be dangerous, and they know where you live."

"A lot of people know where I live. Every time Mom speaks at some conference, her bio ends the same way: Dr. Durant Cooper lives in Castleview, Massachusetts with her husband, Orphion Technologies CFO Jason Cooper, their two kids, and a lovable Golden Retriever. It's easy to find our house."

"Okay. But we still have to find out who sent the note and why."

Abbie liked that he said we. *We* have to figure this out. They were a team, and that thrilled her.

"The envelope might be a clue," Abbie said. "It came from Washington, DC, but I don't know anyone who lives there."

Ty considered that for a moment. "Whoever mailed it might not live in DC. They could live in Maryland or Virginia. A lot of people from those states work in DC, or they could have had someone else mail it from there. Weren't you born in Maryland?"

"Bethesda. Mom was a postdoctoral fellow at the NIH when I was born. We left Bethesda when I was four. I don't see how there could be a connection after all this time."

"So you think this has something to do with your mom?" Ty asked.

Abbie sighed. "It could. She's been acting funny lately."

"Funny how?"

"Like something's bothering her. Something big."

"Did you ask her what it was?"

"Not yet. But she knocked over a cup of hot tea when we were at Pennybaker's the other night. Then she got a call from

Aunt Vivian and suddenly had to use the bathroom. She was gone for a while. That was weird."

"What's weird about it?" Ty asked.

"You know Aunt Vivian and my mom are practically sisters. They grew up together. Why couldn't she just talk to her right there in front of us?"

"Maybe it was girl talk. You know how you women are."

Abbie play-punched him in the arm. "When did you become an expert on women?"

"Wouldn't you like to know?" he said coyly.

The mischievous glint in his eyes told her he was joking, but Abbie's analytical mind couldn't help but wonder if that one sentence held more meaning than he meant to let on. What happened over the summer? And now he was chasing after Kerri Wheeler. Why couldn't he have picked someone else? What did he see in Kerri, anyway?

"Oh, puh-lease," Abbie said, rolling her eyes at him. "But you're right. Mom made some lame excuse about Aunt Vivian meeting a new man and the conversation being X-rated. I don't believe her, though."

"Why not?"

"She jumps every time her phone rings, like she's afraid of whoever's calling. Plus, she's extra annoying. She sends me like fifty text messages a day, just to check in. She does the same thing to Miles."

"That is strange," Ty said. "The note sounds threatening, though. Are you going to tell your parents about it?"

"Heck no. They'll put me on twenty-four lockdown and take away my phone, possibly my computer. I want to see if I get another note. No point in getting them worried right now."

Ty edged closer to her. "I know you, Cooper. There's something else you're holding back."

Tell him everything. He has your back.

"I got a couple of strange calls after the note arrived."

"You mean like a stalker?"

"I guess. Whenever I pick up, there's just silence; then the person hangs up."

Ty's lips formed a grim line. "It's probably the same person who sent the note. I don't think you should keep this from your parents. The guy could be a psycho and try to hurt you."

Before Abbie could respond, the infectious pop tune that was her ringtone sprung from her phone.

She answered. "Hello."

Silence.

She looked at Ty.

"Who is it?" he mimed.

She signaled for him to stop talking.

"Is anybody there?" Abbie asked. "Say something."

"Hello, Abigail. Don't be afraid."

It was a man's voice. One she'd never heard before, and it was oddly soothing. "Who is this?"

"Don't you worry about that, angel. Did you get my note?"

"What do you want from me? Why are you stalking me? I'm telling my parents."

"You won't," he said.

Abbie swallowed hard. She would be brave, despite the chill in her spine that told her this person meant harm.

"You know nothing about me. You don't know what I would or wouldn't do."

He chuckled. "I know more than you think, little one. So much more."

"What's your name, and why did you send that note?"

"We'll be in touch, Abigail. And remember, it's our little secret or else."

"Or else what?"

He ended the call.

Ty eyed her intently. "Well, who was it?"

"It was *him*."

Abbie relayed the conversation to Ty.

"I don't like this. Did you mean it when you told him you would tell your parents?"

She looked Ty dead in the eye. "No. I said that to scare him. He's up to something, and I want to know what it is."

"He could be setting a trap."

"What for?"

"Who knows? Aren't you scared? This guy called your cell phone and doesn't want your parents involved."

She poked him in the ribs. "You're just a kid, but you worry like an old man."

"I'm not a kid, Cooper. And this is not the time for jokes."

He reached over and tucked a loose lock of hair behind her ears. "You know how much I care about you, right? I don't want anything bad to happen to you. I couldn't take it."

Warmth flooded Abbie. His words reminded her of a lazy summer afternoon, curled up in a hammock with a good book. It meant she was still special to him, still his number-one girl, even if they were the only ones who knew it.

"I'm sure he's all talk. I just don't know why he's contacting me, though."

Ty said, "Promise me if this nut calls you again, you'll tell your parents and let them handle this."

"I can't do that," Abbie said.

"Why not?"

"Because I want to know what he's up to. Whatever it is, he needs me to make it work."

5

HEAVY SNOWFLAKES PELTED The Planner when she exited her parked car at the Sheraton Framingham Hotel. The blustery November wind whipped her blonde hair across her face, forcing her to pull up the hood of her coat.

The Planner took the elevator up to her suite, a temporary living arrangement until her apartment was ready. She'd set the stage. Time to watch the dominoes fall. Her visit to Castleview earlier was the final piece of her master plan. The first time she visited the town, she thought she had stepped into a postcard, complete with rolling hills and a European-style town center dotted with independent markets. The town was loaded with sprawling colonial and chateau-style homes with backyards that could double as football fields.

She'd slit her wrists within twenty-four hours if she lived in a place like that. Castleview was the kind of lily-white upscale suburb where nothing much ever happened, but when something did, the town residents would demand answers, a fact that could be advantageous to her plan.

The Planner tossed her coat on the king-sized bed next to the outfit selected beforehand and stripped down to bra and panties. She hurriedly pulled the cashmere sweater over her head. Skinny jeans and designer ankle boots completed the look. The all-black ensemble was a perfect contrast to her blonde hair and unusually bright green eyes, acquired by contact lenses.

Three quick raps on the door announced her guest had arrived. The Planner assessed him after opening the door: early fifties with slightly graying black hair, dark eyes, and glasses. He resembled a college professor, dressed in a multi-colored argyle sweater vest, dress shirt, and khaki slacks. He didn't have a coat or jacket on, even though snow had been coming down hard when she got back to the hotel.

She sat across from him on a striped, burgundy couch, tucked her legs under her, and reached for her e-Cigarette.

"I trust everything went as planned?" she said.

He removed his glasses. "Yes. I did everything as you scripted."

"And?"

"She's a spitfire, as you Americans say. She accused me of stalking her and threatened to tell her parents."

A slow, devious smile spread across The Planner's face. "She won't. Trust me on that."

He said, "She wasn't afraid. In fact, she displayed outright defiance."

"Oh, she'll be plenty scared. Just remember what I said. I need her alive and unharmed."

Her guest raked his hand through his hair and chewed nervously on the leg of his glasses.

"Do you have something on your mind?" The Planner asked.

"I thought you liked Abigail. I don't understand why you want her scared, especially since she's not the real target."

The question annoyed her. The Planner inhaled and let out a long puff of mint-flavored vapor.

"I thought the answer would be obvious to a man of your intelligence. Ever heard the phrase 'destroy your enemy from within?' A scared, confused, and frustrated teenager can cause chaos and uncertainty. Let's just leave it at that. Now, how did it go with the target?"

"She won't go quietly," he stated. "She'll fight back."

"I'm aware of that. You don't come from where she did and achieve what she has without knowing how to fight and claw your way out of the gutter. But she'll be out of my way soon enough."

"What do you mean, clawing her way out of the gutter?"

The Planner untucked her legs, planted them on the thick carpet, and leaned forward with great urgency.

"Perhaps you haven't been paying attention, which concerns me when I think about the scale and importance of this project. Shelby Durant Cooper is not who she says she is. She's a fake, a phony, and a poser. My family has suffered because of her. I intend to see justice served. My way. Now, are you ready for phase two?"

Her guest retreated in his seat like a startled rabbit. "Do you have an empty glass I could use to get some water from the washroom? My throat feels parched."

"Not a problem. But I can do better than that."

She walked over to the large desk drawer with the flat screen TV perched on top and removed a twenty-ounce bottle of spring water from the left drawer. Her guest guzzled it down in one go.

The Planner returned to her sitting position and resumed smoking her e-Cigarette. Then she said, "Do I need to remind you of the stakes? You can have your life back, the life she stole from you. A position worthy of your experience and accomplishments, money, prestige."

"She had no compassion," the guest complained. "I begged her not to say anything, even after I promised to stop. Everyone makes mistakes, but my pleas fell on deaf ears."

The Planner egged him on. "And for what? Because you tried to make some extra income? Give your family all this country has to offer to hardworking, driven people?"

"Exactly. That's all I was trying to do. I didn't hurt anyone. Innovation is what this country is about, isn't it? What I did spurred the innovation race. It was simply a matter of which company would win in the end."

"Absolutely," The Planner said. She stood and then walked toward the north-facing window. "Think about your current circumstances. Slaving away as an instructor at some obscure college, barely getting by on what they pay. Plus, a wife who deserted you in your time of need and children who are ashamed to call you their father. When you left your home country to study at Harvard, is this the life you envisioned?"

"Not at all."

"Good. Whenever you have an attack of conscience, I want you to think about Shelby Cooper."

His eyes popped wide. "Why?"

"Because she took everything from you. And look what she's gained. Speaking at conferences all over the world, the large consulting fees venture capital firms pay her for her advice. Think about her training the next generation of scientists in her lab. I believe you once had that privilege. But most importantly, she has a family. A husband and kids to go home to every night. Where's your family?"

The Planner turned away from the window and pointed an accusing finger at the nervous man. "So don't you dare question me or my methods. Focus on what the success of this project could mean for you."

The man nodded.

"Stick to the plan," The Planner said. "I can do wonderful things for you. I can also make your current life seem like a picnic on the grounds of Topkapi Palace. Never cross me," she warned. "Not even by accident."

"You can count on me," he said, eager to please. "I won't let you down."

"Good."

Her guest stood up to leave, and she escorted him to the door. His hand reached for the handle, and then he turned around, as if he forgot something. "I don't suppose you're going to tell me your real name?"

She knew he'd ask and was prepared for it. The Planner extended her hand to him. "Lansing. Mia Lansing."

After her guest left, Mia yawned. She had slept little in the past few days, staying up until dawn and eating even less. She pulled out a photo from her handbag on top of the dresser and held it up to the light.

"Why couldn't you see through her act?" she said to the image. "Don't you know she's evil? Now look what you're making me do. It's the only way to make things right. But you'll understand, won't you, sweetheart?"

Someone clapped loudly. The deafening sound startled Mia and ricocheted off the walls. "Who's there?" Mia shouted. "What do you want?"

You really think you're going to get away with this?

It was the old woman again, mocking Mia. It was only a matter of time before the woman appeared.

Mia placed her hands on her temples and squeezed. "Shut up! Shut up!"

Mia hadn't heard from that visitor in a long time. She thought she had banished the old woman, but here she was, trying to mess with Mia's plans.

This will end badly for you. Heed my warning.

"You don't know what you're talking about. She'll get what's coming to her. I'll make sure of it."

And then what? You'll take over her life? You're living a fantasy, girl.

Mia paced around the room. Sweat ran down her back.

"You're too late, old woman. The plan is already in motion. You can't stop it. You can't stop me."

You're nothing to her. Why spend all this energy on someone who couldn't care less if you exist or not?

That statement enraged Mia. She grabbed the bouquet of flowers off the small desk and smashed the vase against the wall.

"She will know me," Mia screamed. "I'm going to destroy Shelby Cooper. I'll take away everything she loves—her children, her husband, her life. I'll take back everything she stole from me with her lies."

Maybe. But be prepared. Don't say I didn't warn you.

"Who asked you, old woman? No one asked your opinion about a damn thing. Stay away from me. Stay out of my business."

The only response came from outside the room, the hum of traffic on Route 9.

6

JASON ARRIVED AT Bellos restaurant in Waltham a few minutes before eight in the morning. Waltham, Massachusetts, was part of the Route 128 corridor, a cluster of suburban cities and towns with a large high-tech presence. The restaurant was only minutes from Orphion headquarters. The place hadn't changed much, he observed.

A series of blackboards along the wall displayed the menu, hand-written in chalk. Matching red stools lined the L-shaped counter, and light-blue vinyl covers draped the tables. Jason snagged a table for two without much trouble amid the noisy breakfast crowd.

A waitress came by to take his order, but he opted for coffee only. He wasn't hungry, anyway. After she took off, Jason spotted Charlie Summers through the crowd and waved him over. At just under six feet tall in a simple dress shirt and well-pressed but expensive khakis, Charlie looked more like a prep-school headmaster than the fiercely competitive and ruthless CEO he was.

Charlie sat across from Jason. "Thanks for meeting here. Sometimes it's good to get away from the office."

"What's this about, Charlie?" Jason asked. He couldn't stand the suspense any longer.

The waitress returned with his coffee, placed it on the table between them, and turned to Charlie with a bright smile. "What can I get you?"

"Just some lemon tea and toast, please," Charlie said. "What about you, Jason?"

"Nothing else for me, thanks," he said, eying his coffee.

"One lemon tea and toast coming right up," the waitress said. Her perkiness grated on Jason's nerves. His anxiety about the meeting had run unchecked on the drive in, and he was ready to burst out of his skin.

Charlie rubbed his hands together. "Look, I know you're curious about why I wanted to meet here instead of the office."

"You must have good reason. Let's hear it." Jason sat up straighter in his chair and leaned forward.

"The board is nervous. With the IPO in the works, they don't want anything getting in the way."

"I don't see why anything would," Jason replied with confidence. As he uttered the bold-faced lie, he mentally crossed his fingers.

The role of chief financial officer of Orphion Technologies, a multi-billion-dollar global powerhouse in the hardware and software space, was a major coup for Jason's career. He was barely forty years old when he assumed the role. His performance made Orphion the envy of every competitor, and a couple of those competitors had tried to lure him away.

Jason's instincts when it came to acquisitions and investments had paid off exceedingly well. Under his financial leadership, Orphion had become one of the top ten technology companies in the world, although it wasn't a publicly traded company. Not yet.

Charlie visibly relaxed. "You've always been straight with me, Jason. That's one of the reasons I want you to succeed me when I retire next year. The board agrees."

The waitress arrived and placed Charlie's toast and tea on the table. When she asked Charlie if she could get him anything else, he politely said no. Charlie picked up a knife from the table and spread butter all over his toast. Jason lightly tapped his shoe against the linoleum floor. If Charlie had bad news, he would have said it instead of treating the meeting as a casual get together.

Charlie put down the knife and took a bite of his toast.

"You made the right choice, Charlie. But are you having second thoughts about me taking over?"

Charlie turned red in the face. "Not at all. You're the best person for the job, and everybody knows it."

"Then what is this meeting really about?"

Charlie said, "The board wants guarantees you don't have skeletons in your closet that could come tumbling out at the worst possible time. They want to be certain there is nothing in your past that we overlooked when you joined the company."

Jason observed how carefully Charlie chose his words. *They* or *the board*, implying that none of it was his idea. Jason knew that. Charlie was playing peacemaker. He suspected all these questions came from a specific board member, Bob Engels, a retired pharmaceutical executive, and former lobbyist.

Bob had tried to derail Jason's candidacy for the CFO position years before in favor of his son-in-law Alex, who in Jason's humble opinion wasn't qualified to run a lemonade stand, let alone the finances of a multi-billion-dollar corporation.

"Charlie, if there were issues in my past that could hurt the company, they would have surfaced by now, don't you think? You can tell the board, or rather, Bob Engels, that if he has an issue with me taking over as CEO, we should discuss it like men."

Charlie pulled a face. He hated conflict among the leadership team. Jason almost felt bad for his outburst about Bob, but Jason wasn't about to let anyone snatch the opportunity from him. He had worked too hard to earn his position, and even harder to forget the circumstances that led to him becoming a millionaire in the first place.

"I told the board they had nothing to worry about," Charlie said reassuringly. "You're the right choice, the only choice to lead Orphion into the future. I have every confidence you will do great things."

"Thank you, Charlie," Jason said. "You won't regret it."

7

I STAND NEXT to the kitchen island, assessing the mess I've made: open drawers, cabinets, and ceramic jars; a refrigerator at a slightly awkward angle; my recipe books strewn all over the countertops; and still not a single clue surfaced. No evidence of anything that would point to a bug or camera hidden anywhere. Not a hint about the madman who's after me and using my kids as leverage to keep me in line.

Did he stake out our home? Disarm the security system and break into the house in the middle of the night while we slept? That could explain why he knows so much about my family. Dale, the IT guy at work I asked to identify the source of the calls, confirmed my suspicion that the stalker is most likely using several burner phones, which makes him difficult to track.

In a matter of days, Alessandro and his daughters will be whisked out of the country on a private jet I've chartered on their behalf. After they leave, I can focus all my attention on stopping *him*. I don't have a title I can assign to the psychopath. The phrase "stalker" seems to give him the upper hand somehow, like I'm his helpless victim. I don't intend to become anyone's victim ever again.

Leaving the kitchen and the mess behind, I head to the living room, dragging my suspicion and paranoia along with me. I stand in front of the fireplace. Above it sits a gigantic painting of my favorite wedding photo. Jason, kissing the back of my hand, and me, gazing up at him with a wide, adoring smile.

An idea strikes me as I stare at the painting. I dash to the kitchen to grab the tallest chair I can find. I stand on the chair directly in front of the fireplace and gently lift the painting from the wall. I examine it for any listening devices or cameras. Nothing. I painstakingly replace it and straighten it out so it doesn't look messed with.

When I jump down again from the chair, I almost knock over the glittering pair of crystal swans atop the fireplace. Jason presented them to me as an anniversary gift. He said he drew inspiration from the swans that live at the edge of the reservoir in our town because they reminded him of us, mates for life. If anything happened to them, he would never forgive me.

Frustrated by my lack of progress, I head to our bedroom. I lie face down on the bed and close my eyes, hoping to calm my anxious nerves. My thoughts are still swirling, so I open my eyes and flip over on my back. The chirping sound from my phone on the nightstand lets me know that I have a new text message. I read the message, then jump up from the bed like someone lit a fire under my butt.

(Unknown) What's right with this picture?

A second text follows. A photo of the family taken at Gillette Stadium during a New England Patriots football game. My head is missing from my body.

Rage and fear rise up in me, sudden and thick. I delete the offensive photo and message. There's no reason to keep a reminder that someone is watching my every move and now wants me decapitated. Perhaps there's a simple solution. We could disappear and start a new life somewhere. But as I think about it, I know how silly the idea is.

How do I respond to the increasing threats? Jason bought me a gun for protection when he's away on business trips, not that anything ever happens in Castleview. He trained me how to use it, and I've never had a reason to. But a threat is a threat. I decide to remove it from the closet and hide it in the glove compartment of my car.

It occurs to me there's one place I haven't looked for clues. I can't rule out any possibility, so I dive under the bed, hoping to hit the jackpot.

"What are you doing?"

I'm startled and bump my head as I crawl out from under the bed. Abbie, hands on her hips with major attitude, looks like a school principal reprimanding a not-so-well-behaved student.

"I can't find my iPad and thought it might have ended up under the bed," I explain.

"Under the bed, Mom?" Abbie can't conceal the suspicion in her voice. "What's really going on?"

"Nothing is going on, honey," I say casually. I stand to my full height of five feet nothing and fluff her hair.

"Something *is* wrong, and I'm worried. So is Dad. You've been acting weird lately."

"Did your dad say something?"

"No, but I know when you're not yourself. Like when you found out Dad cheated on you."

"What?" I ask innocently.

"I know what happened, Mom. I thought you and Dad were going to split. You guys had some pretty awful fights about Stephanie Hunt. Right after that, you had your motorcycle crash and almost died on us."

I can't lie to my daughter, and even if I do, she won't believe me. I hug her tightly. She's growing up too fast. Or maybe it's just the way fifteen-year-olds are these days.

I sit on the bed and gesture for her to join me. I say, "Your dad and I love each other. We have issues like most married people, but all you need to know is that you and your brother are our top priority. I don't want you to worry about grown-up problems. You'll be an adult soon enough."

It sounds like a lecture, though I'm grateful for the change in subject. How can I explain to my daughter that I'm scared to death, and some psychopath is threatening to do disgusting things to her if I don't cooperate in some evil plot he has yet to reveal?

"But I'm not a kid, Mom," she points out. "In three years, I'll be old enough to vote, go off to war, run a business, live on my own, get married..."

Married? Where did that come from? I hope she's not doing anything I don't want to think about her doing.

I drape my arms around her shoulders. "You came looking for me for a reason. What's going on with you, and why all the questions about your father and me?"

Abbie gets deathly quiet. She's running a risk-benefit analysis in her head right now, deciding if she should tell me her real reason for coming to find me. She scrambles off the bed and stands in front of the full-length mirror in the corner near the window.

"Do you think I'm pretty, Mom?"

The question surprises me. Abbie is not one of those teenage girls obsessed with her looks. She's levelheaded and keeps the drama to a minimum.

"Of course, Abbie. Why would you ask me that?"

She turns away from the mirror and approaches the bed. "This is important, Mom. I need you to be honest with me and not feed me some cliched platitude."

"Okay," I say hesitantly. "I don't think you're pretty."

Abbie glowers at me as though she can't believe her ears. I make the time-out gesture with my palms.

"I don't think you're pretty. I think you're gorgeous." It's the truth and not just my protective instincts talking.

Abbie inherited my eyes and petite frame, though she's much taller than I am, thanks to her father's genes. At fifteen, she's already five feet seven inches tall. She got lucky and dodged teenage acne all together, and with a dazzling smile that could melt the polar ice caps, Abbie needn't worry about her appearance.

"Really? You're not just saying that?"

"No, Abbie, I'm not just saying that. Go see for yourself. Look in the mirror again. You have an inner glow that comes through to the outside. That's true beauty. No amount of cosmetics, plastic surgery, or any other artificial enhancement can compete with that. Why are you so concerned about your looks suddenly?"

She grabs a throw pillow off the bed and stares at it aimlessly.

"What is it, Abbie? You can tell me. And if you don't want me to tell Dad, I won't."

Her eyes go wide for a second or two, and then she says, "I really like Ty. I mean, like, I want us to date."

The revelation hits me like a thunderbolt. Then I say, "Well, you could do worse, believe me. What changed? You two have been the best of friends for a while."

"That was before. I mean, we're still good friends, but he's just different now. And when I'm with him, my heart beats faster. I feel funny, like I'm catching a fever. Is that weird?"

"No, it isn't, sweetie." I hug her and let out a deep sigh. "You're falling in love for the first time, with your best friend."

Abbie looks at me sheepishly, searching my face for some clue that tells her there's nothing wrong with her feeling this way. In theory, it's fine. But I also know what it's like to be her age and madly in love, at least what I thought was love, and no one could convince me otherwise. What I thought was love had life-altering consequences for me. I walk around fearful that one day those consequences will come looking for me. But I won't allow my past to ruin what could be a wonderful experience for my daughter. When she's ready.

"Does Ty feel the same way? Have you told him?"

Her response is swift. "Heck no! I mean … no, ma'am. I'd rather die than tell him."

"Oh. I see. So you're just going to suffer in silence?"

"No. He needs to put his cards on the table first. Then we'll see."

I burst out laughing, and soon we're both cracking up. As the giggling subsides, I wipe a tear from my eyes and put on my serious face.

"I won't lecture you, Abbie, but I would really like for you to take this slowly. Real intimacy is serious business, and I don't want you to do anything you'll regret. You're a smart girl. I know you can think for yourself and not give in to peer pressure."

"I can think for myself, Mom. You and Dad have been teaching me to have an independent mind before I could walk or talk. I know you're scared, but don't be. I won't be doing anything I'm not ready for. Besides, there might be complications."

"What do you mean?"

"I think Ty likes someone else. Kerri Wheeler," Abbie says with disgust.

"Did he tell you that?"

"He didn't have to. They've been texting each other, and he's trying to get a date with her."

Now I see the real problem. Abbie has a rival for Ty's affection, and she's worried about competing. "Is Kerri beautiful? Is that why you're concerned about your looks?"

Abbie rolls her eyes. "She's a short Beyoncé look-alike with a serious head of hair that won't quit. My friends and I nicknamed her Rapunzel."

"Are you afraid if Ty gets involved with Kerri, the two of you won't be as close as you are now? Because I don't think that will happen. The Kerri Wheelers of the world will come and go, but there's only one incredible, super smart, super special Abbie Cooper. Ty knows that, and when the time is right, he'll recognize it."

"So I'm just supposed to pretend I don't have feelings while he does goodness knows what with Kerri?"

"No, honey. Keep your friendship strong. You two have a special bond. The best relationships often begin with a strong friendship as its foundation. Let things unfold naturally."

I'm trying to do damage control before she may need it. If Ty is into this Kerri girl and Abbie eventually confesses her feelings, she could get hurt. That would be the end of her friendship with Ty.

"Thanks for being cool about this, Mom. Glad you didn't get all judgy."

"I was once a teenager, Abbie, strange as it sounds."

"You're not going to say anything embarrassing, are you?"

"Hey, your parents are people, too. People who make mistakes."

8

THE POTENT SMELL of brand-new tires bombards my nose when I enter the customer center of National Engine and Bodyworks. A stocky man with a bald head and glasses stands behind the black granite countertop. His nametag says *Russell.* He tries to shore up a smile, but doesn't quite succeed. Maybe customer service isn't his calling.

"May I help you?" he asks.

"Yes. I need a mechanic to take a look under my car."

"Care to be a little more specific about what they should be looking for?"

"I will if you give me a chance." I let out an exaggerated sigh and shoot him a dirty look. "I want them to see if there's a GPS tracker on the car. If there is, I need it removed. Today."

I've become obsessed with my stalker and finding out how he knows so much about me. I'm sure he did some online research, but when he tried to run me off the road, he knew I would take that route. I hadn't said a word to anyone about where I was headed that morning, not even Inez.

"Anything else?" Mr. Friendly asks, eyes narrowed.

"No. If there's anything else, I'll be sure to let you know." A couple of customers behind me witness our exchange and shake their heads as though I'm the one being difficult.

Mr. Friendly picks up the gray phone and dials an extension. I stare at the wall behind him. It's covered with the pricing menu, a giant map of all the states in which they have locations, and several certificates for outstanding customer service. Obviously, those certificates were awarded before Russell came on board.

Another employee comes through the glass doors connecting customer service to the mechanics' work area. After a brief exchange about the problem and the filing of some paperwork, I hand over the car keys and head to the waiting area.

I scroll through my phone and check my email. It's the usual, a few bioinformatics newsletters I subscribe to and a plethora of other junk clogging up my inbox. Then my screen lights up. I hit the answer button, take a deep breath, and dive headlong into what I'm sure will be another confrontation.

"I said I would think about it," I say, irritated.

"He wants to go, but he's waiting on you. He's got no more business on this earth except you."

"I'm sorry, Michael. I can't get away right now."

He knows I swore never to go back. But yet here he is, making demands, trying to force me to make a commitment I can never keep.

"I doubt he remembers me," I say. "Our business ended on a summer night many years ago."

"No use holding on to something you can't change. Meanness won't make you feel better about it, either."

"What do you want from me? You want me to feel bad that he's dying? Tell him all is forgiven?"

"Let it go," Michael says, his voice impatient. "Don't punish him because of what she did. She's the one you're really mad at."

"He made his choice. I adjusted to that reality in ways you can't imagine."

"What about your children, your husband?" he asks.

"What about them?"

"When are you going to tell them who you really are? I'm tired of carrying your secret."

"Are you threatening me, Michael?"

An older woman takes up the seat next to me in the waiting area. I turn away from her, a reminder to keep my voice down.

"No. I'm saying that fancy life you're living up north with your rich husband and spoiled kids… well… it could be over just like that. Life is funny that way."

"Go pound sand, Michael!"

"After you, darlin."

I'm spitting mad, but before I hang up on my brother, I need information.

"Has anyone contacted you, asking questions about me?"

"No. Why?"

"Are you sure? Nobody asking questions about the past they shouldn't be asking? No strange calls?"

"Nobody has said anything to me. I could ask—"

"Don't! Please don't say a word to her. I mean it."

"You can't change your past," he says.

"I'm going to try, anyway."

"If you say so. Why are you worried now?"

"I'm not," I snap. He knows I can't go back as long as *she's* alive.

"I'm sorry. I just can't make it. Please try to understand."

I hang up on my brother, the only connection to a past I'd rather stay buried. The pain is as much a part of me as my limbs or my face or head. I've tried to do away with it, like a box of unwanted things you store in an attic. But it's there. There's no escaping it. And I know one day it will destroy me. For now, I don't need the distraction. The present has enough demons trying to slay me.

Sometime later, Dominic the mechanic comes into the

waiting area to hand over the keys to my car and inform me that he removed the GPS tracker.

"It was near invisible where they hid it under the rear bumper."

He places a small, round device the size of a quarter in the palm of my hands. I find it offensive and want to ditch it as soon as possible. Dominic must have sensed my mood.

"I guess your husband can't keep tabs on you now that you've busted him."

The casual statement strikes terror in my heart. What if Jason knows what I did and is trying to teach me a lesson? But Jason isn't the violent type. The stalker had violent tendencies. Jason wouldn't do that. He can be ruthless, but he's also kind and sweet and caring.

The man who took such good care of me after my motorcycle accident left me with two broken legs and a broken arm wouldn't do this to me. The man who bathed me, dressed me, combed my hair—even applied my makeup if we had to go out some place so I wouldn't go stir crazy in the house—wouldn't send a stalker after me. *He just wouldn't.*

I thank Dominic and make a hasty exit for my car already parked up front and waiting for me.

I'm on Route 9 heading west to my Westborough lab. I call Inez to let her know I'm only minutes away so we can go over my schedule for the day when I arrive. After I hang up, my phone rings. Michael can be so stubborn. He won't let this go, and I'm getting tired of it. I come to a traffic stop at the intersection of Route 9 and Edge Hill Road in Framingham.

"Michael, I'm on my way to the lab and can't discuss this now. Please. Give me a break already."

But it's not Michael on the line. The sound of an infant crying comes through the phone, pitiful and neglected. My hands clutch the steering wheel. My breath quickens. "No. Please stop. Stop it. I didn't mean to." The wailing continues until I'm in a full-blown meltdown, unable to think or move.

Somewhere between my anguish and the fog blanketing my mind, horns blare faintly in the distance. As I try to focus, they get louder and louder. The traffic light had turned green, the reason the drivers behind me are honking. I floor it until I pull into the parking lot of a McDonald's down the street.

With a trembling hand, I reach for the bottle of water next to me and chug it down in one long gulp. My heartbeat slowly returns to normal. I can never erase the guilt and shame that has consumed me for over twenty years. My stalker must know this. He was willing to dig up my past—a past I thought I had buried.

9

YOU UNDERSTAND WHAT'S at stake, don't you? If you don't go through with the plan, it could spell disaster for you and your girls," I say.

"Take the children and run was never supposed to be a thought, let alone a plan," he says.

Alessandro sits across from me in a wellness room in GeneMedicine's Westborough office. He's aged. New wrinkles appear on his forehead, as though they sprung up overnight. It's been less than a week since he came into Pennybaker's and asked me to meet him out back to pitch the idea of leaving. I chose a wellness room for this meeting because no one, not even Inez, would think to look for me there.

"Sometimes decisions are made for us. Your daughters need a safe upbringing that only you can provide. Second guessing your decision is the surest way for the whole thing to fall apart."

"Perhaps I'm not as brave as you, Shelby."

"Nonsense. What you're doing takes guts and courage. Would it make you feel any better if I told you I know firsthand what's waiting for Anna and Morgana if you don't take them away? If you don't see this plan through to the end?"

"What are you saying?" he asks, leaning forward.

"The trauma will never leave them. They will resent you for

not saving them from their abusive mother. And it will haunt you forever. Is that what you want?"

My intensity scares him. Alessandro slinks back into the chair and crosses his arms. He says nothing.

When he finally speaks, he says, "I worry about you. All the trouble you've gone through to help my daughters and me at great personal risk. I don't take that lightly."

"I've covered my tracks. Not to worry."

"And what about Jason?" he asks. "It would hurt me if he finds out, and it causes problems in your marriage. No need to tempt fate."

"Don't worry about Jason or me. You gave me something far more valuable than money. I can never repay the debt I owe you for helping me reclaim my life. That motorcycle crash could have left me permanently disabled. Because of you, I made a full recovery."

My reassurances have the desired effect. He's calmer. I ask the question I've been afraid to ask. "Is Isabella suspicious?"

"No. She's happy to have the girls out of her hair and me out of her sight. I've taken them on trips before."

I shiver despite the comfortable room temperature. I can't help but think about the fallout. What will happen once Isabella Rossi discovers her husband and children are gone? If my first and only introduction to her is any indication, she might think "good riddance."

It happened a few months back when I ran into them in the parking lot of the Whole Foods supermarket in Framingham.

After I had placed the groceries in the trunk of my car, I came around the front to open the driver's side door. I spotted them parked across from me. Isabella was pounding on Alessandro's chest with both hands. He tried to deflect the blows as best as he could. At first, I opened my car door and pretended I didn't see them. Another car cut in front of us and temporarily blocked my view. After the car disappeared, I took a closer look and that was when I noticed the children in the back seat.

I snapped. I crossed the small parking lot, ignored the adults, and knocked on the passenger's side window. The twins, Anna and Morgana, were in tears. The teenage girl seated next to them stared straight ahead, her body rigid.

The front passenger window came down, and for the first time, I stared into the face of Isabella Rossi.

"What do you want?" she asked. She didn't bother to mask her rage.

"I'm sorry to come by like this, but I noticed the kids crying in the back seat. Is everything okay?"

Alessandro, in the driver's seat, wouldn't look at me. This would be an awkward time to make an introduction.

"This is none of your business," Isabella hissed. "Leave us alone."

"You're in a public place. People can see you."

She looked at me defiantly. "Get lost."

I leaned in closer. "Ma'am, you're scaring the children. Would you prefer someone calls the police?"

"Dr. Cooper, please don't do that," Alessandro said, his speech tense and rushed. "We're fine. Just a little disagreement, that's all."

Awkward or not, introductions were called for. I was a patient, he told her, who needed intense physical therapy back in early spring after a motorcycle crash almost killed me.

Isabella looked at me like something unpleasant she found at the bottom of her shoes and then said something to him in Portuguese. Alessandro started the engine. I took the hint and went about my business.

After that incident, Alessandro confided in me he spent as

little time as possible at home, just to avoid Isabella. He would go home at night to have dinner with his girls, tuck them into bed, and then return to his office and work until all hours. When he wasn't working, he spent his time with his daughters outside of the house or played soccer with other Brazilian friends and acquaintances in the area.

"So she doesn't care at all?" Even now, I have trouble believing everything I've learned about Mrs. Rossi.

"Isabella never wanted children. I was the one who insisted. She only married me to please her parents."

I know all too well what it's like to be stuck in a loveless relationship, but I don't share that thought with him. Instead, I reach over and squeeze his hand. "It's going to be okay. It's a new beginning for you and the girls. You're finally free. You should be celebrating."

Alessandro says, "It feels like a funeral. The death of everything I have built and known since I came to America as a young teenager."

"But look at what you'll gain."

He nods. "You're right. But I may never see you again."

"I have to be okay with that, and so do you."

He cocks his head to one side. "Yes. I believe it will be okay."

I turn my attention to the back of the couch and retrieve the gift bag I stashed before he arrived. "I got these for the girls. Maybe it will keep them company on the long flight."

He opens the bag and takes out two dolls made in the likeness of his daughters.

"I don't know what to say. Thank you. My girls will cherish these dolls."

I stand and so does he. "Are the girls excited about the trip to New York?"

"Yes. Anna wants to visit the Statue of Liberty, and Morgana wants to go to Dylan's Candy Bar."

"I took my kids there when they were younger. I'll never do that again. They were the roadrunner on steroids, and I was Wile E. Coyote with my tongue hanging out trying to keep up with them after the sugar high."

"I'll remember that when I'm chasing Morgana around the store."

The plan is to take his girls for a day trip to New York. No bags, just the clothes on their backs, cash in a nondescript overnight bag, and the best fake passports money can buy. Before the end of the day, a limousine will pick them up from the city and take them to an airstrip where a chartered private jet will be waiting for them.

The pilot will drop them in Panama, where they will lie low for a few months, maybe Buenos Aires afterward to throw the authorities off the scent before they enter Brazil. The whole thing could take up to a year.

A gloomy aura takes over his features. "I can never repay your kindness."

"Will you stop? We've already been over that. And who knows, I might accidentally run into you on the streets of Rio during carnival one of these days."

Alessandro grins, and the sparkle I love returns to his eyes briefly. "That would be wonderful."

"I'll be praying for you and the children to have a safe journey."

He opens his arms wide, and I hug him tightly. "*Adeus*, Alessandro," I say, and step away from him.

"*Eu amo você*, Shelby."

10

CRANKING UP THE heat as I zoom down the Mass Turnpike heading west, I think of Alessandro and his daughters. Despite my reassurances that leaving was the right thing to do, there's a small part of me that wonders whether my motives were pure, whether taking the girls away from their abusive mother is my way of getting back at *her*. I couldn't stop *her*, but I could stop Isabella Rossi. My mother would never qualify for Mother of the Year, even if she were to cure cancer.

I glance in the rearview mirror. My spine jerks upright on its own. A Massachusetts State Police cruiser is on my tail. I recognize the navy-blue and gray sedan, different from local cops. I breathe in and out slowly. Was I speeding without realizing it?

The siren wails. I pull over in the breakdown lane just before exit eleven, near the Westborough Service Plaza. It's roughly three in the afternoon on a weekday, so the traffic in both eastbound and westbound lanes moves at a steady pace.

I reach for the registration in the glove compartment, careful not to disturb the gun I now carry for protection against a stalker who has me on edge. The officer taps the driver's side window, which I roll down with the push of a button.

He says, "License and registration, please." He's appears to be in his mid-forties, tall, with a moustache and buzz cut.

I hand him the two items. The nameplate above his left shirt pocket says Hannon. "Was I speeding, officer?"

"Is this your car?" he asks.

"Yes. What's wrong?"

"Wait here, ma'am."

Officer Hannon takes off for the cruiser just a few feet behind me. I tap my fingers on the steering wheel in a pattern of random beats. A couple of minutes go by. I explore all possibilities. Why did he pull me over? I wasn't speeding. I have no broken taillights. The registration is current. The car is fully insured. He only wanted to know if the expensive German import was mine.

I glance at the clock on the dashboard. Ten minutes have already gone by, and the officer still hasn't returned. Fear prickles at my scalp, and I can't keep the feeling of dread from seeping into my bones. I call Jason and speak the moment he picks up.

"A state trooper pulled me over. I don't know why. He's taking too long. Why can't he just give me the ticket and my license back so I can go home?" I draw in a frustrated breath and take a few seconds to calm myself.

Jason says, "Tell me from the beginning what happened. Stay calm and don't say or do anything to set him off. What did he say when he pulled you over?"

"He just asked if the car was mine and took off with the license and registration. You need to stay on the phone with me, okay?"

"Of course, baby. Where did you get pulled over?"

"Westborough. Here he comes now."

"Ma'am, do you know you have a broken taillight?" Officer Hannon asks.

I'm stunned by the question and give him a blank stare. "No, I didn't. This car is only a few weeks old, and I haven't had any accidents or anything." I'm babbling, but I think I would have noticed a broken taillight when I drove off to work this morning.

"That's why I pulled you over. See that you get it fixed."

I breathe a sigh of relief as the officer hands me my license and registration. "Yes, Officer, of course I will."

I wind the window up, place the registration in the glove compartment, and then slip my license into my wallet.

"All set, honey," I say to Jason. "It was just a broken taillight."

11

AFTER I PUT the car in gear, I merge into traffic. A broken taillight. That's what the officer said, although I don't know how it could have happened. Perhaps another car backed into mine in the garage, and I was in too much of a hurry after I left work to notice. I've been known to do that. I'm always running from one place to the next with little downtime.

Between the demands of my job, the kids' activities, family time, Jason's job—including the part where I have to be the perfect corporate wife—I rarely have time to just sit still. It's also the reason I'm low maintenance: hair styled in a short pixie cut, make-up minimal, just mascara and a little rouge now and then and a simple but high-end wardrobe in vivid colors that compliment my dark brown skin. I complain little because a busy life helps me to forget the things I'd rather stay buried in the past where they belong.

My phone rings. Maybe Jason forgot to mention something when I called him in a panic earlier. However, when I check the caller ID, it says unknown. It's *him,* my stalker. I contemplate ignoring the call but decide I'd rather find out what he's up to, so I answer.

"What is it now?" I bark. The car in front of me slows down unexpectedly, and I lightly tap my brakes.

"That's no way to greet an old friend, now is it? Are you

having a bad day, Shelby? It could get worse."

"For you maybe."

"No, Shelby. Your day is about to explode like a nuclear bomb. There's no telling how far the damage will extend. I have a feeling the police aren't done with you yet."

He may as well have spoken in Mandarin. Dominic, the mechanic at National Engine and Body Works, removed the GPS tracker from the car. How does the stalker know the police pulled me over, and why does he think they would arrest me? And for what? My mouth goes dry. The inside of the car is blazing hot, so I shut off the heat.

"I'm not playing this ridiculous game with you right now. You're a weak coward who hides behind anonymity and threats, a raging psychopath with no conscience."

Silence. Then he belts out a loud, piercing, thunderous laugh, as if I'm an imbecile who couldn't possibly comprehend the gravity of who or what I'm dealing with. I don't. I don't know who he is or what he wants.

Is this stalker someone I once crossed paths with? Did he develop an irrational hatred of me and wants me to suffer? Or perhaps the truth is far simpler. I'm just a pawn in a game.

Jason ran his own successful software company for years before he sold it to IBM in an eight-figure deal. Could this situation have something to do with Jason's past? Threatening someone's family is an easy way to gain their cooperation, although I can't think of any reason this could be connected to my husband or his past business dealings.

"I was trying to warn you. Instead of thanking me, you shower me with insults," he drones. "All you have to do is cooperate, Shelby, and everything will be fine. Think about what could happen to Abigail and Miles if you don't."

"What are you talking about?" I ask, trying to disguise the

tension eating away at me like a ravenous horde of locusts. He doesn't answer my question and ends the call.

The loud, high-pitched wailing of police sirens startles me. I glance in my rearview mirror. Flashing blue lights get closer and closer, the sound louder and louder. Why are they following me again? *Breathe*, I tell myself. Maybe they're not after me. Officer Hannon said it was a broken taillight, and I intend to get it fixed right away. *Everything is fine. It's just nerves.* My stalker has my imagination working overtime.

I turn on my signal and move into the left lane to get out of the way of the state police cruiser. Bad move. He's right on my tail. Next thing I know, the deafening noise of a bullhorn slices through the afternoon air.

"Pull over. Now!" the hostile voice instructs me.

My hands tighten on the steering wheel to stop them from wobbling. It hurts to breathe, as if someone set my lungs on fire. I pull over into the breakdown lane and wait.

Officer Hannon raps loudly on the driver's side window. His face is as hard as a three-day-old, stale bagel. I slide the automatic windows down again.

"Ma'am, step out of the car, please."

"Why? What's going on?"

"Ma'am, it would be best for everyone if you did this voluntarily."

If I stay in the car, he could drag me out by force—not that it would take much effort on his part. I'm barely five feet tall and might weigh a hundred pounds soaking wet. I grab my cell phone and purse as I exit the car.

"Can you tell me what this is about?" I ask. My hands are clammy. My breath bursts in and out.

He doesn't answer. Chaos ensues. No less than six squad cars with blaring sirens and flashing lights roll up behind his cruiser.

Officers exit their cars, weapons drawn. My heart races at an unnatural speed, and I'm afraid it will explode. I greedily suck in the cold November air, afraid it might be my last breath.

Officer Hannon directs my attention to the trunk, and that's when I notice the broken taillight and the bloodstain on the bumper.

"Can you open the trunk, please, ma'am?"

"Huh?" The stress must be getting to me because I can't form coherent words. Officer Hannon stands next to me, feet wide apart, arms folded. The other officers form a semicircle, still with their weapons aimed at me.

"Are you refusing to open the trunk, ma'am?" Hannon asks, his tone harsh.

My legs feel like they will buckle any minute. Dizziness and nausea battle for dominance. I manage to squeak out the words, "No, I'm not refusing. I'm just confused."

Hannon says, "We have reason to believe someone used this vehicle to commit a crime. Please open the trunk, ma'am."

The ludicrous idea must have triggered an adrenaline spike. I say, "A crime? That's ridiculous. My car has been in an underground garage all day. I just came from work. I don't know where the blood came from, but I'll show you there's nothing in the trunk except my gym bag and some bottled water."

I hit the remote on the key chain and pop the trunk. "See, there's nothing in there."

But the expressions on the officers' faces tell a different story. I inch closer to the trunk and peek inside to see what has them looking as if they just lost a comrade.

My legs are about to give way. I can't control my breathing, and my chest is tightening. *I'm having a heart attack at forty!* Alessandro Rossi is inside the trunk with a gaping hole in the middle of his forehead.

12

THREE ADDITIONAL POLICE cruisers pull up. Officer Hannon is speaking, but I can't make out his words. I want to scream, but my voice won't work. Hannon pins both my arms behind my back and snaps on cold metal bracelets that bind my wrists together. I'm escorted inside a police cruiser. I throw up all over the floor.

We arrive at the Weston Police Barracks. The long, narrow, white structure right off the Mass Turnpike looms before me like a disapproving parent about to dispense punishment. I'm ushered inside the main lobby with stark white walls, a bench, plaques on the wall, and an officer behind a plexiglass window who is swimming in an ocean of paperwork. I'm instructed to remove my coat, and then a female officer pats me down. She escorts me to an interrogation room, and then I'm left alone.

A rotten stench permeates the air. Vomiting in a police cruiser was not one of my finer moments. The mess made its way to my blouse. The room is impersonal, fluorescent lights embedded in the ceiling, walls bare and uninviting.

The back of my eyelids burn, and I hunch over in my seat, holding my stomach. The past hour comes back to me in a montage. Flash: Mass Turnpike. The conversation with Jason. Flash: the stalker saying the police aren't done with me yet. Flash:

police sirens and guns drawn. Flash: popping the trunk.

I squeeze my eyes and will the image to clear out of my brain, but it won't. Alessandro. Bullet hole. Blood. Dead. He's supposed to be in Panama with his daughters. How did the stalker get him to make a detour? That psychopath stalker threatened to kill my children if I didn't cooperate. Did he kill Alessandro to show me he means business?

The door swings open, and two detectives walk in: a strapping fifty-something male, well over six feet, slightly balding with graying facial hair and world-weary eyes that say he's seen it all. His partner is a fortyish brunette, attractive but serious, hair up in a ponytail, black pantsuit, white shirt.

The man speaks first. "Dr. Cooper, I'm Detective Eric Van Dorn, and this is my partner, Detective Tess McCall."

I nod in their direction. Van Dorn asks if I need a drink before he takes the seat across from me, while McCall stands against the wall, her eyes assessing. I rub my left wrist, the mark from the handcuffs visible and itchy. The fog that hijacked my brain earlier is lifting, slowly. I have an idea how this is going to go, and I will cooperate, up to a point.

Van Dorn clears his throat. "Dr. Cooper, we have a homicide on our hands, and we're hoping you can help us understand what happened." He removes a small notebook and pen from his jacket pocket. McCall, arms folded, looks on. "We're not accusing you of anything; we just want to ask some questions."

Right. And Alessandro is just a little bit dead.

"What do you want to know, Detective?" I ask Van Dorn. The steady calm of my voice surprises me.

"Do you know the victim and how he got into the trunk of your car?"

"Yes, I know him. He was my physical therapist. No, I don't know how he ended up in the trunk of my car."

"Where were you today between the hours of 11:00 a.m. and 3:00 p.m.?"

"At work. I left at two."

"Where were you headed?"

"Home."

"What route did you take?"

"I left my office in Cambridge and then got on the Mass Turnpike, taking it all the way west until state police pulled me over near the Westborough exit."

"Did you leave your office at all today, prior to heading home? Maybe to grab some lunch, run an errand?"

"No, I didn't leave the office at all. Several colleagues can vouch for me."

Van Dorn writes something in his notebook. "What kind of work do you do?"

"I'm a research scientist, Director of Bioinformatics at GeneMedicine."

"Wow. Bioinformatics. Never heard of it. What do you do in your lab?"

I can't tell whether he's impressed or just pretending to be to establish a rapport.

"I build algorithms and use mathematical modeling, computer simulation, and a bunch of other technology-related tools to organize and interpret massive amounts of biological data. The idea is to extract information that could help lead to a cure for diseases like cancer and Alzheimer's."

"Sounds complicated."

I don't answer. McCall joins in on the fun. "Did anyone see you leave work?"

"I don't know."

"Where was your car parked?"

"In the underground garage."

Van Dorn writes in his notebook again.

McCall continues, "Did you notice anything unusual about your car when you left work?"

What she really means is *how could you not know there was a dead body in your car?*

"No. I was in a hurry to get home, so I just left."

Two sets of eyebrows arch with curiosity.

McCall presses on. "Why were you in a hurry?"

"My son has a bake sale at school tomorrow, and I'm supposed to make Petit Fours and cupcakes."

"What school does your son attend?"

"The Carlisle School in our hometown. Castleview."

Van Dorn takes notes. He'll no doubt check out my story.

"Do you own a gun, Dr. Cooper?" Van Dorn asks.

This is where the interview ends. I'm no legal expert, but I know I can't say another word to the police without a lawyer present.

13

ALESSANDRO IS DEAD. The finality of it hits me with brute force. It wasn't supposed to happen this way. He's dead because of me. There's no escaping that fact. A raging psychopath targeted Alessandro because he wanted to demonstrate how far he was willing to go to keep me trapped in his evil web. With no way out. No way to expose him. Feeling helpless, defenseless, and desperate. I'm afraid for my family and what will happen to me. By the time my attorney walks into the interrogation room, my tears are pooling on the table.

Alan Rose pulls out the chair across from me. He places his gloves neatly on the table, removes his coat, and then hangs it on the back of the chair. I watch him open his briefcase, remove a notepad and pen, and finally take his glasses from the pocket of his suit jacket. His presence is commanding and calming. He reminds me of actor Gregory Peck as Atticus Finch in the movie version of *To Kill a Mockingbird.*

"First things first," he says, taking charge. "What did you say to the detectives?"

"Not much." I give Alan the run-down on the brief interview. He hands me the silk handkerchief from his pocket to clean my face, for which I'm thankful.

"From now on, you talk to no one. All questions and

requests come through me. So far they haven't charged you with anything, so I'm going to try and get you out of here on personal recognizance. But I have a few questions of my own."

"How bad is it?" I ask.

"Right now this case is a felony homicide. It carries a maximum sentence of life in prison, with the possibility of parole in fifteen."

I lean back in my chair and let my arms dangle at my sides.

"I didn't do this," I say.

"It doesn't matter what I believe. What would be helpful right now is your recollection of events, with as many details as you can remember."

Alan Rose is a high-powered attorney who has never lost a case. I met Alan and his wife Bree, on a few social occasions. Jason's company is a client of Lockerbee, Rose and Nash. I'm sure that relationship is the reason Alan got here so quickly.

"Okay," I say. "My day was unremarkable until the police pulled me over for a broken taillight. At first."

"The only thing linking you to the crime is the discovery of the body in your car," Alan says. "There's no proof you put it there and no eyewitnesses. Jason said the victim was your physical therapist?"

"That's right." I explain how Alessandro came into my life after my horrific motorcycle crash, the torture of physical rehabilitation, and how Alessandro's patience and understanding had as much to do with my recovery as the strenuous routines I endured. I can barely get the story out in between the tears, anger, and hiccups.

"Take your time," Alan says.

"Sorry. It's so unfair. So wretchedly unfair."

"Were you friends outside of the patient-provider relationship?" Alan asks softly.

"Casually. We ran into each other at Whole Foods occasionally. Once in a while, he enlisted my help with some computer-related problems."

I squirm in my seat. The fluorescent lights must be giving off some extra heat. I dab sweat from my forehead with Alan's handkerchief.

"When was the last time you saw him?"

"I didn't see him much once I stopped going to physical therapy."

"Do you know his family?"

"Alessandro has two young daughters: Anna and Morgana. He brought them to the center sometimes. He's married, and his wife came by his workplace a few times while he was treating me, but he never introduced me to her." *Not while I was a patient, anyway.*

"Can you think of anyone who would want him dead?"

"No. His employees and patients liked him. He was an all-around good guy."

"You speak as if you had some affection for him."

Did I say that?

"We got along. I'm grateful for what he did for me."

"That's it?"

"What else is there?"

"You're holding back," Alan says, with certainty. "Look, Shelby, I need all the facts. We can't be blindsided by some crucial piece of information you neglect to tell me. It could come back to haunt us later on."

Alan's eyes bore into mine. I struggle to maintain eye contact. My stomach is churning, and I feel like throwing up again. I cover my mouth with my hand.

"What's wrong? Are you sick?" he asks.

I swallow hard and then breathe in and out slowly. "No," I squeak. "I'm having a hard time with this. With… everything that happened."

"That's understandable under the circumstances. But now is

the time to nail down critical information while it's still fresh in your mind. Okay?"

I nod.

"Let's talk about the timeline," Alan says. "I want to know everything you did today. The coroner will establish a time of death. We have to be certain investigators can't place you anywhere near the vicinity of the murder."

"I woke up at my usual time."

"What time would that be?"

"Six in the morning. I went downstairs, worked out for a half hour, and then showered and got ready for work."

"What time did you leave the house?"

"Around seven."

"Did you check the trunk of your car before you left home?"

"No. I had no reason to."

"Anything unusual about the car? Did it seem heavier somehow? Was anything out of place?"

"No. I backed out of the garage like I always do."

"What route did you take to work?"

"Route 9 heading east, exited on Route 30 in Framingham, and then got on the Mass Pike. Took exit eighteen toward Cambridge."

"Did you stop anywhere?"

"No."

"Where did you park when you arrived at work?"

"In the garage."

"Did you notice any strangers or suspicious individuals looking at your car?"

"Not really."

"Do you own a gun?"

I blink rapidly and then stare off to the side. I breathe mathematics for a living and see the equation clearly: a clever adversary who's always one step ahead of me, plus Alessandro found dead in my car with a bullet to the head, plus the fact that I own a gun, which equals viable suspect.

"Yes," I confess. "Jason bought it for me for protection when he's away."

"What kind of gun is it?"

"A Smith & Wesson revolver. The .357 Magnum."

"Where is it?"

"In the glove compartment of my car."

Alan winces and drums on the table with his fingers. "The car that the police have now impounded; the car that the crime scene techs are processing as we speak?"

I stare at him. My earlier math equation tightens around my neck like a noose. If everything follows its logic, the gun would have been fired. My prints will be all over it.

"Give it to me straight, Alan. What are my chances of getting out of this mess unscathed?"

"If I had to use an analogy," he says, loosening his tie, "I would say the Thanksgiving turkey is far from cooked. There are many unanswered questions, which make the state's case purely circumstantial if they charge you. It's going to be difficult to pinpoint exactly where the killing took place, which means they can't place you at the scene. Your alibi is solid, and that will be ironclad once we go over the security footage of the garage where your car was parked. Plus, you have no motive as far as I can tell. Is there anything else you neglected to mention?"

I can't exactly confess that I aided and abetted in a kidnapping, and that action may have had fatal consequences for Alessandro.

"No, I told you everything I know."

Alan says, "If the district attorney pursues you as his number-one suspect, you and I will spend a lot of time together. If you don't trust me to provide a vigorous defense and act in your best interest, this case will be a difficult climb."

"I understand what I'm up against."

"Do you? This meeting is a precursor to a toxic storm that could rage for months."

I find a spot on the table and focus all my attention on it. My mind keeps churning with all kinds of questions, mostly terrible ones. Do I have a future? How do I prove my innocence, especially since I've been keeping secrets that make me look guilty? What about my family, how will they cope if anything happens to me? Most importantly, who is setting me up and why?

"I'm innocent," I say to Alan.

"Then let's get on with the business of proving it," he responds.

He has no idea that the task will be damned near impossible.

14

ABBIE WAS FINISHING up her homework when she heard a helicopter approaching. She frowned and closed her math textbook. She stood up from the desk and walked toward the window. Abbie drew the curtain aside and looked out across the lawn. The roar of the chopper got closer, as if it were about to land on their doorstep. She ran out of her bedroom and yelled for her father as she slid down the long, winding staircase.

"Dad. Dad. Do you hear that?" She arrived in the kitchen, almost out of breath.

Abbie found her father sagging against the island in the middle of the kitchen. He looked like if he didn't lean in for support, he would end up flat on his face.

Abbie slowly walked over to him. "Dad, what's going on? Why is a helicopter hovering over our house?"

Before her father could respond, Miles appeared with Mahalia, the family Golden Retriever, in tow. The canine whimpered and wagged her tail. The LAN line rang, and her dad wouldn't answer. It was right next to him. The phone kept ringing. Abbie couldn't stand it anymore, so she reached for the phone.

"Don't pick that up," he barked.

"Dad, what's going on? Where's Mom?" Abbie had a gut feeling something terrible had happened.

"Take a seat," her dad said. "You too, Miles."

They did as he asked. Mahalia sat at her usual spot at Miles's feet, whimpering. The dog's anxiety wasn't lost on Abbie. Their dad was about to deliver terrible news.

"Come on, what is it?" Miles asked impatiently.

"There was an incident this afternoon involving your mother." Abbie noticed her dad hadn't moved an inch.

"What incident?" Abbie probed.

"The state police took your mom in for questioning. About a murder."

Abbie and her brother exchanged frightened glances. "Why do the police think Mom knows anything about a murder?" she asked.

"Because they found Alessandro Rossi's dead body in the trunk of her car."

Miles whimpered like Mahalia had only moments before. He held the canine's collar in a death grip. Abbie squeezed her eyes shut. Her thoughts raced. She recalled the anonymous note she received and the phone call while she was in the chapel with Ty last week. *The storm is gathering speed and will explode with a bang*, the note had said. Abbie had ripped it into tiny pieces and thrown it away. *What if he shot Mr. Rossi and framed Mom?*

Abbie breathed hard, as though she'd just run the Boston Marathon. She couldn't make eye contact with her father, but she had to ask, had to be sure that this wasn't some sick coincidence.

"Abbie?" her dad asked, frowning.

She wrung her hands in despair. "It's just awful. How did Mr. Rossi die?"

"A bullet to the head," her father said.

Abbie clutched her stomach. "Excuse me," she whispered, and then bolted from the kitchen.

Abbie sprinted up the stairs and barely made it to the toilet in her bathroom before she emptied her stomach. She rinsed her mouth with mouthwash afterward and splashed cold water on her face.

Abbie left the bathroom, grabbed her phone lying on the desk, and made a call. He answered on the first ring.

"Mr. Rossi got shot and the police are holding my mother for questioning," she said breathlessly. "What the stalker said in the note came true, Ty. The storm exploded with a bang. I'm in so much trouble. My mother is in so much trouble. I don't know what to do."

"Slow down, Cooper. What are you talking about? Who got shot?"

"Mr. Rossi, Mom's former physical therapist. Are you deaf? Someone shot him in the head. He's dead. They found him in the trunk of my mom's car, and the police are holding her. They think she killed him."

"Are you sure? Maybe they mistook your mom for someone else and it's not Mr. Rossi who got shot."

Ty's reaction told Abbie everything she needed to know about what she and her family were about to face. His shock couldn't have been more obvious.

"Should I tell my dad about the note?" she asked in rasping breaths.

"I don't know, Cooper. This is too crazy to be real. Okay, let's think about it for a minute. I mean, we're just kids; we don't have answers."

"I know that, idiot."

"I'm not an idiot. You called me, remember?"

"Sorry. I'm freaking out."

"Me too. This stalker guy took it to another level. Tell your dad and let the police deal with it."

"I can't. I'm too scared. You see what he did to Mr. Rossi.

He'll come after the rest of us if I tell."

"Yeah, maybe you're right."

"I gotta go. I'll call you back. I'm heading downstairs and see what else is going on."

After Abbie hung up on Ty, she headed back downstairs to find Miles in tears and her dad watching him with overly bright eyes. They both sat at the kitchen table.

"I had to go to the bathroom," Abbie blurted out. She took a seat too.

"Alan Rose, your mom's lawyer, just called," her dad said. "She won't be coming home tonight, Abbie. They've charged her with killing Alessandro Rossi. Her arraignment is set for tomorrow morning."

Terror stabbed at every cell in Abbie's body. The sound of her heartbeat thrashed in her ears. She covered her face with both hands. If she told her dad about the note, the stalker could get even angrier and try to hurt them. Abbie decided her father couldn't find out this bad guy had been contacting her anonymously. The risks were too high, although she didn't understand why he would pin this murder on her mom or why he would warn her in advance.

How was she supposed to know what he meant by *the storm would explode with a bang*? Why did he hate her mother so much? And why kill poor Mr. Rossi? He was just her mom's physical therapist. None of it made any sense. It was too much to take in. They had to focus on proving her mom wasn't capable of murder.

Miles clung to their father after he got up from the table. Abbie did the same. Their dad embraced them in his strong arms.

"It's going to be okay," he soothed. "You know your mother is innocent. The police made a mistake. Once it's all cleared up, she'll be home with us where she belongs. Alan is with her right now. She'll be home soon. I promise."

15

JASON HEADED TO his study on the first floor of the house, the place he retreated to in a crisis. The LAN line and his cell phone rang non-stop, and he had refused to answer either, only picking up his cell phone for family and Alan Rose.

He was glad that awful news helicopter had left. The noise had been deafening, shattering their serene, suburban existence. They lived on a quiet country road, with a private cobblestone path leading to the house. He hoped the news media wouldn't trespass, but he wouldn't hold his breath. They would wait to ambush him at some point.

He instructed the kids not to watch the evening news, not that he planned to follow his own advice. There were many calls to make, starting with another call to Alan Rose, and then his sister Robin in Atlanta, and his mother, who would have to leave Connecticut tonight to stay with the kids so he could be there for Shelby at the arraignment and bring her home.

Jason stood in the middle of the room and turned on the TV to Channel 8. No surprise Alessandro Rossi's murder was the lead story.

"A shocking murder in MetroWest leads our broadcast tonight," the young female anchor said. A picture of Alessandro Rossi in his office flashed on the screen. They gave the vital stats: his name,

age, marital status, where he lived, and that he was the sole owner of Rossi Physical Therapy & Rehabilitation Centers, with four locations across the state and one in Rhode Island.

The anchor continued, *"State police confirmed they have arrested a suspect in connection with the crime, but have not officially revealed his or her identity. However, WBCY News has received unconfirmed reports that the suspect in custody is Dr. Shelby Cooper, a top researcher at Cambridge-based GeneMedicine."*

A photo of Shelby at last year's company picnic flashed on screen.

"Dr. Cooper is one of the most vocal advocates nationwide for women and girls pursuing careers in the STEM—Science, Technology, Engineering and Math—fields. Dr. Cooper is married to Orphion CFO Jason Cooper, who we have interviewed several times on this station."

He'd heard enough.

ABBIE WATCHED LITTLE TV and mostly used the set to stream her favorite shows on Netflix. She wanted to catch a few minutes of the local news to see what they said about her mother, despite her dad's warning to the contrary. Abbie decided against it when she had to keep an eye on Miles while Dad made some calls.

They sat together on her bed. "What are we going to do, Abbie?" Miles asked. His eyes brimmed with fresh tears. "What if Mom doesn't come home tomorrow or the day after?"

"She will, Miles," Abbie answered, and rubbed his shoulders. "It's just a mix-up. Remember the time you brought home Max Mitchell's backpack by mistake because the two of you had the same bag? And you almost got in trouble the next day, but then they figured out what happened."

Miles nodded.

"Well, it's like that with Mom. It's a mistake. Once the police find out she did nothing wrong, she'll come home and they'll look for the real bad guy."

"But what if they don't find him? Does that mean Mom will never come back to us?"

"No matter what happens, she'll find her way back to us. But we all have to say extra prayers when we go to bed. Mom would like that, wouldn't she?"

Miles grinned for the first time since their dad delivered the dreadful news about their mom. "Yes. She wouldn't yell at me for skipping my prayers."

"That's right. You would score major cool points from her."

Abbie hugged her little brother tight. She had to keep an extra eye on him. Their mother spoiled him rotten, and he would be lost without her. They all would.

16

I SIT NEXT to Alan Rose at the defendant's table in courtroom three of the Worcester Superior Court.

My clothes are disheveled, the same outfit I had on yesterday. Charcoal-gray wool slacks, a pink open-front cardigan sweater and matching blouse, and high-heeled ankle boots. I haven't slept. My bones hurt. I need a shower. I look straight ahead, avoiding the glare of the cameras and the stares of the few reporters who snagged a seat for the arraignment. I glance back at Jason seated in the gallery, his face expressionless.

Alan runs through the proceedings that are about to take place. Once they call the case number, I'll be brought before the judge. The judge will read the charges against me. The prosecutor will give the specifics of the case, at which point I enter a plea of not guilty.

I shiver as I recall my stalker's vile threats. *Rule number one: do not repeat a word of this to Jason or anyone else. Consequence of breaking rule number one will be your children in matching coffins. I will not be kind in my methods. All you have to do is cooperate and all will be well with Abigail and Miles.*

He wants me to go down for Alessandro's murder, or my kids will pay the price. He murdered a husband and father in cold blood to show what he was capable of, what would happen to my children, my family, if I disobey his orders.

Tears prickle at the back of my eyes. For the first time since I became an adult, I'm no longer in control of my destiny. Judge Susan A. Donnelly enters the courtroom, a middle-aged woman with a short bob and blue-rimmed glasses. The bailiff calls the case number, and we move to stand before the judge. So does the district attorney to our right. It doesn't matter what transpires in the next few minutes. My fate is sealed.

I plead not guilty to felony homicide, improper disposal of a body and improper transfer of a body. Assistant District Attorney Frank Barrows, a slightly overweight man in desperate need of a haircut and a shave, makes his case against bail.

"Your Honor, law enforcement discovered the body in Dr. Cooper's vehicle while she was driving said vehicle. She knew the victim personally. And she owns a gun. The Coopers are wealthy, and Dr. Cooper has access to resources that would allow her to flee the state or the country and stay away indefinitely. Due to the heinous nature of the crime, the Commonwealth requests that she be held without bail and her passport confiscated."

The cameras go off in a symphony of clicks and flashes. Then it's back to the hushed silence, daring my lawyer to trump the ADA's argument.

Alan's rebuttal is just as compelling. "Your Honor, there is no proof that my client murdered Mr. Rossi or dumped his body in her vehicle. There are no eyewitness accounts of the crime, and the police have yet to establish where Mr. Rossi was killed; therefore, they can't place my client at the crime scene.

"Everything that means anything to her is here—her husband, her children, and her work. She's been a law-abiding citizen and is anxious to clear her good name and reputation, which have been severely damaged by this tragic circumstance. We ask that you grant bail and Dr. Cooper be given the opportunity to prove her innocence and restore her good name."

"I've heard enough and have made my decision," the judge says. "Based on the circumstances of the case, I grant bail in the amount of one million dollars, and Dr. Cooper will be required to give up her passport."

The gavel comes down. Alan cheerfully stuffs some papers into his briefcase. The prosecutor levels an incredulous stare at the judge. The determined jut of his chin says this is far from over. Jason cracks a smile. The reporters are ready to pounce. This is a critical victory in the fight to clear my name, but I feel as though someone just ripped my heart out of my chest.

I grow dizzy under the weight of the impossible choices before me: walk out of this courtroom a free woman and put my children's lives at risk or cooperate in the scheme to frame me and hope it will keep them safe while I work to prove my innocence.

I put on a brave face as Jason and Alan usher me out of the courtroom. I stop and turn to Jason. "You know how much I love you and the kids, but I can't come home right now. Tell them you can't afford the bail. If you pay it, that will be the end of our family."

17

HOW ON EARTH was he supposed to deliver this baffling, tragic news to his children? How could he explain it to them when he didn't understand it himself? *Tell them you can't afford the bail. If you pay it, that will be the end of our family.*

Jason still reeled from the bombshell Shelby dropped this morning after the arraignment. Something dark and twisted had descended on his family, and she was caught up in the thick of it. He needed to stay focused on the kids, however. The unraveling of the mystery surrounding his wife's warning would come later.

"Shelby is one of the most levelheaded people I know," his mother, Naomi, said. "She wouldn't do something like this for the heck of it. She wouldn't put you and the kids through that kind of hell. I don't like this, Jason. Something terribly disturbing is going on here."

"I know that, Mother."

Jason sat at the kitchen table with his head bowed. His mother squeezed his shoulders and then pulled out the chair across from him and sat. Naomi Cooper was a force to be reckoned with, someone who rarely heard the word *no* based on the sheer force of her personality and wisdom. The retired advertising executive in her mid-sixties ran a Bed and Breakfast in Ridgefield, Connecticut. Wrinkles barely registered on her round, delicate face.

"I'll help you deliver the news to the kids," she offered. "I know you wanted to do it alone, but they need to be surrounded by all the love their little hearts can hold. This won't be easy for them. It will tear them apart. We have to make sure we're there to keep them together."

Jason strained to keep his voice even and upbeat, to hide the emotional mushroom cloud that had erupted in their lives. He gathered the kids in the family room to deliver the dreadful news.

"Mom will be away a little longer. It's going to take some time to sort out the legal issues surrounding the case."

Abbie said, "What? How is that possible, Dad?" Despair was plain on her face.

A fleeting glance passed between Jason and his mother. The dog already knew. Mahalia's whimpers grew louder and more intense as she lay in a defeated heap at Miles's feet.

"Mahalia, cut it out!" Miles yelled.

The dog's whimpers grew in volume. Mahalia left her spot at Miles's feet and entered the kitchen, pacing from one end to the other, wagging her tail. She eventually stopped in front of the large stainless-steel refrigerator and scraped against a photo with her two front legs. It was a picture of Mahalia, Miles, and Shelby building a sandcastle on the beach last summer.

"Mom isn't coming back, is she?" Miles asked, his lips trembling.

"Come here, babies," Naomi said. "Come sit with Grandma."

Miles and Abbie obeyed. Jason could barely stand it, the sheer terror wrapped in devastation etched on their faces.

"Mom is temporarily detained," Jason said.

"Detained where?" Abbie asked. She wanted answers, and Jason knew there was no sugarcoating anything with her. His mother gave him an encouraging nod.

"They took Mom to jail today."

Abbie said, "She's innocent. How could they take her to jail?"

Jason needed to be up front with his kids about an illogical situation. If he didn't, they would get their information elsewhere, in a way not necessarily kind or accurate.

"Abbie, I don't know what went wrong. She pleaded not guilty, and the next thing I knew, she'd been carted off to the women's prison. They granted bail, but she asked me to say we couldn't afford it."

"So Mom did it? Is that what it means?" Miles asked.

"No, Miles, your mother is not a murderer," Naomi said. "We all know that."

Jason looked from Miles to Abbie. It tore him apart to see their world crumble before them. He would swallow his own grief for now. Shelby and the kids needed him focused to reunite the family.

"I know this looks bad, kids," he said. "But whatever your mother is afraid of is the key to bringing her home. Something scared her so bad that she thinks going to jail is the only answer. We have to find out the connection between Alessandro Rossi's murder and your mother being framed for it."

"This bites," Abbie said, her face twisted into a scowl. "I thought yesterday was the worst day of my life, but today just took first place. I should just die now and be done with it. You know that Mom's life is over, don't you? Even when she comes home, her career is over.

"All the hard work she put into her research, gone. Her company is going to pretend she never worked for them. They're going to find every paper she ever published and start a bonfire or wipe their servers clean. Good thing we're rich because Mom will never earn a living as a scientist again."

How could he argue with that? Even he had to worry about his job. The crisis communications team kicked into high gear and put out a press release. *Jason Cooper is a valued member of the senior management team of Orphion Technologies. The company stands by him while he and his family go through this horrible crisis.* Blah blah.

"I understand you're worried about your mom's reputation," Jason said to Abbie. "I am, too. But the first priority is getting her out of Bayport."

"What are you going to do?" Miles asked. "How are you going to get Mom back? Jail is horrible, isn't it? And only bad people go to jail. Are they going to hurt Mom?"

His mother jumped in. "Nobody is going to hurt your mother, sweet pea. They punish people who do that in jail. Your mom is safe."

"I got Mom the best lawyer, and we'll hire our own investigator," Jason said. "If either of you," he said, looking from Abbie to Miles, "hears anything or sees anything or something doesn't make sense, please come to me.

"For the next couple of days, I'd like you guys to stay home from school. I spoke to your teachers and headmasters, too. They will email homework. Please stay off the internet, especially social media. We have a lot of work to do, but it will be worth it when Mom walks through the door with a big smile on her face."

18

I ARRIVE AT the pre-trial unit of Bayport, a correctional institution for female offenders in Framingham. I'm on the second floor of the health admissions building. That's all I'm capable of knowing for sure. The rest is a slow-moving fog of linoleum floors, white walls and blue doors. A corrections officer behind a plexiglass window is yelling instructions at me. I can't keep up, and I'm not moving fast enough for her, so she yells louder.

However, the worst is yet to come. The female guard assigned to get me through processing looks like she feels sorry for me, but the pity disappears quickly. Maybe I imagined it. She records information regarding my case. My property is searched, a small leather handbag holding my wallet and some makeup items. I take off the earrings I wore to court. The guard looks at my hand. "The rock comes off, too."

I hand over my wedding and engagement rings. My brain goes into survival mode and finds a way for me to deal: numbness. The guard sends me behind a plastic shower curtain and instructs me to strip. She photographs my naked body. I'm asked to hold my arms up and open my mouth while the guard pokes around. She asks me to squat, spread my cheeks, and cough.

I'm weak with humiliation and don't have the strength to cover up my body with my hands. I must shower, but not before throwing up in the sink. Afterward, I receive my new belongings and change into the prison-issued uniform: blue shirt with matching pants and a white t-shirt. I'm issued a military-style blanket, sneakers that are too big, a towel, soap, toothbrush, toothpaste, cheap bra and panties, and a comb.

I'm escorted to my cell, where I already have a roommate. I must look a fright to her.

"It ain't that bad. Takes a few days to adjust, that's all."

She's a few inches taller than me, but everyone is. Long, brown, wavy hair; large, brown, glazed-over eyes; lashes for miles; too skinny. Looks like she's in a perpetual state of misery. That's going to be me if I don't get out of here soon. I collapse on the bottom bunk with the thin cheap mattress. I didn't even ask her name or which bunk was hers.

ABBIE'S FRIENDS, WHO lived in the dorms, had agreed to check in via video chat. The quartet included Anastasia Cruz, who hailed from Columbia, a Selena Gomez look-alike from a soccer-obsessed family. Callie Furi, a free-spirited California girl who was not blonde and didn't care for sand and surf (Abbie's mom said Callie resembled a young Elizabeth Taylor), and Frances Lin, a first-generation Chinese American, who had an opinion on everything, like Abbie did. Abbie was black and the only local girl in the group. They called themselves the Rainbow Posse because of their diverse ethnic backgrounds.

"Dish," Frances ordered. "What's going on with your mom?"

"It's not good, ladies. They took her to jail today."

"What?" they asked in unison, eyes bulging from their sockets.

Abbie adjusted the computer on her lap. "She told my dad not to post her bail."

"That makes no sense," Anastasia blurted out. "It must be a conspiracy, and the real killer is behind it."

"Yeah," Frances chimed in. "No way, Mrs. Cooper is a murderer. Somebody set her up. But what kind of psycho would do something like that to her?"

Abbie shook her head and kept her suspicions about the stalker to herself. "I don't know, Frances. I'm freaking out and so is my brother."

Tears pooled in Callie's eyes. She sniffled and looked away for a brief moment. Anastasia squeezed her hand. Then all three, their faces solemn, stared back at Abbie from the screen.

"What does your dad say?" Frances asked.

"He's in shock, like we all are. He says he got the best lawyer for Mom, and he'll hire his own private investigator, but I don't know if it'll be enough. If somebody went to all that trouble to set her up, he won't make it easy to get caught."

"They always make a mistake," Callie said. "On all the TV crime shows, the killer slips up just once, and that changes everything."

"Callie's right," Frances said. "It takes a lot of work to set up somebody. There's a clue out there that could turn everything around."

"Don't be sad, Abbie," Callie said. "You have to believe they'll catch the real killer. A positive attitude is half the battle."

"Thank you, guys. I appreciate the support."

"Are you coming to school tomorrow?" Anastasia asked. "A couple of reporters came snooping around yesterday. Ms. Winthrop kicked them out."

"I don't know. My dad wants to keep us home for a few days until the craziness dies down a little. There are still reporters hanging out in the area, trying to get the neighbors to say something that will make the evening news."

The girls talked for a while longer, about classes, the upcoming Platinum Ball, and how ridiculous the amount of homework was. After they signed off, Abbie called Ty. She needed to hear his voice.

"Check your email," he said.

"Why?"

"Just check. I'll hold."

Abbie accessed her email from her phone and saw a message from Ty. When she opened it, a meme of a roaring tiger appeared with the caption: *Because You're Fierce!* Abbie bolted to the bathroom and locked herself in. She sat on the cold tile floor, leaning up against the tub for support.

"Cooper, are you there?"

She couldn't answer because she was crying so hard, convinced one of the blood vessels in her eyes would pop. But sweet, wonderful, supportive Ty understood the state she was in and stayed with her on the line, soothing her battered soul.

19

THE EARSPLITTING SOUND of an announcement over the PA system ricochets off the walls and shocks me into consciousness. I slowly open my eyes to find out what the ruckus is about. The air smells of stale urine and something rancid I can't identify. I sit up and take in my surroundings, and it all comes flooding back to me. The nightmare is real. *I am in a jail cell.* The steel bars. Ugly gray walls, toilet, sink. The woman I met yesterday, my new roomie, is staring at me like some strange specimen under a microscope.

"You're one of them college girls, ain't you?" she asks.

My eyes are sore and tired from crying. If I'm going to survive in here, I have to make friends. Isn't that what's portrayed in all the prison movies?

"What's your name?" I ask, sitting up.

"Elsa."

"Why are you here?"

She's confused by the question.

"What are you in for?" I ask.

She looks up at the ceiling, then back at me. "What you wanna know for?"

"Just making conversation."

"None of your business then."

"Okay. What's with the noise?"

"That's our own personal fancy alarm clock."

"Well, it's obnoxious."

"Better get used to it."

"Why? I'm innocent."

She laughs at me, showing yellow, rotting teeth. If I had to guess, I'd say she was in for dealing crystal methamphetamine. Or maybe I've watched too many crime dramas on TV.

"Why is that funny? I *am* innocent. Do I look like I belong here? What do you think I did? Don't answer that." I'm bombing here. "You have kids?" I ask, eager to change the subject.

"One."

"I have two. A husband. A dog. A nice house."

Wretchedness puts me in a chokehold. Saying it out loud draws a sharp contrast to what my life was and what it is now. I am an inmate, a number in the system. I belong to the Commonwealth. Until they find Alessandro's killer, I'll be told when to wake up, when to eat, when to go to sleep, when I can have visitors, when to go to the bathroom. Suddenly, my head spins. Heartbreak. Despair. Then blackness.

JASON LED DETECTIVES Eric Van Dorn and Tess McCall to the living room. He had a raging headache that wouldn't quit, and he had barely slept since Shelby's arraignment. He ran on fumes and was in no shape for police questioning, but he wanted it over with and to cross it off his growing to-do list. It was ten o'clock, the morning after the arraignment. A shaft of sunlight pierced the window. The sun must not have received the memo about his current mood. Or maybe it didn't care.

Van Dorn's sharp gaze meandered around the space, and Jason could see his mind running like a calculator. McCall was younger and intense, with a wide-legged stance. She looked like she wanted to string someone up by their eyelids.

The detectives sat next to each other on the sofa, and Jason took the armchair opposite them. McCall wasted no time.

"How well did you know Mr. Rossi?"

"I didn't. He was my wife's physical therapist after she suffered major injuries from a motorcycle crash."

"When was that?" Van Dorn asked, producing a pen and a small notebook from his jacket pocket.

"Earlier this year. Late winter."

"Can you be more specific?" McCall asked.

"I'll get back to you on exact dates. The insurance company would have the records of her treatment, and the names of Mr. Rossi's staff at the center."

Jason stretched out his legs and relaxed his body. He was dressed in black from head to toe. It was appropriate, though his wardrobe choice had not been deliberate. Jason chose to have the detectives question him without his attorney present. He had nothing to hide. He wanted to be accessible to the investigation but wasn't about to allow them to railroad him, either.

"When was the last time your wife had contact with the victim?" Van Dorn asked. An unspoken agreement had apparently passed between the two detectives. Van Dorn would take the lead for now.

"As I mentioned, her therapy went on for most of the spring. Occasionally, she mentioned running into Mr. Rossi at the store. Nothing worth thinking about."

Van Dorn asked, "Did Mrs. Cooper exhibit any strange behavior or change her routine in any way? Anything seem to be bothering her in the weeks leading up to the murder?"

Jason reached back into his memory bank. That night at Pennybaker's back in late October, Shelby was jumpy. She spilled her drink all over the table and left for a long bathroom break. But he wasn't about to mention it to the detectives.

"No. Nothing changed about her behavior or her routine."

McCall crossed her legs, her eyes two orbs of hot coals. Van Dorn stroked his chin and concentrated on something he had written in his notebook. This must be their good-cop-bad-cop routine.

"Where were you between the hours of 11:00 a.m. and 3:00 p.m. on the day of the murder?" McCall couldn't help herself.

"In my office. Several individuals can vouch for my whereabouts. I was also on the phone with my wife when state police first pulled her over."

That nugget of information animated the investigators. Van Dorn pounced. "Is that so? Care to tell us what you talked about?"

"Shelby was afraid, distraught. She didn't know why she was pulled over. She asked me to stay on the phone with her."

"We'll look into her phone records," McCall said.

"You do that," Jason snapped.

Van Dorn shifted around in his seat. "Your wife must have spent a lot of time with the victim because of her therapy. Would you say they were close?"

"I'm not sure what you're getting at, Detective. Are you close with your doctor or any other person who provides a service to you?"

Van Dorn grinned. "Touché. But did your wife have a relationship with Mr. Rossi, outside of therapy?"

"Are you asking me if my wife was having an affair? That's outrageous, and I resent the question."

"No need to get bent out of shape, Mr. Cooper. No one said anything about an affair. People get close when they spend a lot of time together. Sometimes it's sexual, and sometimes it isn't. Just trying to cover all the angles here. Nobody's accusing your wife of anything."

"It sounded like you were."

McCall wasn't about to let it go. "Did you and your wife

have any marital problems?"

"No."

"Didn't she file for divorce at the beginning of the year but then withdrew the petition?"

"That was a lifetime ago." Jason sighed heavily, annoyed by the line of questioning. Then he said, "Every marriage has challenges. We worked things out."

"Did Dr. Cooper have any enemies or anyone she may have angered or had a beef with?" Van Dorn rejoined the interview.

"No. Everybody likes Shelby."

"Any gambling problems, debt, financial issues?"

"None."

Van Dorn appraised the living room again. His eyes landed on the baby grand piano off in the corner near the window. He moved on to the expensive art lining the walls, pieces Vivian had recommended and bought at auction. He looked up at the coffered ceilings, the crystal chandelier, and finally the fieldstone fireplace before he flipped another page in his notebook.

"I see. Did she have many friends?"

"A few, mostly the women in her motorcycle club. Her best friend, Vivian, lives in Chicago."

"We're going to need all their contact information and addresses," McCall said. Jason ignored her.

Van Dorn flipped through his notebook again. "You're currently the chief financial officer at Orphion Technologies?"

"That's correct."

"I hear the company is going public soon. Should I buy some stock?"

Jason looked at him, expressionless and silent.

Van Dorn cleared his throat, mostly out of embarrassment, and McCall jumped in. "Rumor is that you're the next CEO of Orphion. Your wife's arrest must put a damper on things."

"No, it doesn't," Jason responded, his voice flat. "Whether I become CEO is irrelevant right now. Next question please," he said, looking at his watch. "I have somewhere I need to be."

"We're trying to establish a motive here, Mr. Cooper," Van Dorn said. "By all accounts, Alessandro Rossi was a good man and had no known enemies. It seems odd that someone would kill him so violently. Aren't you at all concerned that the police found his body in your wife's car?"

"Not at all. Whoever is setting up my wife obviously put it there. Do you honestly think a person of her size and height could put a dead body in the trunk of a car?"

"Maybe she had help," McCall offered.

Jason ignored her again and abruptly ended the interview. "Detectives, I really must go. If you have additional questions, please call me. I'm even willing to come down to the station and save you the trip."

"Can we look around a bit?" McCall asked.

"Not without a warrant, you can't."

"Okay. We'll get one, then."

Jason knew a warrant to search the house was already in the works and could be executed later in the day. But he'd had all he could take. Everyone stood.

"If you think of anything, call me," Van Dorn said, handing Jason his business card. McCall didn't bother. Jason escorted them out of the house, knowing this was only round one.

20

LATER THAT DAY, a uniformed guard behind the desk of the pre-trial unit of the Bayport Women's Correctional Facility took Jason's driver's license and asked him to empty his pockets. A pudgy, frowning guard searched him.

Jason had done his research on visitor policies for the prison. The cell phone stayed in the car. He adhered to the clothing rules as well, wearing a simple sweater, jeans, and sneakers. After a pat down, another unsmiling guard ushered him into the visitors' room, a sparsely furnished area with white plastic chairs, tables, and a soda and snack machine along the wall. There was only one other visitor waiting for an inmate. Jason pulled up a chair. His nerves were on the verge of shattering.

When Shelby appeared, it took all the energy he had not to fall apart. She'd only been in for twenty-four hours, but jail had already taken a toll on her. Dark circles shadowed her large, sable brown eyes, which looked like enormous pools on her oval face. She wore a hideous prison uniform, many sizes too big for her tiny frame. She looked so out of place.

Shelby pulled up a chair. Three uniformed guards lurked strategically around the room.

"Not exactly couture, but it will have to do," she said, pointing to her prison-issued uniform.

He was glad she could joke about it because he couldn't. "I have a million questions. Has anyone threatened or mistreated you? What are you eating? What do you need? I'll get it for you. I don't care if Alan has to throw his weight around or ruffle some administrative feathers, whatever it is…" He trailed off to catch his breath.

"It's not pleasant in here, but that's the point. It's scary and depressing, and I just want to come home."

Jason curled and uncurled his fingers, desperately trying not to reach out and touch her, which was against the rules.

"How are the kids?" she asked. "What is this doing to them?"

"It's hard. Miles is confused. He doesn't understand why you're here when you didn't do anything wrong. He cries at bedtime. Abbie, well, you know our daughter. She's angry and scared. She's playing tough, mostly for my benefit. Abbie thinks it's her job to keep the family together until you get home."

"She told you that?"

"No. She didn't have to. She's been spending more time on the phone with Ty than she does her girlfriends."

Shelby smiled. And for a fleeting moment, it felt to Jason like their usual end-of-day conversation at home, about the children, work, things that might be bothering them, something funny that happened that day. But the harsh arm of reality promptly slapped him silly.

"What's so funny?" he asked Shelby.

"Abbie and Ty. She's falling for him. Hard."

"When did this happen?"

"It's been building for a while. But she would rather die than tell him."

Jason smiled, too. He knew this day would come, but he always thought Shelby would be there to help Abbie navigate the trials and tribulations of first love.

He said, "She could do worse. Ty is a good kid."

"I told her the same thing. Just focus on the kids, Jason. I don't want you worrying about me in here. Let Alan do his job. You need to be strong until I can come home."

He had to ask the question that had been burning a hole in his brain since the arraignment. Two questions actually. "What happened in court, Shelby? We could afford the bail, so why did you choose to be here instead of home where you belong?"

"It's better that I'm in here. As long as I am, and Alan is working to prove I didn't kill Alessandro, everything will be fine."

Her response bewildered him. Jason rubbed his temples with both hands. "What are you talking about? Did somebody threaten you? Do you know who killed Alessandro Rossi?"

"Let it go, Jason. Job one is keeping the kids safe and happy. That will help me survive in here until they find the real killer."

Someone or something has a grip on her so tight she actually believes it's better for her to be in here. How am I supposed to break through that wall?

"It's also my job as your husband to protect you. How can I do that if you won't tell me what's going on?"

He had to press a bit more. The mist gathering in her eyes said it wouldn't take much for her to crack.

He lowered his voice. "What is it, baby? Please tell me. If it's something you don't want Alan to know, it will be our little secret. We'll figure out another way to get you out of here."

Shelby hesitated. Then she said, "I may have stuck my nose in where it didn't belong, and the person got even."

"What are you talking about? Who is this person?"

Shelby sighed loudly. Jason braced himself. "Alessandro's wife used to beat up on him. A bad case of domestic abuse."

Jason leaned back in his chair. That was not what he'd expected to hear, not that he had any clue what was about to come out of Shelby's mouth.

"That's awful. How did you find out?"

"He told me."

Jason had heard of Battered Husband Syndrome, but why would his wife know such intimate details about the life of a man she only saw for health reasons?

"I feel terrible about what happened to him, but confiding in you about his domestic problems was crossing the line."

"He needed somebody to talk to. I had therapy every day until I recovered from the accident. We talked. That's a difficult burden to carry, and he needed a listening ear. Nothing strange about it."

Her explanation sounded plausible, but something was missing.

"So he felt comfortable revealing his darkest secret to a married woman he barely knew? Why not one of his employees or a friend? Why did he pick you?"

Shelby looked down at her hands, unable to meet his gaze. Her body language spoke volumes, and Jason didn't like what it was saying. His anxiety radar went into overdrive. The wool sweater he wore itched. Jason would rather stay in the t-shirt worn under the sweater, but trying to remove the sweater might set off the armed guards. Not a good idea, after all.

"I don't know why he picked me," Shelby said. "But one day last month, I saw proof of what he had been telling me all along."

Jason let out a puff of air after Shelby told him the story of how Alessandro's wife attacked him in the Whole Foods parking lot, and how she tried to stop it.

"You think she had him killed, then put the body in your car as payback?"

Shelby nodded.

Jason pondered that for a moment. A wife wanting to get rid of her husband does so and frames someone else for it, because that someone threatened to report her for domestic abuse. The theory had some teeth, but it still didn't explain the larger, more pressing issue at hand.

"That still doesn't explain why you didn't want me to pay your bail. Why are you sabotaging your freedom, dragging the family through this nightmare? Why won't you come home, Shelby? What's keeping you here?"

"I love you, Jason. Kiss the children for me."

She tried to end the conversation, but he wasn't quite done with her. "Who called you at Pennybaker's the other night?"

"Vivian. Like I told you then."

"I love you, too. But I don't believe Vivian called you that night."

AFTER JASON LEAVES, I slink back to the concrete box I now call home. If only he knew how badly I want to go home, to hold my children, to sleep in my own bed in his strong, soothing embrace. To be free, to do all the things I took for granted before coming here.

I won't ask Jason to bring me pictures of the family to keep me going, however. I'll find the strength to survive so I can spit in the face of the monster who's determined to break me. Reaching under the thin mattress, I remove the note that came in today. Corrections officers can only read incoming mail if there's a "Mail Cover" placed on it. That's usually used to track organized crime or gang members. My stalker is meticulous in his research and knows how the system works. From now on, whenever I feel my spirit waning, I'll whip out the typewritten letter.

Dear Shelby,

Abigail and Miles are such wonderful children. I know how devastated you would be if any harm came to them. Your continued cooperation will ensure their safety. Any attempt on your part to undermine this process will have grave consequences.

On the other side of the letter are two 3D hand drawings of coffins, labeled with my children's names.

21

AFTER ABBIE SAID good night to her grandma and her brother, she went to find her dad. He wasn't in the master suite, and she figured right when she found him in his study, on the sofa, staring into space.

"Dad?"

Abbie sat down next to him. He wouldn't look at her at first. She knew he was trying the tough-guy act because he didn't want her to know he was falling apart. But she liked this side of him. It showed Abbie how much her father adored her mother, and that made her feel secure.

"Dad, it's going to be okay. Mom is strong. And stubborn."

He turned to look at her. "When did you get to be so smart?"

"I've always been smart, Dad. It's in the genes."

He chuckled and kissed her forehead. "So you don't think I'm lame for sitting here, barely functional?"

"No. Your wife is gone, and you don't know when she's coming back. That's serious, Daddy. What did Mom have to say for herself anyway, about why she refused bail?"

"She only said it would be better if she stayed in jail until the police find the killer, and that I should focus on you kids."

Abbie shivered. "What is it, sweetheart?" her dad asked, his tone sharp. "Do you know something? Do you know why your mother refused bail?"

She wouldn't say anything. Keeping her mouth shut about the stalker was the only way to make sure things didn't get worse for the family, although she couldn't see how they could. Abbie stared at her dad, wide-eyed and tongue-tied. He placed his hands on her shoulders and searched her face. "Don't be afraid, sweetheart. Whatever it is, you can tell me."

"I don't know anything, Dad."

"Are you sure? For a moment there, it looked like you thought of something that could be helpful."

"I got nothing. This whole mess is one big jigsaw puzzle. We're all trying to understand how the pieces fit."

"You would tell me if you knew something, right? If someone reached out to you or you heard something?"

"I would, Dad. For sure."

Abbie needed to get out of there. She hugged her father tight and bid him good night. He was the only parent she had for now. She returned to her room.

Abbie had left her phone charging on the nightstand. She peeked at it before climbing into bed and immediately regretted the decision. A series of text messages appeared on the screen.

(Unknown) I know you're hurting. Consider me a friend.

(Unknown) Your mother is a deceiver. That's why she's in jail. She won't tell the truth.

(Unknown) I know you understand. You're smart.

(Unknown) Are you there? I know where to find you.

The phone trembled in Abbie's hands. Of course, he knew where to find her. He knew her cell phone number, where she lived, and probably what she had for breakfast every morning.

Abbie hated feeling trapped and helpless, like some evil, invisible puppet master controlled her life. Her fingers typed fast before fully formed thoughts escaped her brain.

(Abbie) Is this how you get off? Scaring children?

(Abbie) You're disgusting. Die already and leave me alone.

She climbed into bed, pulled the covers up under her chin, and ignored the droplets hitting her pillow.

"WHY ARE YOU jumpy?" Mia asked. "Did you do something you weren't supposed to?"

"Of course not," the man said, adjusting his glasses. "I didn't see you coming, and when you got into the passenger seat, it startled me. It's dark out and no one's around."

He's afraid of me. Good. Mia arranged for them to meet in the abandoned lot behind Henry's Steak House in Framingham.

"First, congratulations are in order. You're competent after all."

He beamed at the compliment.

Mia said, "The hard part is over. The rest should be easy."

"The rest?" The man repeatedly adjusted his shirt collar.

"Yes. You didn't think this was it, did you? I didn't spend two years planning this just to walk away after the hard part was over. The next phase is just as important, if not more so. It's what I've been working toward all this time."

"I see."

"Do you? I'm finally about to have everything I want. Now that the imposter is out of the way, it's time to ramp it up with the rude teenager."

"Abigail?" Trepidation rang in his voice.

"What, do you have a thing for her? Touch her and I'll bash your head in," Mia threatened.

"No, that's not it. Just wondering if this is the best way to get the results you want. She's determined. Angry. Defiant. She won't easily break."

"I'll deal with her petulance when the time is right. Keep up the pressure."

Shame, shame, shame. She's not stupid, you know.

It was that damn old woman again. "Why can't you just stay dead?" Mia shouted.

"I beg your pardon?" The nervous man practically bolted from his seat.

"Not you. It's the old woman who won't shut up."

"What old woman?"

"Get out of the car."

"But it's my car."

"Okay. You can stay. Do you have questions? You know what needs to be done?"

"Aren't you afraid Abigail will tell her father we've been communicating?"

Mia took a long, exasperated breath. "Sometimes, you're so useless. She's a child. How hard is it to message her and keep her frightened? Must I do all the hard work? Her mother is already in jail for murder. She's scared to death. Don't you think she would have already told her father if she was going to rat you out? She's afraid she'll end up as dead as Alessandro Rossi if she says anything. Keep up the pressure. And if she gets out of line, you know what to do. Are you clear now?"

"Yes."

"Good. And don't screw up. For your sake."

22

ALAN ROSE IS not a man to beat around the bush, one of the qualities about him I admire most. I pull out the chair across from him in the tiny, claustrophobic room with bare walls and no personality, the room set aside for inmate meetings with their attorneys. The furniture is minimum: a table and two chairs.

"Help me keep you out of prison," Alan says. "And in case you forgot, anything you tell me falls under attorney-client privilege. I can't be forced to disclose any of our communication, not even in the court of law."

I take a deep breath as my heart beats wildly. "What happened?"

Alan removes a folder from his briefcase and hands me several sheets of paper. A quick scan reveals they're my cell phone records.

"What am I supposed to be looking for?" I ask.

"Look for the incoming call to your cell phone on October 28 at 5:23 p.m."

I peek at the number. How could I have been so careless? How could he have been? We were always meticulous, no calls on private cell phone numbers, only the burner phones.

"I can see why this looks bad."

Alan says, "Until now, the district attorney couldn't connect you to the victim other than the fact that he was your physical therapist. This call strengthens his circumstantial case."

Part of me cringes when he refers to Alessandro as *the victim*, as if he was a nobody, some random John Doe. I shift in the uncomfortable chair as Alan waits expectantly for my response.

"We were friends," I say.

Alan remains silent. His stoic expression tells me to continue, and I'd better tell him the whole truth.

"I didn't say anything to you earlier because I thought it would make me look guilty. I'm not. Alessandro called me on the day in question, the date on the phone records."

"What did you discuss during that call?" Alan grabs a small notebook from his briefcase and a pen.

"His plans to leave the country."

Alan's expression hasn't changed. "Do you know why he wanted to leave?"

I don't want to betray Alessandro, even in death, but my future has a big question mark next to it. If I don't tell my lawyer what he needs to know, and the police and district attorney find out, it could be the end of me. I have to play this smart.

I tell Alan about the plan, how Alessandro wanted to protect his children from their abusive mother, the abuse she inflicted on him, how he asked for my help, and that I gave it willingly.

Alan doesn't flinch. He expresses no emotion. His face is as unruffled as his finely tailored Italian suit.

When he speaks, his tone is cool and composed. "The fact that you were helping him escape a violent domestic situation works to our advantage. You were trying to help him, so that makes it unlikely that you killed him. However, you abetted in the kidnapping of minors, a felony." He removes his glasses and places them on the table.

"Can't we argue that I didn't know he was planning on taking his children with him?"

"On a jet chartered for three passengers?" Alan counters.

"Why not? Maybe some friends were going with him." As I say it, I know how ridiculous it sounds. No jury would buy that.

"I need every detail of this plan, the name of the service you chartered, who you spoke to, when and where the plane was supposed to take off, and where it was headed. I assume you used a fake name and paid cash?"

"Of course, I'm not that dumb. It may surprise you what people are willing to overlook for the right price." The statement comes off as bragging. I apologize for the faux pas.

Alan rakes back his hair, then returns his glasses to his face. "Okay. We have an abusive wife and mother, and a victim who was planning to escape. You admit you were friends. I need the names of everyone at the center with whom you had contact while you were in therapy. They can substantiate your friendship with the victim. Without a motive for the killing, there is a gaping hole in the prosecution's case. Did you tell anyone about the plan to help him escape, anyone at all?"

He's asking whether I told anyone, a potential corroborating witness. Only problem is, it's not a good idea to go blabbing when you're committing a felony.

"I told no one."

Alan takes additional notes. Then he says, "There's still the issue of the gun, which the prosecution's case hinges on. Ballistics came back. The bullet that killed Alessandro Rossi came from your gun. They found one set of prints. Yours."

I wince, confusion clouding my brain. How did my stalker get the gun from the glove compartment, shoot Alessandro, and return it to its place? I saw the gun while searching for the car registration when state police pulled me over. The GPS tracker had been removed from the car prior. Unless he installed another one while the car was parked in the garage at work.

"I touched the gun. As I told you when the police brought

me in for questioning, Jason taught me how to shoot, so that's how my prints got there."

I place my face in my hands. One bullet. One set of prints, one gun, all belonging to me. The killer obviously used gloves. I feel that noose getting even tighter around my neck.

When I remove my hands from my face, Alan stares at me. "I know it looks bad, but this is far from over. We can win."

"What's our next move?" I ask.

"I'll file a motion for a pre-trial hearing. I prefer to take our chances with a judge in the courtroom where he or she can decide if there's enough evidence to move forward with a trial. It's preferable to the district attorney convening a grand jury. They're notoriously friendly to the prosecution, and the defense is not invited to that party."

"I see."

Alan asks me a bunch of additional questions about acquaintances, friends, anyone who may wish me harm, and then we circle back to the gun.

"Did you leave the gun anywhere other than the usual place you kept it? Did anyone know where you kept it besides your husband, or could anyone have discovered it by accident? Were there any unusual visitors to your home in the past couple of months, a contractor, a plumber, anybody who would have had reason to be in the house besides family and friends?"

Alan is in lawyer mode, lobbing questions faster than I can keep up. There's no doubt in my mind that the stalker got to my car somehow, used the gun, returned it, and dumped Alessandro in the trunk.

"I know who took the gun," I blurt out.

"Now would be a good time to tell me."

"Someone was stalking me, before Alessandro got killed."

"Is that so?"

"You don't believe me?"

Alan sits ramrod straight in his chair. He swallows, his Adam's apple bobbing up and down.

"Why would you not tell me this from the beginning?" he asks. "Do you enjoy being in jail?"

"Of course not. He said if I told anyone about the phone calls and notes, he would kill my family. I believed him. That's why I haven't discussed the situation with Jason. He'll want to fix it, and I'm afraid it will tip off the psychopath.

"This guy knew everything about me, Alan. Where I lived, my kids' names, and where they go to school. For all I know, he could be watching the house. As long as he thinks I'm obeying his orders, they can stay safe. Unfortunately, it means the bulk of the work to get me out of here will fall on you and maybe even Jason."

"What did this stalker want?'

"He kept saying I had to pay for my sins." I fill in Alan on my history with the stalker: the calls, texts, the photo of Abbie, the notes, and the GPS tracker. Alan writes furiously, like some artistic genius with a sudden burst of creativity.

I say, "Look at my phone records again. He was using a burner phone to contact me. Perhaps more than one, so you can't trace the calls. I had one of the IT guys at work try, and he couldn't get a trace."

"Do you have any idea what he meant by paying for your mistakes?"

"Not a clue. He sounded unhinged, and I thought he had the wrong person. When he started naming my children and my husband, that's when I knew he was serious."

"Do you remember anything about his voice, an accent, how often he called?"

"I detected a faint foreign accent he was trying to disguise. He sounded well educated."

"I need to know when and where these incidents took place," Alan says.

I recounted to the best of my ability the details of the incidents in question.

"I need the name of the mechanic who removed the tracker from your car. We can also get a copy of the service order to substantiate the strange coincidence of being stalked and only days later, framed for murder."

"I remember a guy named Russell because he had a major attitude. He was a jerk, frankly. My mechanic was Dominic. I don't know his last name."

Alan takes a few more notes and then gathers his belongings to leave. He touches my arm. "Don't quit on me. You did great today. But I have one other favor to ask."

"What is it?"

"Don't ever keep anything from me again. It could cost you your freedom if I'm blindsided."

23

DR. SINGER ASKED, "How are you feeling today?"

"I'll be a lot better if you give me something so I can sleep," Mia said.

"Perhaps we can review your sleep journal together."

"How is a sleep journal going to get me eight hours of sleep so I'm not up at all hours of the night? You may as well tell me to count sheep," Mia raged. "I don't pay your exorbitant fees so you can give me pointless exercises."

Dr. Singer didn't react. He never did. Mia had started seeing the prominent Harvard psychiatrist at his home office in Sudbury several weeks before. She had chosen him carefully, not only because of his credentials. After observing him at several lectures and interacting with students, she deemed his persona and appearance the right combination. Grandfatherly, with mostly white hair, kind eyes, and non-threatening. He would make an excellent expert witness on her behalf. His eldest daughter once did a stint in a psych ward, a major plus. *Doctor, heal thine own.*

Mia grinned at her own joke. Her eyes meandered around the room and landed on a photo of Rachel Singer with her parents, younger sister, and brother on a boat on Cape Cod. They looked like the perfect American family. Everything in this home office was perfect: Persian rugs, a large bookshelf, plants, photos, and paintings, even the dog that sat at his feet sometimes. Mia hated that damn mutt. He was always staring and growling at her, so she told Dr. Singer it made her uncomfortable and she hadn't had to deal with it since.

"Well, let's exhaust all possibilities before we go the medication route," Dr. Singer said. "Are you willing to do that? I'm sure you're aware medications don't always work the way we would like them to. If we can get you to fall asleep for several hours by using positive behaviors that don't require drugs, that will go a long way toward healing."

Jerk!

"I've suffered enough. If I don't get some sleep soon, I may not be responsible for my actions."

Dr. Singer leaned forward. "What are you getting at, Mia?"

Oh, you're all concerned now.

"I need to sleep to function properly, so I don't have to listen to that freaking old woman shooting off her mouth. I need to sleep so I can get out of bed in the morning like a normal person instead of wanting to jump into the Sudbury River and never come out."

Dr. Singer wrote something in his notebook. Mia wanted to grab it and hit him over the head with it. Her frustration grew by the minute. She glanced at the letter opener on the desk drawer next to him. Mia was asking for something simple, but no, he had to make it complicated. *Damn shrinks, they're all the same.*

Mia took a deep breath to calm herself. She couldn't go off the rails. There was so much more to do.

When Dr. Singer looked up from his writing, Mia saw concern in his eyes, like she was worse off than he originally thought. She had to offer reassurances. She didn't want him poking his nose where it didn't belong. That would spell trouble for them both.

"I'm sorry. I didn't mean to flip out on you. That's what I've been trying to tell you. Not sleeping makes me crabby. And then I have thoughts I shouldn't have."

"What kind of thoughts, Mia?"

"Like Shelby Cooper deserves everything that's happening to her and worse."

"You're not sympathetic at all? You believe she's guilty?"

"Is there any doubt?"

"How can you be so sure?" Dr. Singer removed his glasses and held it between his thumb and index finger.

"I know her. I told you before what she did to my family."

"You only said that she lied about something, but you didn't say what. Would you expand on that point?"

"She's a thief, a liar, and a destroyer. That's not enough for you?"

"Mia, I'm really concerned," he said, and returned his eyeglasses to his face. "The only way to get to a place of calm and peace is to work through the difficulties in your life. Based on our previous sessions, you spend a lot of energy focused on Shelby Cooper. That isn't healthy for your psyche."

"You know, for what I'm paying you, I'm not seeing results. I expect results when I pay for a service." Mia got louder. "I told you Shelby Cooper took something precious from me, and she's a fraud. How do you expect me to have sympathy for someone like that? She got what she deserved. The only way I'm going to be at peace with what she did is when she's rotting in a prison cell forever and ever and ever. Got it?"

Dr. Singer held up his hands. "All right, no need to get upset. I hear you. Your feelings are valid. If Shelby Cooper hurt you, it's understandable that you would want her punished. But it's for the law to decide her guilt or innocence in Mr. Rossi's death."

"They're idiots," Mia said.

"Who?"

"The police."

"Why is that?"

"It's a straightforward case, but they'll mess it up."

"Have you tried yoga or meditation?" Dr. Singer asked, switching subjects.

Mia looked at him like he had horns. "What?"

"What is your experience with yoga and meditation?"

"Yoga isn't so bad. I used to do it almost every day."

"Why did you stop?"

"Too busy."

"It sounds like it could be a valuable routine to return to. I'll give you a handout and some online resources to get you started."

"You better pray this works."

"Does threatening people get you the results you want, Mia?"

She cocked her head to one side, considering his question. "Some people only respond to threats. If they did what they were supposed to, I wouldn't have to resort to threats."

"Perhaps we can work on a healthier perspective. The world doesn't work that way."

"It does for me."

24

WE'RE OFFICIALLY IN the registration phase of the IPO," Jason said. "After auditioning five investment banking firms, it came down to Goldman Sachs and Credit Suisse. The ball is in your court now, Bruce, to draft the prospectus."

Jason was back in the office for an important meeting. He could have conducted a conference call from home, but he wanted to squash any lingering doubts about his ability to be effective at his job, despite his family crisis. The IPO was the company's top priority, and he would continue to lead the charge.

Jason had gathered the team most intimately involved in the details of the IPO in the executive conference room. He glanced around the table at the company's chief legal counsel, Bruce Cunningham; Susan Crawford, Head of Investor Relations; Will Landers, Treasurer; and Chloe Grace, Director of Financial Analysis and Planning.

"That's great news, Jason, just what we were hoping for," Bruce said. "In anticipation, I already put together a preliminary draft of the prospectus. It's with Charlie now, but I'll send you a copy shortly."

Bruce, a loyal company man in his late fifties with a thick head of platinum-colored hair and a pack-a-day cigarette habit, loosened his tie and poured a glass of water from the jug at the center of the table. Jason tried to squash the anxious thoughts swirling around his brain. The kind that made him feel like a pigeon just pooped on his head and then pecked him in the eye for good measure. *They're trying to throw me out of Orphion, slowly and subtly, so I won't notice.* But he had. There was no plausible reason for Bruce's lack of communication, why he didn't inform Jason that the prospectus had been completed. This IPO was Jason's baby. Charlie and the board had given him full autonomy in its execution. Bruce knew that. He should have taken Chloe more seriously when she tried to warn him things were happening behind his back. He'd been distracted, trying to ensure his wife didn't end up in prison for the rest of her life.

"See that I get that prospectus ASAP, Bruce," Jason said icily. He didn't give Bruce a moment to respond. He continued, "Susan, set up a meeting with Matt and his team in marketing to get those slides ready for the road show. It's important we get the positioning and our story perfect for potential investors. And I'll be attending that meeting."

"Sure thing, Jason," Susan said. She shrank back from the table, as if someone had poured a bucket of ice water down her blouse.

Jason didn't micromanage and knew his staff was proactive. Susan most likely had that meeting already set up, but damn it, he needed to remind everyone he ran the show.

Was he giving in to paranoia? Would the board force him out? Jason's worries weren't financial. He didn't need to pawn Shelby's jewelry collection to keep the family afloat. This was about his legacy.

It was about his children who looked up to him. Being forced to leave a job at which he exceled would have a negative impact on their already fragile psyches. It would signal that their dad couldn't hold on to his job and therefore, couldn't hold the family together. Jason would not allow that to happen.

Will Landers spoke up, bringing Jason out of his depressing musings. He said, "I don't mean to step out of line, but have you considered that your situation could put the IPO at risk? Once the roadshow starts, potential investors might get nervous about investing in a company where the wife of the CFO is in jail, accused of murder."

Jason knew his team had questions they were afraid to ask. He also knew the gossip mill worked overtime. He hoped the news of Alessandro Rossi's murder and Shelby's supposed involvement would remain a local story, confined to the state of Massachusetts, although common sense told him that was naïve thinking. Orphion was a global company with operations in more than sixty countries. Then there was the internet, social media, on and on. Yet, Will putting it so bluntly rattled Jason.

"You shouldn't concern yourself with my wife's current legal woes, Will. As for the IPO, Charlie and I and the rest of the senior management team will do what's best for the company, with the board's input of course." Jason stood. "This was a productive meeting. Thank you, team. I'll let you get on with the rest of your day."

Chairs scraped against the floor, and pens, notebooks, and paper coffee cups were grabbed off the table. Everyone scrambled out of the conference room as if wild beasts chased them. Except for Chloe Grace. In her mid-thirties, Chloe was a bright, ambitious, capable woman who joined Orphion as a newly minted MBA straight out of Babson College. She worked her way up from an entry-level job in the finance department and now reported directly to Jason.

"What is it, Chloe?" Jason asked.

"Watch out for Will. He could be a problem."

"I can take care of myself. I've handled far worse than Will Landers."

"Sorry. I know it was a rough meeting. Coming in here

couldn't have been easy."

"It's my job, Chloe." He didn't mean to raise his voice. There was a lot swimming around in his head. Getting Shelby out of jail took precedence. Then how her supposed involvement in Alessandro's murder was playing out in the press and the impact it was having on his kids, his current job and future ambition to become CEO. This latest face-to-face meeting had been quite revealing.

"The world doesn't stop because I have problems. What I said to Will applies to you as well. You don't need to concern yourself with what's going on in my personal life."

"They're out to get you, you know," Chloe said, blatantly.

"They?"

"You know what I mean, Jason. We need you to guide this IPO and run the company when Charlie retires. You must stay, no matter what they throw at you."

"You're a real cheerleader, Chloe. But nobody controls my destiny except me. Now, I really must go."

"Can I get you anything? I'm heading to the cafeteria. It's lunchtime. I bet you haven't had anything decent to eat since Shelby… well, you know."

He's been living on copious amounts of coffee and not much else. He'd even lost several pounds, which he only noticed because he had to buckle his belt tighter.

"No time for lunch; I'm off to another meeting."

JASON'S OTHER MEETING was a near collision in the hallway with Bob Engels on the way to the kitchen to grab more coffee. "Excuse me, Bob. I didn't know you would be here today."

Bob reminded Jason of Uncle Pennybags from the Monopoly game every time he saw him, a portly man with an untidy moustache.

Bob slapped Jason's shoulder as if they were old war buddies. "These are exciting times for Orphion. Thought I'd stop by to chat with Charlie."

"I'm sure Charlie keeps you up-to-date," Jason said. "And you know everything is running smoothly and on schedule."

Bob dropped his hand from Jason's shoulder. "Do you have a few minutes? I won't keep you. Something has been weighing on my mind. I wanted to get your perspective. Shall we meet in your office?"

Bob sat one chair away from the desk. Whatever was "weighing" on Bob's mind would have Jason playing defense. He took the chair opposite Bob.

"How are you coping, Jason? I can't imagine what this is doing to you and the kids. Abbie and Miles must miss their mother terribly."

In Bob-speak, that meant he doubted whether Jason was focused enough and still capable of doing his job after such a tragic, personal blow.

"Mistakes occur every day, Bob. This is a clear case of wrongful arrest. Shelby will soon be vindicated. Then we'll put this mess behind us and move on with our lives."

"Good. Good." Bob nodded his head as if in complete agreement with Jason.

Awkward silence followed. Bob tapped his left foot.

Jason said, "You mentioned wanting my perspective on something? I have a full schedule planned for the day, so if you wouldn't mind, please let me know how I can help you."

"Of course. I didn't mean to hold you up." Bob stopped tapping his foot. "How would you feel about getting extra help?"

Jason blinked. "I don't follow."

"Family is everything to you, Jason. You're living a nightmare and your children are watching it play out. That's inconceivable to most of us, an unimaginable scenario. It's only right that the board does everything in its power to see you through these tough times."

Jason sat perfectly still and refused to allow a single word to escape his lips. The tactic served him well in negotiations. Say nothing. Your opponent gets uncomfortable with the silence. Then nervous because he doesn't know what you're thinking. When he can no longer stand the silence, he has to say something. He will usually make allowances that benefit Jason's stance in the negotiations.

Luckily, he was fluent in Bob Engels' opaque language: *Jason, you're diminishing the company's reputation with your family scandal and legal problems. It would be best if you slowly faded into obscurity. We can hire an army of consultants to make this IPO happen without you.*

"What I mean is—" Bob scratched his arm like someone suffering from a bad case of the chicken pox. "Your attention is divided, and rightfully so. It couldn't hurt to have a couple of consultants come in to ease the pressure. They would report directly to you, of course."

"Does Charlie share your concern?"

"No. I thought I would run the idea by you first."

Jason leaned forward. "Have you received any complaints about the way I've been handling the IPO?"

"None."

"Good. So what does that tell you?"

"No offense intended here, Jason." Bob broke out his snake-like charm, baring his perfectly bleached and bonded teeth—his wrinkled face the embodiment of sincerity. "It was only a suggestion. We're all impressed with the way you've been pushing forward."

"Your support is touching, Bob. I'll be CEO of Orphion in a year, so I'm invested long-term. We all know how important this milestone is in the company's history."

Bob started scratching again. This time his ears, like a dog trying to get rid of troublesome ticks. Jason mentally prepared himself for whatever would come next, although he couldn't imagine what could be worse than Bob sitting in his office, blatantly trying to force him through the exit doors.

"I have to level with you. There's another reason I wanted to meet privately. Frankly, it's a troubling matter." Bob stopped his itching and focused squarely on Jason.

Jason balled his fists. "What is?"

"A few days ago, I received a phone call. One that could affect your tenure as chief financial officer, not to mention the company. It could bring all kinds of scrutiny, scrutiny that could be dangerous to the IPO. We're already working overtime to minimize any damage caused by your wife's incarceration but this… Orphion will take a serious hit if this comes out."

"What are you talking about, Bob? No need for theatrics. Plain language will do."

"I received a call from one Nicholas Maza. He said his business is real estate and imports/exports, and that the two of you have done business in the past. He made it clear his interest in purchasing a substantial amount of Orphion stock once we set the price. That simply cannot happen, Jason."

Pandora's box had officially opened. Jason wished he could shed his jacket and tie and down an ice-cold drink before he suffocated under the weight of his guilt and shame.

"I don't recall that name, Bob."

"Sure you do. We both know Nicholas Maza's true enterprise is not real estate. I don't have to explain to you what could happen if your past association with him gets out. Do the right thing before it's too late, Jason. Resign from Orphion. Immediately."

25

WHAT IS THIS insanity, Jason? How could this be happening?"

"I don't know, Vivian. It makes no sense to any of us. And what's worse, the media frenzy hasn't let up. This morning I barely made it down the street to drop the kids off at school. News vans and cameras everywhere."

Shelby's best friend, Vivian March had arrived at the house an hour earlier. Dressed in a dark red V-neck designer sweater and slacks, Jason could tell she was falling apart like the rest of his family. Vivian's sweater draped loosely on her body. She was always a thin girl, but the V-neck style of the sweater emphasized her protruding collarbone. Her usually long, elegant fingers looked skeletal, only skin and bones.

They huddled in the family room off the kitchen. "What are you doing to bring our girl home, Jason," Vivian asked?" "It sickens me, thinking about her being in jail. She won't survive. It's like the universe went and lost its damn mind."

"I hired a private investigator to look in places the police wouldn't think to, since they're convinced Shelby is the killer. They searched the house, took her iPad and her laptop."

"I had no idea all of this went down. Why didn't you tell me sooner?"

"I couldn't tell you all this over the phone."

Vivian rubbed the back of her neck, and Jason went to the kitchen, returning with a bottle of spring water he handed to her.

"Thanks. This feels like it's happening to someone else, not Shelby. Did they say why they think she did this? Sounds like they have a case built on nothing but air."

"Well, besides finding the body in her car, her gun was fired. The bullet that killed Alessandro Rossi came from her gun. It was in the glove compartment of her car."

"What are you saying, Jason? That Shelby did this?"

"There's a simple explanation for her prints being on the gun. I taught her how to use it. It's her property."

Vivian took a few sips of the water, then placed the bottle on the large coffee table, strewn with copies of leading fashion and travel magazines. Her eyes lingered. Perhaps it was too much. The reminder of what Shelby's life had been before steel bars replaced glossy magazines in a place where she was treated as barely human.

Vivian asked, "How are the babies doing? This must be unbearable for them."

"Abbie is on an emotional rollercoaster."

"How do you mean?"

"The timing couldn't be worse. She's struggling with romantic feelings for Ty, and her mother isn't here to help her."

"Ty, her best friend?"

"Yup. See how cruel the universe can be?"

"You said it. And Miles?"

"He doesn't understand. He keeps everything bottled up," Jason explained.

"So what's next?"

"Keep pressure on the investigators to pursue other suspects. Get Shelby out of Bayport."

"How can I help?"

Jason pondered the question. He had seen enough true crime programs to know there was always a connection to the past. People didn't randomly frame other people for murder. There was always a personal connection. Yes, Shelby and Alessandro Rossi had a connection, but what does his role as Shelby's physical therapist have to do with this case? Did Jason really know his wife? He mentally scolded himself. Of course, he knew his wife. Eighteen plus years they'd been together.

"Did Shelby ever mention anybody she may have been close to growing up in Louisiana? Before your family took her in?" Jason asked Vivian.

Vivian took another sip of her water and placed the bottle on the coffee table. "I can't think of anybody. You know Shel doesn't like to talk much about her childhood. It's as if that part of her life died with her family in the fire."

"I suppose you're right."

"You think there's a connection to her past? I don't see how. She left Kenner as a teenager. I don't see what that would have to do with what's happening now."

Jason said, "Just grasping at straws, I guess."

"Wait a minute," Vivian said. She stood and folded her arms. "I just remembered something. It was a long time ago, and I forgot about it. Shel only mentioned it once, so I figured it wasn't important."

"What is it?" Jason asked, his voice anxious.

"Mia Lansing."

"Who's Mia Lansing?"

Shel said they used to be friends growing up in Kenner. They went to the same high school."

"What else did she say about this Mia person?"

"Nothing much. She said after a while, Mia stopped coming to school and nobody knew why. That was the end of the friendship

I guess, but she's the only person Shelby's ever mentioned from that time."

Could Mia have information that would lead to Shelby's freedom? Was it too much to hope? One name wasn't a lot of information, but Jason figured it was better than nothing.

26

JASON'S MOTHER FOUND him in the living room, staring at the gigantic painting above the fireplace. "Honey, why don't you go to bed? Tomorrow is another day, and you'll feel better after you rest up."

"I will, Mom. Soon."

"You know, that photo was always my favorite from your wedding," Naomi said as she stood beside him. "The two of you look so happy. The only thing missing is a halo around your heads."

Jason said, "It was the happiest day of my life. No exaggeration. I owe Vivian. If it wasn't for her, I never would have met Shelby."

"So you keep saying," his mother said. Her voice oozed with skepticism. "But fate has a way of bringing people together. What's meant to be will come to pass, no matter what anybody does, or doesn't do."

"I'm just saying Shelby saved me, and she doesn't even know it."

"You never told her about the Mazas?" his mother asked.

Jason moved away from the photo and plopped down on the leather sofa. The threat from Bob Engels had been painfully circulating in his head. Jason hadn't had a chance to come up with a defensive strategy. He knew Bob would make a lot of noise among the board and executive ranks about his latest finding, the smoking gun he'd been looking for to kick Jason out of Orphion. Nicholas Maza handed it to him. But why?

His mother joined him on the sofa and grabbed his forearm. "What is it?"

"It's nothing for you to worry about, Mom."

"Boy, don't patronize me. I'm your mother. I could still give you a good whipping."

Jason laughed out loud. He didn't doubt his mother would attempt to do just that.

"Nicholas Maza is no longer a skeleton in my closet. He slithered his way out, and now he's running around, talking to people he has no business talking to."

Jason filled in his mother on the tense conversation with Bob Engels from earlier in the day.

Naomi sighed and placed her hands on her knees. "I wish your father were here. He would know what to do."

"I know you still miss him, Mom. I do too. But I can handle Bob."

"What are you going to do?"

"I don't know yet. When I took over as CFO, I thought I'd left the Mazas in my rear-view mirror for good. Sebastien Maza was dead, and I figured if Nicholas wanted to expose me, he would have done it decades ago. Once Charlie tapped me to be his successor, I started having doubts again about whether the past would stay there. Now Bob Engels is using my secret to bully me under the guise of protecting Orphion. He won't get away with it. Not as long as there's breath in me."

"That Bob Engels is a disgrace," his mother said. "You've been nothing but loyal to that company, but I guess you're too good at your job. People like Bob Engels can't stand it."

"Jason nodded. "Perhaps you're right."

"But what about Vivian?" his mother asked.

"What about her?"

"Come on, Jason. Crises have a way of bringing people together and not always in a good way. I don't like it, especially given your history."

"You're overreacting. Vivian is looking out for Shelby. As for our past relationship, it's just that—the past. It has no bearing on the present."

"Is that why you never told your wife about the two of you?"

Jason shook his head. "What good would it have done except cause a rift between them? You know Shelby had a tragic childhood. Why would I want to destroy the only familial relationship she has left? Besides, Vivian and I happened before Shelby and I got together. That period in our lives became irrelevant the moment I fell in love with Shelby."

"You're vulnerable now, Jason," his mother said. "I don't want you doing something stupid in your grief. Don't get your loyalties confused. That's all I'm saying."

27

WHAT ARE YOU doing here?" I ask Vivian. I'm surprised to see her. I was certain Jason would have mentioned I don't want to see anyone except him and Alan Rose. Now that she's here in the visitor's room, I'm not sure how to react to her presence.

"You didn't think I would stay away, did you? How could you even think that I would?"

"I don't know, Vivian. Didn't Jason tell you about my bad attitude?"

"He did. But I'm stubborn, too."

Vivian March is the closest I'll ever come to having a sister. We don't see each other as often as we'd like, but we couldn't be closer if we lived next door to each other. Vivian is based in Chicago and hangs out with celebrities and business tycoons, thanks to her high-flying career as an art buyer for the rich and famous.

I barely know what day it is, but by her clothes, I figure it's still winter. Vivian is all about glamor and even when she keeps it casual, the aura of glamor and style are ever present. Today, she sports a royal blue cashmere top with her hair styled in two thick cornrows braided asymmetrically, bringing a more youthful, playful appearance to her flawlessly made-up face.

Despite her bravado, she's stunned to see me in this condition. Hearing someone is in jail and seeing them there are two different things. Vivian's way of dealing with it is to talk to me as if we're home, sipping expensive Bordeaux on the patio.

"I think we should take that trip to Dubai we always talked about, just the two of us," she says. "One of my clients lives there and would treat us like royalty."

"Yeah? An exotic vacation sounds good right now. Not like the vacation in here. Can you believe they don't even have a pool? And no room service? Don't get me started on the accommodations. The thread count on the sheets is in the single digits. No ocean view from the room and no spa. How do they expect people to live under these horrible conditions? It's just awful, I tell you. I'm writing a strongly worded letter to the management when I leave."

Perhaps I took our little game too far; Vivian bursts into tears, then quickly wipes them away with the arms of her sweater, an odd move for her. Vivian is meticulous about her clothes, chiefly because they cost a fortune.

"I don't want you to be sad," I say. "Just look out for Jason and the kids."

"I wish I could do more. I want you to come home so we can resume our lives and forget that you were ever in this awful place," she said, looking around. "You don't belong in here, Shelby."

"How is Jason? I mean really?"

"Barely holding on."

"I figured that was the case despite his protests to the contrary."

Vivian's eyes land on my hands. "Where is your wedding ring?"

"They took it."

"That's just plain wrong."

"It's a prison, Vivian. A medium-security facility for women serving criminal sentences or awaiting trial. I have no rights here. No one in here cares—or believes—that I'm innocent."

My plight slowly sinks in for her. For a woman like Vivian, this is an unthinkable, unbearable situation. If we were to switch places, she would be on suicide watch from day one. She grew up a pampered, spoiled girl with a father who overindulged her and a mother who couldn't control her. Hardship and difficulty are two words she can't spell, let alone comprehend.

"I can't take this, Shel. I can't see you like this," she announces, her breathing uneven as she tries to control her emotions. "Can't the police find the real culprit? What's taking so long? And I don't understand why you told the court you couldn't afford to post the bail. That was a lie. It makes you look guilty, and I want to know why you did it."

I want her focused on keeping Jason sane and making sure my kids are okay. I love her to death, and we have an unbreakable bond, but I cannot tell her the truth. She will go running to Jason, and then my children could pay the price. Over the years, we've kept each other's secrets, but some secrets should stay buried. It's time I end this visit.

"Don't worry about me. As long as my babies are okay, I'll make it. Help keep Jason together. And yes, I will go to Dubai with you when I get out of here."

She cracks a smile for the first time since she entered the visitor's room. "I'll hold you to that. And you're paying for the trip. It's your punishment for getting arrested. Just saying."

I stand to let her know the visit is over. "Please don't come back here. I mean it. I'll see you in Dubai."

She pushes back. "You're scared. Why?"

"What do you mean?"

"I know you, Shelby. There's something you're not telling me."

"You know everything you need to."

After Vivian leaves, I shuttle back to my cell, escorted by my prison guard. Seeing her here, under these conditions, is a not-so-subtle reminder of the twist of fate that brought Vivian and me together. I haven't thought about it in a while, but from time to time, it likes to pay me a visit. Taunting me, taking me back to that day, that place. Reminding me I can never fully escape. That I can never erase the shame that led me to the awful thing I did. Perhaps my arrest and incarceration are the Universe's way of trying to even the score.

28

AL GREEN'S HIT "Let's Stay Together" played on the sound system as Jason slid into a corner booth at Pennybaker's. Long lines formed at the front of the restaurant as patrons waited to be seated. Jason had an all-important meeting with Tom Bilko, the investigator he hired to help with Shelby's case.

Tom had retired from the Worcester police force and became an in-demand private investigator who also had expertise in security. It helped that he had old friends inside a few police departments in the state. At six-foot-five, with biceps as big as a python and a fiery red goatee that said *don't mess with me if you value breathing*, Tom inspired confidence.

"What are your contacts at the state police telling you?" Jason asked.

"Not much. The district attorney has political ambition, and taking down your wife looks good. The case still has holes they need to close, like where he was killed. There's no crime scene other than your wife's car, and no motive or opportunity has been established. Until they do, state police homicide has the case."

Jason said, "I have additional information. I don't know if it means anything as far as exonerating Shelby, but I'm not willing to discount anything at this point."

"Let's hear it."

Jason told Tom what Shelby said about threatening to report Isabella Rossi for domestic abuse. Tom didn't seem fazed at all. Jason figured a battle-worn veteran like him had seen and heard it all during his crime-fighting years.

"Does her lawyer know?" Tom asked.

"I gave him the basics, and Shelby filled in the rest. He's happy to hand the police another suspect, a popular strategy with defense lawyers."

"I'm sure they'll pursue that lead also," Tom added.

"Do you know the detectives assigned to the case?" Jason asked.

"Van Dorn is a good guy. His real gift is looking beyond the evidence. His thinking can be unorthodox, but that's what helps him crack his cases wide open. McCall can be a hothead, but she's a smart, highly capable detective. But my guess is you're not buying into it, otherwise you wouldn't have hired me."

"Nothing against the police," Jason said. "They have a job to do, and I respect that. But I also have a family to protect and an innocent wife to get out of jail. I have to do something."

Tom nodded. "I get it. You must do what's best for your family."

Jason asked Tom for his honest assessment of the case.

Tom lobbed a question at Jason instead. "Did your wife have a beef with anybody? Outside of what you just told me. Something only close friends and family would know about. The more leads and possible suspects we have, the harder it could be to prosecute Mrs. Cooper."

Jason remembered his conversation with Vivian about Mia Lansing, but he wasn't ready to share that yet. He wanted to see where Tom was headed.

"Nothing comes to mind. Why do you ask?"

"They targeted your wife for a reason. People don't drop dead bodies in random cars. We're talking some seriously twisted hating going on, full-on psychopath here."

"I'm not aware of anyone who hates Shelby enough to go to these lengths. It's sick."

"That's my point," Tom said. "To you and me, something might be insignificant, not warranting a second thought. To somebody who's not right in the head to begin with, anything could be construed as an insult or rejection, and they blow it out of proportion. The poor victim usually never sees it coming."

Tom continued, "Maybe in passing, without even thinking about it, your Shelby may have said something or done something to someone. It was no big deal to her. But to the other person, that perceived wrong festered over time. Then, they saw an opening and took it."

Jason rubbed his tired eyes. What Tom said made no sense to him, but neither did the situation. Vivian's parents, Rita and Daniel March, took Shelby in after her parents and brother died in a fire. She had few friends, mostly the ladies in her motorcycle club and a couple of mentors in her field.

What Tom suggested was something far more sinister than Jason could wrap his head around. He was the one harboring a devastating secret that could destroy his family and get him kicked out of Orphion before he could take over as CEO. If Shelby had a dark past, too, he didn't know how he would handle it.

"That's a lot of speculation that produces nothing of substance we can use," Jason remarked.

Tom asked, "How much do you know about Dr. Cooper's relationship with her physical therapist?"

"What are you getting at?" The cops asked Jason the same question back at the house.

"Just covering all the angles. I'm wondering why they picked Rossi to frame Shelby. Don't tell me the thought never occurred to you?"

"I haven't had time to think through anything, Tom. Shelby was pretty banged up after the accident. Couldn't walk for weeks. I give Alessandro Rossi credit for the work he did with her. That was the nature of their relationship."

But you can't say for sure, can you? Jason's spine tingled, and his heart skipped a beat.

"Maybe it's nothing. Maybe it's something," Tom continued. "You asked me to leave no stone unturned, so I had to put it out there. What about her past?"

"I've been more focused on the present. We don't know who's behind this, so I must assume my children could be targets. As for Shelby's past, we met when she was a senior at Duke University, and we've been together ever since."

"I can say from experience," Tom said, "that whoever framed her is highly motivated and had help. It takes more than one person to pull off a crime of this magnitude. All we have to do is find one of them, then watch the dominoes fall."

"Then you and I are taking a trip to Kenner, Louisiana," Jason announced before he had time to think about it.

Tom arched an eyebrow. "The only thing I remember about Kenner is that a plane crashed into the town in the 1980s. Killed all passengers and crew on board and eight people on the ground. Why are we going there?"

"Shelby grew up there. I have a name. Someone who could possibly give us some clues that would point to the real killer if this is connected to her past."

29

"THIS SEAT'S TAKEN," Frances said.

"Says who? I always sit here." Abbie was in no mood for games.

"Not today. Never again," Frances insisted.

"Really? How about I shove this tray of food down your throat," Abbie threatened. "Then can I sit?"

The three girls at the table burst out laughing, and Abbie breathed a sigh of relief. She couldn't take it if her best friends turned on her because of her mother's troubles. The St. Matthew's dining hall buzzed with the usual lunch crowd, students meeting with their advisors, and friends and classmates catching up. Footsteps echoed over the wooden floors and trays clattered on the long wooden tables. Portraits of important alumni and mounted deer heads watched the commotion from the walls.

Abbie placed her lunch tray loaded with a chicken sandwich, salad, and bottled water on the table and then pulled out a seat.

Anastasia wasted no time. "What's new, and how are you doing?"

"Fine," Abbie said, then took a bite of her salad. She knew her friends were eager for fresh details of the ongoing investigation straight from a trusted source, and not from the media reports, rumors, and flat-out malicious gossip.

"My mom is hiding something, and she's scared but won't say why," Abbie confided.

Callie touched Abbie's arm. "This is just awful. Mrs. Cooper doesn't deserve this."

"Yeah. It took a lot of planning to pull this off," Frances added. "It's the work of a pro. According to the news, Mr. Rossi was shot in the head, execution style."

Abbie could always count on Frances to be blunt.

"I'm confused right now," Abbie said.

"Who wouldn't be? It's strange that they picked Mr. Rossi, though," Frances mused.

Abbie's antennae perked up. "What do you mean by *picked Mr. Rossi?*"

"Think about it. There had to be something about Mr. Rossi and your mom that made him a target for the killer," Frances explained.

"You're not making any sense," Abbie said.

Frances leaned in closer. "The killer had to make it look convincing that Dr. Cooper was capable of killing Mr. Rossi. Otherwise, the frame wouldn't work. So the question is, what did the killer know about Mr. Rossi and your mom that no one else does?"

Abbie reached for her bottled water, and in her haste, knocked over the tray. She quickly picked it off the floor. Frances drummed on the table. Callie looked at Abbie, worry etched on her face, and Anastasia chewed on a carrot stick from her lunch tray. Frances broke the awkward silence.

"What's going on, Abbie? Tell us the truth. Do you know who framed your mother and why?"

"No. Why would you ask me such a stupid question, Frances?"

"It's not a stupid question. You just freaked out for no reason."

"I didn't freak out. Stop exaggerating."

"Yes, you did. And you've been holding out on us. You know something, don't you?"

Abbie's irritation grew by the second. "Cut it out, Frances. I knocked over the tray by accident."

"I don't believe you."

"Frances, stop it," Anastasia pleaded. "This is hard for Abbie, and you're not making it any better."

Frances had the decency to look away, embarrassed. "Sorry. I forgot to take my chill pills today."

Abbie didn't want to spend another second talking about her mother's legal problems.

"Have you guys seen Ty around? I haven't heard from him since yesterday."

"Did you two have a fight?" Frances asked slyly.

"No," Abbie answered, twirling her scarf.

"That's why you have on a new outfit, isn't it? You were expecting to meet up with Ty today."

Abbie winced. Though Frances's comment embarrassed her, it was true. She had picked out her outfit carefully: black skinny jeans, a sapphire-blue zip front cardigan in a cute winter floral design, and on her wrist, she wore a simple black onyx and gold charm bracelet.

"Ty and I are friends. My appearance has nothing to do with him. Everything in my life is not all about Ty, Frances.

"You always look beautiful, Abbie," Callie interjected. "Frances, stop it."

"Ty!" Anastasia blurted out. "We didn't see you."

Abbie went still, her heart thumping against her ribcage. Anastasia and Frances sat against the wall, while Callie and Abbie were on the opposite side, their backs to the diners across the aisle. Anyone could creep up on them, and they wouldn't know it. Apparently, Ty had. Abbie hoped he didn't hear what Frances had said about Abbie dressing up for him. She would be mortified and would probably jet out of the dining hall to go die of humiliation in the student lounge.

Abbie turned slowly to see Ty grinning down at her. She couldn't help but smile back at him. At least he wasn't ignoring her.

"Hi," she said, trying to sound cool and in control, and not like the blubbering mess she really was.

"You got a minute?" he asked.

"Sure. I'll meet you down the hall."

After Ty left their table, Abbie turned around to two pairs of brown eyes and one pair of blue trained on her. "Awww," they said in unison.

"You guys make me sick. Frances, take care of my tray, will you?"

WHEN ABBIE ARRIVED at the chapel, Ty was seated already. She stopped directly in front of him. They exchanged no words. Next thing she knew, he stood and pulled her into his arms. She went willingly into his embrace and allowed herself to be caught up in the moment. He felt so good and smelled even better; a mix of musk and exotic spices wrapped in a perfect summer breeze, even though it was early December.

She didn't want the hug to end, but of course, he broke away first. *Damn you, Kerri Wheeler.*

"How are you holding up?" he asked.

They sat on the bench in the first row and turned to face each other. "If my mother goes down for this, my dad won't make it," Abbie said.

"What happened?"

"Dad moved out of the master bedroom. He says it's too hard to sleep there without Mom next to him. He's overwhelmed, Ty."

"I thought he hired a private investigator to help find evidence to free your mother."

"He did, but that can't help him deal with his wife being

in jail. Plus, investigations move slowly, I found out. I've been reading up online on what life is like in prison, and it's awful. Did I mention the police searched the house the other day? And, just to make sure my entire existence is one big suckfest, Mom doesn't want us to visit her in jail."

"I'm so sorry, Cooper." Ty began pacing, hands in his pockets. "This case is strange. The stalker had to know something about your mom, something big enough to kill for. I hate to say it but Mr. Rossi was just collateral damage."

"That's what everyone keeps saying," Abbie grumbled.

"How much do you really know about your mother's past?"

Abbie glared, letting him know he'd better tread carefully.

"I don't mean anything bad by it, Cooper. I'm just saying maybe there's a part of your mother's past she never shared with you. The note said something about loved ones deceiving, right?"

Abbie's eyes popped wide. "Are you saying my mother has secrets and this guy knows what they are?"

Ty nodded. "Something like that."

She stayed silent for a few beats, letting Ty's words sink in. They made sense.

"What a mess, huh?" he said. Ty stopped his pacing and stood beside her.

"I'm scared." Abbie didn't think about the words. They simply came from that place where vulnerability co-existed with raw emotions she tried hard to suppress.

"I know." He leaned over and brushed away her tears with his thumb. "It will get better. You can't quit, Cooper. Stay strong for your mother. Besides, who's going to be my go-to girl if you crash?"

"Sorry," Abbie said between sobs. She wiped away her remaining tears. Ty was right. She needed to be his go-to girl, the way it had always been. But she sensed there was something more behind his comment. Or was she reading too much into it?

"Is everything okay with you?" she asked.

"Fine. I'm worried about you."

"You got all your applications in?"

He stared into the distance, his eyes not landing on anything in particular. "I don't want to talk about it."

Abbie stood and joined him in the aisle. She shook his shoulders. "What is it? Tell me. Why are you freaking out?"

"I'm not. I'm a little stressed, that's all."

"About Yale?" Abbie forced him to look at her. "You'll get in for sure. No one has better grades than you."

"It's not enough. Everyone in our graduating class has good grades, takes a ton of AP classes, volunteers, and plays sports."

Abbie knew the pressure seniors faced to get into top-tier colleges and universities, especially the Ivy League. Ty planned to apply to all eight, but Yale was his first choice, so he applied early action and sent his remaining applications to meet the regular deadline. Abbie knew in a couple of years she'd be sitting in that same seat. Her parents had high expectations. A lot of pressure came from parents, but the school also wanted to uphold its reputation and its high college matriculation rate.

"I get it, but you're putting way too much pressure on yourself. No matter what, you're going to get into a great school."

"Who wants to get into their safety school and not their first choice?"

"Ty, your safety schools are some of the top universities in the world. You'll do just fine. Unless this is about more than college admission. What's really going on?"

"Stop making a big deal about it. Everything is fine."

Everything was definitely not fine, but she knew when he had reached his limit and pushing him would just lead to a fight. Abbie pulled out her smart phone and realized she'd be almost late for class. Christmas was three weeks away. She would have to pray harder than she ever had in her life for a miracle, a Christmas miracle that would have her mom walking through the door and decorating the Christmas tree, baking her amazing gingerbread cookies, and making homemade eggnog.

"What are you doing for winter break?" she asked.

"Heading home for Christmas. After that, the Bahamas for a week, and then I'm not sure after that."

Ty's mother Jenny was originally from the Bahamas and his father Bobby from Guyana. The Ramballys visited Jenny's family home once a year, during the winter. For the first time since Abbie fell for Ty, she wouldn't be seeing him for over a week. Between missing Ty and her mother being in jail, this would be the crappiest Christmas she had ever spent.

"Tell me the truth. Did your parents tell you to stay away from me because of all the news coverage?"

"Cooper, I'm here talking to you right now. No one is going to keep me away from you."

"It's okay if they did. If it were me, I wouldn't want the press finding out my kid was friends with the daughter of an accused murderer. I can't pretend it doesn't hurt because I think your parents are cool. But I understand if they did."

Ty tinkered with a charm on her bracelet. "Stop it. My parents haven't said anything like that to me. They asked how you were doing. They know how I feel about you, so they wouldn't tell me to stay away from you. Even if they did, I wouldn't listen."

How I feel about you?

"What do you mean, how you feel about me?"

"Come on, Cooper. You're my best friend. We tell each other everything."

Abbie felt like a deflated parachute after a landing. Her eyes stung, but instead of letting the tears flow, she faked a yawn and told Ty she had to go. She was late for class.

30

THE PRISON CHAPLAIN is waiting for me in the visitor's room. However, when I arrive, I'm in for a surprise. The chaplain has pulled a disappearing act, and in his place is the pastor of my church, Anton Devereaux. My heart beats like a drum in my chest. *So much for my past staying buried.*

"What are you doing here, Anton?" I ask, my tone measured, controlled. Why pretend the hostility between us is in the past?

He cracks a nervous smile and then rushes headlong into a series of questions and thoughts, tripping all over each other.

"How are you doing? The congregation is praying for you and your family. Some members are even fasting. Has your brother Michael come up from Louisiana to visit you, to offer moral support? How are Abbie and Miles dealing with this situation? What are the police doing to bring the real killer to justice?"

He removes a handkerchief from his pocket and dabs the sweat sprinkled on his forehead. Anton has been nervous around me ever since our old pastor announced his departure this past summer and that Anton would be his replacement. I had to come to terms with the fact that the man who almost ruined my life was now pastor of my church. This was all before my stalking began. Once I got arrested, everything that caused me distress in my life prior paled in significance.

"Tell the congregation I'm grateful for the prayers. Thank you for spearheading that effort. My lawyer is working overtime to get me out of here. No, Michael hasn't come to visit me, and I don't want him to."

"Why not?" he asks, too loudly. One of the guards levels a dirty stare in our direction. He must be having a rough day. The chatter of family and friends visiting other inmates is all around us. There was no reason for the guard to zero in on Anton and me.

"Too painful. You shouldn't come back either," I tell him.

"I can't do that, Shelby."

"The fewer people who see me in here, the better it is for my psyche. Now, if you came to pray for me, that's great. Let's do it, and you can be on your way."

I've hurt his feelings. He silently flips through his Bible. After the shock and rotten coincidence of discovering Anton would replace Pastor Briggs, I did everything I could to avoid him. When services ended, I always had an excuse for rushing out instead of socializing the way I had in the past.

Anton had questions I didn't want to answer, years' worth of deeply buried anger focused on him, anger I didn't want to address. I stopped going to mid-week services all together, further limiting any contact with him. I dodged him for two full months. Now, I have nowhere to run. He has me cornered like a rabbit.

"You took time out of your day to visit me in jail. Sorry I snapped at you. Let's pray that my release happens quickly and the authorities zero in on the real culprit."

After fervent prayers for me, my family, and all those affected by Alessandro's murder, Anton sits still. He's not ready to leave. He's been waiting for an opportunity to get me alone, and he's going to take it. What did I expect from him? Just because he now wears the label *pastor* doesn't mean he changed. For years, I hated him. I blamed him for what happened. I blamed him for using me and then discarding me at the first sign of trouble.

"Why did you choose the name Shelby?"

My mouth pops open. I snap it shut when I realize he isn't joking. He's dead serious.

"You came to visit me in jail to ask me this irrelevant question?" I almost shout the question at him.

"It's a good way to break the ice," he says. "Plus, you've been avoiding me."

"I have good reason to avoid you."

"I'm not that selfish boy you knew. I'm sure you're not the same person you were back then either."

He makes a good point. I'm not about to admit it, though. "Are you sure you're not the same selfish, snotty brat?"

"People change. I've changed, and so have you." His voice is soft, pleading with me to understand. Maybe he had changed. The old Anton didn't care what I thought or wanted.

"Fine. I picked Shelby because my daddy's favorite car in the world—"

"Was the 1964 Shelby Cobra Roadster," he finishes.

I remain silent for a few seconds. Why would he remember that? I figured he'd never give me another thought, let alone remember my daddy's favorite car. Why is he trying to score points with me? What does he want?

"You're surprised I remember that."

"I am. Why do you?"

"I recall everything you ever said to me," he says. "The things that were important to you, anyway. I remember you and your daddy were close. That he owned a mechanic shop, and he taught you about cars and motorcycles. That the two of you would go through his stack of *Popular Mechanic* magazine, and that his dream car was the Shelby Roadster. It was your way of holding on to him? The name, I mean."

I don't want to talk about my daddy or go down memory lane with Anton. If he thinks that'll make me agreeable to whatever he's peddling, he has another think coming.

"What do you want, Anton? Why are you really here?"

He's been waiting for this question from me. He leans in eagerly. "I've thought about you a lot over the past twenty-five years. When I saw you in church over the summer, I couldn't believe it. The least I can do is visit, pray for you. I know you grew up in a Christian home and your faith is important to you."

"How would you know what's important to me, Anton? We knew each other when I was fifteen years old. I'm forty now. As far as I'm concerned, we're virtual strangers."

"Don't say that. I know what I did was wrong, how badly I hurt you. I know seeing me might bring back painful memories. I'm sorry if that's the case."

"I don't think about the past. I leave it right where it belongs."

Anton looks me dead in the face. He knows I just told him a bald-faced lie.

31

JOHN KINGSLEY ACADEMY High School stood on Mascot Drive in Kenner, Louisiana. It was the only high school in town. Jason and Tom agreed Tom would take the lead and do most of the talking when they entered the main office. They timed their visit meticulously, after school was already in full swing but before lunch. Tom found an empty parking spot under a tree across from the high school, a nondescript red brick building in need of a makeover.

Tom hit the buzzer and waited for them to be ushered in. Once inside, he and Jason ran smack into the main office. In the empty hallway, a delivery guy pushed a dolly loaded with boxes labeled B&B Snack Foods. A chunky, tired-looking woman about to bust out of her too-small sweater sat behind the desk, a jar of assorted candies next to her.

"May I help you?" she asked. Her voice wavered between curiosity and suspicion.

"Yes, ma'am," Tom said. "We're looking to speak with your principal."

He pulled out his investigator badge and flashed it. "We're trying to locate someone who was a student here a long time ago. We thought your principal could help."

"Kim, get out here," the woman bellowed. "There are some folks here from up north looking for information."

Neither Jason nor Tom had said anything about where they were from. He guessed Tom's thick Boston accent was a giveaway.

A tall, thin woman with curly gray hair and freckles, glasses dangling from a chain, appeared from behind a desk in the back of the office. Tom repeated their story to her.

"I see. Principal Martinez will be back shortly, but perhaps I can help."

Good, Jason thought. They didn't have to wait for the principal's return.

"We're trying to confirm if Mia Lansing attended this school and if her family might still be in the area. We're talking mid-to-late 1980s," Tom said.

"Oh, that's a while ago. I've been at this school for almost thirty years. Lansing, you say?"

"That's right, Mia Lansing."

Jason wished they had more to go on, but Vivian couldn't remember much other than the girl's name and that she and Shelby went to high school together. It would have been simpler to ask Shelby, but Jason didn't want to burden her with the details of his end of the investigation. She had enough to do preparing with Alan Rose for a pre-trial hearing. Alan got wind of some grumblings from the prosecution that they might try for a grand jury indictment. It would be disastrous if the jury came back and found there was enough evidence to indict Shelby.

"Wait here," Kim said and then left them alone with the welcome committee and the clock ticking away on the wall for company. Jason took a seat, and so did Tom.

The woman at the desk asked, "What did Mia Lansing do?" Jason noticed the nameplate said *Esther*, but that didn't mean it was her name. Maybe Esther wasn't in the office today.

"You know Mia?" Jason asked, his eyes sharply focused on *Esther*.

"Never met her. But I remember when I was still in middle school, my cousin Carly talked about a Mia Lansing who stopped coming to school because she got pregnant. I guess she was too ashamed. She wasn't the only one, but the others continued on with school until they had their babies."

Their conversation was interrupted when Kim returned with an old, tattered folder and wearing her glasses. She opened the folder.

"It says here Mia Lansing attended this school freshman year and stopped coming in the middle of her sophomore year, between 1987 and 1988. There's no record that explains why."

"Is there an address in that file?" Tom asked.

"I can't say exactly, but perhaps she lived on Fournier Avenue," Kim said, with a conspiring wink.

"How far is the town hall from here?" Jason asked. It would be easy enough to go through the property owners' records in the town hall.

"Ten minutes," Kim said. "You can't miss it."

When Jason and Tom returned to the parked rental car, Tom plugged the address into the GPS and headed for the town hall.

"So what do you think?" he asked Jason.

"Don't you find it strange she would drop out of school never to be heard from again, even if she were pregnant?"

"That is suspicious," Tom said. "In my experience, when that happens, it means things didn't go too well for the pregnant teen. There are several scenarios. Maybe Mia skipped town. Or someone forced her to skip town."

"What do you mean?"

"Maybe Mia's parents weren't interested in having grandchildren and told her she was on her own. Or the daddy wanted no part of it and took care of the problem permanently."

Jason winced. "Are you telling me Mia Lansing could be dead?"

"It's a possibility."

32

A SUDDEN CHILL ENGULFED Jason, and he zipped his suede jacket all the way up. It was a balmy fifty-five degrees in Kenner, but he couldn't shake the strange feeling that overtook him as he and Tom pulled up to the quaint yellow house with white trim and a red door at 561 Fournier Avenue. The residence looked like a well-kept cottage with flowers planted in the front yard.

Tom knocked on the front door and waited. Jason looked across the street. A mother pushed her baby in a carriage. The wind picked up speed and knocked over a garbage can. Tom knocked again, harder this time.

"Maybe we should try the back," Jason said.

Tom cocked his ears to the door. "I think I hear someone coming."

A light-skinned black woman with major attitude appeared at the door. She would have been a beautiful older woman, except for the look of barely concealed contempt that clouded her face, as if she smelled something downright foul. Her light-brown eyes showed no warmth. Jason had read somewhere that people with brown eyes were the most fun and happy. He remembered laughing out loud at the absurd declaration. They might as well have said shoe size determined intelligence. The woman's mouth was set in a grim line, as if she found the thought of speaking to them distasteful.

"Sorry to bother you, ma'am," Tom began. "We're looking for someone who used to live at this address, and we were wondering if you might know where she is. We came all the way from Boston to look for her." Tom remembered his manners and introduced himself and Jason. He extended his hand. She didn't take it.

"Anyway, ma'am," Tom continued, "we're looking for Mia Lansing. We were told this was her last-known address. Does she still live here?"

The resounding slam of the door was the only response they received to the question. Tom looked at Jason, perplexed. Jason mirrored Tom's confusion with a furrowed brow.

"That tells me we're on the right track," Jason said.

"She definitely knows something," Tom concurred. "What did this Mia Lansing chick do to her?"

"Only one way to find out." It was Jason's turn to knock. He would force Ms. Grim to speak with him. Shelby's freedom might depend on it.

Jason rapped loudly on the door. The woman flung the door open and spoke for the first time. Jason hadn't noticed before that she leaned on a cane.

"If you don't leave my property right now, I'll call the police."

"Why?" Tom asked.

Ms. Grim twisted her face into a sneer, as if Tom were a moron without any sense. "You're harassing a senior citizen and trespassing."

"What don't you want us to know, Betty Lansing?" Jason asked. "We're just two guys from out of town trying to locate someone and asked for help. But here you are talking about calling the police. You are Betty Lansing, correct, a retired nurse?"

Betty looked like she could topple over and used the cane for support. Jason took a small step forward to assist her. She must have sensed his intention and gave him the death stare. Jason pulled back, raising both hands to show he meant no harm.

"Ma'am, we just want to know if Mia Lansing lives here or lived here. Then we'll leave you alone," Tom begged.

"Mia Lansing was my daughter," she said, and glared at them both. "She's dead. Now leave."

33

MAYBE SHE SHOULDN'T have yelled at him. But Mia was more miserable than ever and getting more depressed by the minute. She was paying her psychiatrist to take care of these problems, and instead they kept getting worse.

Dr. Singer had a cup of tea on the coffee table. Mia said nothing, just sat across from him. For a moment, neither one of them spoke. Dr. Singer's nervousness lay thick in the air. Mia liked that he was afraid. He should be. He sipped his tea, then placed the mug down on the table.

"What do you want to talk about today?" he asked.

Mia didn't respond; instead, she stared out the basement window that gave a view of the frozen ground above them. It was a cold, sunny morning. The sun's rays came through the windows, as if they knew this session needed some brightening.

"Why do you think the old woman keeps appearing and talking to you?" Dr. Singer prodded.

"Because she hates me," Mia responded, without looking at him.

"Are you sure?"

"Yes."

"Are there periods of time she appears more often than others?"

She's trying to get me to back off Shelby. Never.

"When I'm busy, going about my day. She likes to make me feel stupid and inadequate."

"Hmm." Dr. Singer wrote on his notepad. "Does she ask you to do anything?"

"What do you mean? Like tell me to jump?"

"What I was getting at—"

"I know exactly what you're getting at," Mia said. Her voice was low and menacing as she turned to look at him.

His phone vibrated. Dr. Singer reached into his pants pocket and looked at the screen. "Could you excuse me for a moment, Mia? This might be an emergency." He left the room.

The notebook he'd been writing in sat on the desk. She'd be a moron not to go through it. Mia stood, walked over to the desk, and began thumbing through from the beginning. Nothing much. Her name, age, why she came to see him. Boring. But she kept going through his notes. Mia was a speed reader, so she should be able to get through the entire notebook before Dr. Singer came back. Then she hit the jackpot. Or maybe not. Anger swelled inside Mia.

Patient exhibits random episodes of rage and hostility. Could lead to destructive behavior. Feelings of entitlement are prevalent. Has difficulty showing remorse or guilt.

Highly intelligent but uses charm and manipulation to get her way.

Patient is obsessed with Shelby Cooper. Unable to process perceived wrongs in a healthy manner. Antisocial Personality Disorder?

Mia wanted to rip the notebook to shreds. Her eyes fell on the shiny letter opener on the desk. She forced herself to remain calm and kept flipping through the pages of the notebook. More psychobabble.

Patient's lack of sleep may be affecting her ability to function.
Don't think sleep aid will help. Need to dig deeper.

Mood swings, thoughts of suicide, made more perplexing by my the belief patient...

Mia heard a noise and turned around, startled. He caught her red-handed.

"May I have my property, please?" Dr. Singer asked, hand extended.

Mia handed him the notebook without a word.

"Why were you going through my private notes? There are boundaries surrounding the doctor-patient relationship."

"I'm sorry. I thought you cared about me as a patient, but I guess not."

"I do care. I want you to get better."

"So what's all that crap in the notebook?"

"Please, have a seat."

Mia obeyed, and Dr. Singer took his usual spot. "Sometimes psychiatry can be like hunting for treasure. We look at all the symptoms and clues and combine them with our expertise to see if we can pinpoint a diagnosis. Only then can we prescribe a course of treatment."

"I don't think I should see you anymore."

"You're perfectly within your rights to make decisions about your mental health."

"I'll think about it."

Mia didn't wait for a response. She left Dr. Singer sitting in his chair, looking somber.

She banged her hands repeatedly on the steering wheel of her car parked in his driveway. She couldn't trust Dr. Singer anymore. That jerk almost seemed relieved when Mia said she didn't want to see him anymore.

34

THEY'D BEEN COMMUNICATING through instant message using TOR, a program that allowed anonymous communication and prevented tracking. Was it dangerous? Sure. But Abbie needed to be on good terms with the stalker, pretend to be some naïve teenager who was no threat to him and gain his trust. If things got weird, she could always ignore him.

(Unknown) How are you today, Abigail?

(Abbie) Sad. Depressed.

(Unknown) Don't be. Sometimes even the ones we love must pay for their mistakes.

(Abbie) I don't understand. What did my mother do that she deserves to be gone from her family?

He didn't respond right away. The seconds ticked by. Did she scare him off? Pushed too hard?

(Unknown) Sometimes, we don't know our loved ones as well as we think we do. Your mother has destroyed lives. She hasn't been truthful about many things. That's why she's being punished.

(Abbie) What are you talking about?

(Unknown) Goodbye, Abigail.

(Unknown) No, don't go! I'm sorry. I didn't mean to upset you.

But he was gone.

Abbie pounded her fists on the desk in frustration and almost fell off the chair when she heard two quick knocks on her bedroom door. If it was Miles, she was going to wring his neck. She loved her brother to death, but he had the worst timing in the world.

She let out a sigh loud enough to be heard two streets over. "What is it, Miles?"

It wasn't Miles. "It's Dad. I have a surprise for you."

Abbie groaned inwardly. Her dad acted like she and Miles were made of eggshells. He always asked if they were okay, how they felt, if they wanted to talk. They always gave him the same answer. When he wasn't satisfied, he would start mumbling about them seeing their school psychologists or he would threaten to take them to a private therapist for adolescents.

All that coddling might be fine for Miles, but not for her. Abbie wanted to help her father bring her mother home, although she didn't exactly know how she would do that.

Abbie walked over to her solid oak antique dresser and pulled open the first drawer. She found a scrunchy from her pile of hair accessories and pulled her hair into a hurried ponytail off her face. Then she opened her bedroom door ever so slightly.

"Dad, I'm fine. You don't need to worry about me. I won't do anything stupid."

"I know, sweetie. But I thought this would cheer you up."

"I'm really not in the mood—"

Abbie took two nervous steps backward when Ty stepped

out from behind her dad, his grin as wide as the Alaskan coastline.

"Ty, what are you doing here?"

Her heart was doing more back flips than a gymnast. She ripped the scrunchy from its ponytail and let her hair fall past her shoulders.

"I asked your dad if I could come over and help you with AP Biology since I aced it last year, and he said yes."

"I'll leave you kids alone to catch up on your *biology*," Jason interjected. "Ty, remember what we talked about?"

"Yes, sir, I won't forget."

"Good." And with that, her dad disappeared.

Abbie's toes curled. She couldn't believe Ty was here, in her bedroom. He'd come over a few times before, but they always stayed in the family room under the watchful eye of whichever parent was around at the time. Her dad must be worse off than she thought to allow them to be alone in her room.

"Are we going to just stand here?" Ty asked. "What's up with you, Cooper? You act like you've never seen me before."

"Oh, sorry. Come in," she said, opening the door wider. "I'm just really surprised, that's all."

"It smells nice in here," he said, jamming his hands in his pockets as he strolled in. "What is that scent?"

"Jasmine oil. It's my favorite."

Abbie watched Ty take in the details of her room. The ivory carpeting that matched the walls, and for contrast, a burgundy rug at the foot of the bed and matching curtains. The ivory overstuffed armchair and mini sofa had burgundy throw pillows for a pop of color. Her father had painted her dresser ivory with gold floral accents.

Black-and-white family photos peppered the wall, but Abbie treasured three photos in particular. In the center of the wall, her inspiration, Doctor Keith Black, one of the leading neurosurgeons in the country, and chairman of the neurosurgery department and director of the Maxine Dunitz Neurosurgical Institute at Cedars-Sinai Medical Center in Los Angeles. Abbie wanted to follow in his footsteps and even exceed his accomplishments.

The second photo was ballerina Misty Copeland, and the third of Lewis Hamilton, the first black race car driver to win Formula One. Her dad's company was a sponsor at that event last year, and Abbie had been thrilled to meet the British hottie.

"I always wondered what your room would look like," Ty said. "It's pretty cool. Very elegant."

Butterflies fluttered in Abbie's stomach and heat rushed to her cheeks. Mostly because he wondered what her room would look like. Abbie needed to calm down and stop making a big deal out of a casual statement.

"Thanks," she said, and gestured for Ty to take a seat. "What did my dad mean when he asked if you remember what you two talked about?"

"Oh that. He said I should keep my hands to myself, or he would chop them off. I told him I would never do anything to mess up our friendship. I respect you too much."

Abbie forced a smile. "I'm glad you respect me. We wouldn't be friends if you didn't. Does that mean you don't feel the same way about Kerri? Rumor has it the two of you were all over each other at general assembly the other day." She sounded like a jealous idiot, but she didn't care.

Ty stared at his shoes for a beat, then let out a puff of air. "I don't understand what you're asking me, Cooper," he said, looking at her. "What does Kerri have to do with you and me?"

"Nothing. I just thought as your best friend you would tell me you had a girlfriend instead of me finding out on social media."

"What are you talking about?" His quizzical expression told her perhaps she made a mistake in bringing up the subject.

"So, she's not your girlfriend?" Abbie couldn't take back what she had started. The genie was already out of the bottle.

He went quiet, his lips pursed in a firm line, his jaw set. "I like Kerri. We hang out. We kissed a few times, nothing to make a big deal about."

Anger and sadness tugged at Abbie. Anger because he insisted Kerri wasn't a big deal in his life when the evidence suggested otherwise, and sadness because he would never see her as anything other than his best friend. It hurt. The type of hurt that made her want to break dishes, rip things out of the wall, and scratch Kerri's eyes out with a cactus.

Jealousy coursed through Abbie. She wasn't sophisticated enough for Ty. Kerri didn't walk around school with confidence; she sashayed. They were probably planning their perfect little lives after graduation, although according to the spies Frances had all around school, Kerri's first choice for college was the University of Pennsylvania. So what? It was only a four-hour drive from Yale. Ty could be there every weekend if he wanted to.

"I'm sorry," Abbie said, squeezing his hand. "You didn't come here to get the third degree. I don't want you to get hurt."

"I like that you care so much about me. That's why you're going to be a brilliant surgeon one day and a great mom, too."

Why did he say she was going to be a good mom? There was no way he could know. During class, she would daydream about their future together. They would marry right after she graduated from medical school; Dr. and Dr. Rambally, since Ty wanted to be a cardiothoracic surgeon. Three kids—two boys, Blake and Lucas, and one girl, Alexis. Abbie quickly dismissed the fantasy and focused on the present.

"What's that crack about me being a good mom? I don't even know if I want kids."

"You do. And you'll have them," Ty said with conviction.

"What about you? Do you see kids in your future?"

"For sure. I want a big family. Being an only child isn't all it's cracked up to be."

"I feel sorry for your wife, having to pop out all those babies so you can have a sports team," Abbie joked.

Ty's face lit up. "She'll be fine, and love having babies."

"Dude, it's the twenty-first century, and that was way sexist."

He leaned in closer, his face mere inches away. Abbie could feel the heat of his breath on her cheeks. Her brain nearly fizzled, not knowing if she should go with the flow or what. For the first time, she noticed flecks of green in his eyes. Abbie always thought Ty had brown eyes. How come she never noticed that before?

"No, it isn't. Not if we're in agreement. Do you know anyone who feels the way I do about family?"

"Maybe," she said, her voice hoarse. "I might know someone." He was going to kiss her. Abbie's senses crackled like Fourth of July fireworks. She imagined herself just melting on the floor in a puddle of raging hormones.

Ty ran his index finger across her lips, ever so gently. Abbie shuddered.

"Abbie, Grandma's back." Miles was on the other side of the bedroom door. Loud, obnoxious banging followed.

Ty retreated to his corner of the sofa, breaking the spell. Miles marched in, his face beaming with excitement.

"Haven't you ever heard of knocking?" Abbie shouted. She tossed a throw pillow at him.

"I did knock," Miles said defiantly. "Were you guys kissing?"

"No," they said guiltily.

"Yes, you were," Mile said, a mischievous spark circling his face. "I'm telling Dad."

The last thing Abbie needed was her little brother telling their dad something that wasn't true, especially since Dad promised to cut Ty's hands off if he didn't keep them to himself.

"You do that, and I'll tell him you've been sneaking your Nintendo Switch in your backpack when you know Mom told you a million times not to take it to school."

"You won't say anything, will you, Miles?" Ty chimed in.

Miles knew he was beat. "I guess not."

"Tell Grandma I'll be right down," Abbie said to Miles's hunched frame.

After Miles left, Abbie turned to Ty, now perched at the edge of her bed, twirling around one of her stuffed animals.

"I guess we won't have time to go over AP Biology," Abbie said. "That was a great excuse to come over."

"It wasn't an excuse. I really thought you could use my help. I know you're doing well in the class, but I figured I could share my study techniques with you."

Abbie's gaze cut sideways. She said, "Studying, huh? Is that what we were doing?"

"I can't help it when I'm around you," Ty said. "I have to keep reminding myself you're my best friend and I shouldn't do anything inappropriate."

"We have to go," Abbie said, not wanting to go down that path. "If I keep Grandma waiting, she'll come find me and have something to say about it."

Ty stretched. "What's she like?"

"You'll see."

35

GRANDMA NAOMI PREPARED dinner in the kitchen wearing perfect makeup, high black boots, a fitted sweater, and a leather skirt with a hemline that Abbie was sure her dad had a problem with. Abbie helped with dinner: grilled pork chops with green beans and tomato in a chimichurri sauce. Grandma added sweet potato fries as a side dish. She said they could use some comfort food since she doubted Dad cooked anything since Mom left.

After everyone took seats at the dinner table, ready to dig in, Grandma said exactly what was on her mind.

"Stop mourning my daughter-in-law. She's not dead. She's in a tough situation right now, but have faith that she'll come back to us soon. And where is that big old tree she puts up every Christmas? Where are the nutcracker soldiers? Jason, do you think your wife wants you and the kids sitting around acting like people with no hope?"

"No, Mother. I suppose not."

After Grandma Naomi was satisfied with that answer, she turned her attention to her next victim: Ty.

"Young man, you must be pretty special if my granddaughter asked you to stay for dinner. What do your folks do? Where are they from? Do they have a good relationship? That will determine the man you'll become. Do you have any siblings?"

A mortified Abbie came to Ty's defense. "Grandma, stop it. He's just having dinner with us, that's all."

Her dad chuckled, and Miles licked his fork with one hand and stuffed a piece of pork in Mahalia's mouth with the other.

"It's okay, Abbie. Your grandma just wants to make sure you're hanging out with people who share your values."

"Handsome and smart. I like him," Grandma said to no one in particular.

Ty continued, "My family lives in Scarsdale. My mother is originally from the Bahamas and my dad from Guyana. I'm an only child. Both my parents are surgeons at New York-Presbyterian Hospital in New York City."

"That's a long commute," Grandma said. "About an hour?

"A little less than that, but they stay in the city during the week and head home on the weekend," Ty explained.

"I see. So you're not a day student like Abbie then."

"No, ma'am. I live in the dorms."

The clanking of silverware provided a backdrop for the continued interrogation.

Grandma then shifted her attention to Miles. "Miles, how is school?"

"Good."

"And?"

"And that's it, Grandma."

"Are you keeping up your grades? Are kids being mean to you about what's going on with your mother?"

"Everything is okay. Mr. Atkins made a big deal about it in class, so everyone knows they're supposed to be nice to me."

She moved on to Abbie. "What about you? Do you have anything to add to your brother's 'everything is okay?'"

Abbie didn't have a chance to respond. An excited Miles

interjected. "The Platinum Ball is coming up soon. I heard Abbie talking to her friends about it."

Grandma's eyes brightened. "Oh really? I hope you're going," she said, turning to Abbie.

"I don't think so."

Abbie noticed her dad shift interest from his dinner to his mother.

"Nonsense. You're a beautiful, intelligent, special girl, and any young man in his right mind would be lucky to take you."

Abbie tried hard not to look at Ty, who became extra quiet.

"It's no big deal, Grandma. It's not like it's the most important thing in my life right now."

"Sweetheart, your grandmother is right. You shouldn't allow what's going on with your mother to stop you from enjoying high school. She would be the first person to tell you that."

Trust her dad to act like she was some fragile flower whose petals would fall off if he didn't say and do all the right things.

"Even if I wanted to go, I couldn't. The ball is for juniors and seniors only and one of them would have to ask. I don't think they would ask a sophomore."

Grandma scoffed. "That doesn't matter."

"Ty is a senior," Miles piped up, his mischievous grin not lost on anyone at the table.

Awkward silence followed. Abbie didn't dare look Ty in the eye. He suddenly found his green beans interesting scientific specimens. Unfortunately, Miles took the silence to mean he should proceed with his particular brand of eleven-year-old wisdom.

"Ty and Abbie, sitting in a tree, k-i-s-s-i-n-g."

Abbie lunged at him from across the table. "I'm going to rip your head off and then feed it to Mahalia. You know she'll eat anything."

Mahalia placed her paws over her face, chagrined. The threat hanging in the air didn't faze Miles, however. He said, "Everyone knows you're in love with Ty and you write his name in your notebook all the time. You shouldn't feel embarrassed, Abbie. I think Ty will be a great boyfriend. He can play video games with me when he comes over."

Miles looked pleased with himself. Abbie's lips trembled, and she could have sworn she had stopped breathing. Her chest tightened, as if constricted by some giant, bone-crushing snake that lived in the Amazon or someplace like that.

OMG, somebody shoot me right now. My life is so over.

Her father and Grandma gave Abbie glances that said, *sorry your brother just embarrassed you in front of the boy you're in love with. You'll live. We promis*e.

Did they not understand that her brother dropped a nuclear bomb on her life?

Get away from the table. Run!

With no apologies for leaving the dinner table, Abbie upped and left, a stream of silent tears the only witness to her complete humiliation.

36

I'M SURE ALAN Rose's people are all over this, but what's your take on Isabella Rossi?" Jason asked his investigator.

He leaned up against the desk in his study while Tom rummaged through his bag. Tom took out his laptop and booted up. He looked up at Jason.

"Before I went to visit her, I checked out whether Alessandro Rossi made any calls to the police or to 9-1-1. Anything to substantiate that she was physically abusive toward her husband. There was one instance where the police showed up at the house, but no charges were filed. That was the end of it."

"How did Mrs. Rossi react when you brought up the subject?" Jason asked.

"She said it was a misunderstanding and married people have those all the time. Isabella wasn't eager to answer my questions. She said she ran into Shelby a few times, and that Shelby was a little too friendly with Alessandro for her comfort level."

"What does that mean?"

"Your wife bought her twin daughters dolls in their likeness. According to the daughters, their dad went to see Shelby the day before they were supposed to go to New York for a daddy-daughter trip. The day before someone murdered him."

Jason's stomach cramped up. What did this new information

mean? That Shelby was generous? Alessandro Rossi helped her walk again. Jason could envision his daughters hanging around their father's workplace from time to time. That was how Shelby knew them. Buying them those dolls is the kind of thing she would do. She loved children, although for reasons Jason couldn't fathom, she was dead set against them having any more kids once Miles was born. After a while, he gave up on the issue and settled into the family life they had until she got arrested for murder. But why would Alessandro Rossi visit her office?

"How old are the twin girls?" Jason asked Tom.

"Anna and Morgana are nine years old."

"Why would their father tell them he was going to visit my wife?"

"Well, it seems that the girls," Tom said, and punched a few keys on his laptop, "like Dr. Cooper. She bought them fancy dolls. And if they've seen Shelby before, it would make sense that they're comfortable with her and their father knew that."

Tom turned away from the screen and looked Jason dead in the face. "I hate to speculate here, but my gut tells me there was more to your wife's relationship with Alessandro Rossi than she let on."

Jason frowned. "I'm not a fool, Tom. Something is definitely going on here, but I don't like what you're implying."

"All I'm saying is Isabella Rossi doesn't like your wife. She wasn't happy about her daughters telling her that her husband visited Shelby at her office. She wasn't happy about the gifts."

Jason didn't like where this conversation was going. He needed time to wrap his head around those facts. The best thing to do was to change the subject without really changing the subject.

"What about the neighbors? Anyone noticed anything strange going on?"

"Nothing concrete," Tom offered. "The older couple who live next door would only say there's something off about Isabella. That her husband and children seemed afraid of her and she screamed at them constantly."

"That proves nothing other than she may be a terrible wife and mother. It doesn't make her a killer or give us a motive."

"Correct."

"Anything on Alessandro's business dealings?" Jason asked.

"I have a guy working on it, nothing yet. What do you expect to find?"

"I'm not sure. Outside of the fact that he's an entrepreneur and helped Shelby get back on her feet, we don't know much about him, do we?"

JASON WASN'T THINKING straight when he pulled up to the white colonial with the blue shutters in Natick, a MetroWest Boston suburb that bordered Framingham. He wanted to look Isabella Rossi in the face, observe her body language, listen to what she didn't say as much as what she did say. It was an impulsive idea, in the middle of the day, but Jason figured her kids would still be in school, so Isabella might be alone. She could very well slam the door in his face the way Betty Lansing had, but he had to try.

Jason parked on the curb in front of the house and took the path leading up to it. He rang the doorbell and waited. There was no response. He impatiently pushed the doorbell again.

The door flew open. He instinctively knew it was *her*. Isabella Rossi wasn't beautiful. She was stunning. Even with her tired eyes glaring at him. From her delicate bone structure to the lustrous, raven-black hair that hung like a decorative curtain, she was the type of woman people noticed. But despite her beauty, Jason sensed something dark inside her. Not because of what Shelby claimed or because the neighbors told Tom Bilko that she constantly yelled at her kids and husband. Jason couldn't describe it. It was just there, like a force emanating from her.

"Can I help you?" Her voice sounded like tires rolling over gravel.

"Mrs. Rossi, I'm sorry for your loss, and I apologize for showing up without an appointment. But I think we need to talk. I'm Jason Cooper. Shelby's husband."

He watched for a reaction. None came. Then she said, "I know who you are."

Isabella led Jason into the living room. Family photos lined the mantel, with a large, autographed portrait of international soccer superstar Cristiano Ronaldo dominating the collection of pictures. A framed photograph of the Brazilian flag occupied the wall above the fireplace. But no wedding photos, Jason observed. No hand around the waist, smiling into the camera shots. He took a seat, and so did Isabella. Her body language said she wanted him gone as soon as possible, so she would not make him comfortable.

"What can I do for you, Mr. Cooper?"

"Please call me Jason. I'll get straight to the point. Your husband died under horrific and mysterious circumstances and the police think my wife did it. You and I both know Shelby didn't kill Alessandro. I'm hoping you can help me get justice for them both."

"I thought that was a matter for the police, Mr. Cooper."

It wasn't lost on Jason that she called him Mr. Cooper to keep him at arm's length.

"Yes. But I believe in the process of elimination to arrive at the right conclusion, Mrs. Rossi. My wife is not a killer. The police can't establish a motive. Your husband helped her walk again. There is no reason for her to want him dead."

"Perhaps, Mr. Cooper," she said with deliberate slowness, "you don't know your wife as well as you think you do."

Jason fired back, "And how well did you know your husband, Mrs. Rossi?"

She glared at him. “All I know is that my husband changed after he started treating Shelby.”

“Changed how?”

“He became secretive. Started spending too much time at work. I went through his things.”

Isabella let the statement hang in the air. Jason wanted to reach out and shake her. She was torturing him on purpose. He silently counted to five.

“And what did you find?” he asked.

A burner phone. I called the last number that showed up in the log. Your wife answered. I hung up.”

His chest rose and fell with rapid breaths. He counted to five again in his head. Jason couldn’t let this woman see she had disturbed his composure. “How do you know it was Shelby and not some other woman? Have you heard her voice over the phone before?”

Isabella shrugged. “I didn’t have to. I knew right away it was her.”

“You seem sure of yourself. Perhaps the woman on the phone was your husband’s therapist. From what I hear, you had unique ways of keeping him in line. Perhaps he didn’t want anyone, including you, to know he was seeking help.”

Jason let that theory sink in for a moment. Isabella was not amused. “You should leave, now! And never come back.”

37

ANTON VISITS AGAIN. I pull up a chair across from him. We pray. I wait for the barrage of questions. That's the way it's been ever since he started coming. I don't know why I do this with him. Perhaps I'm bored. Perhaps I need to unburden my guilty conscience. Maybe I want him to feel the anguish I've lived with for the past twenty-five years, the kind that visits at night, then visits during the day too, and soon, it follows me everywhere.

"You said we're strangers," he begins. "That's not true. I cared for you. I just couldn't let my parents know how I felt. They would have pressured me to stop seeing you. Then I panicked when you delivered the news. I wish I could take it back, all of it.

"A few days after you told me, I went by your house to apologize and make things right. Your mother said you didn't live there anymore, and I should never come back. I'm truly sorry for the pain I caused you, Shelby."

He insists on digging up the past. Maybe he needs to unburden his conscience too.

"Thanks for the apology. But you didn't make the trip simply to apologize. I have a good idea what you're chasing."

"You do?"

"Yes. It's the question you've been dying to ask me ever since you landed in Framingham and saw me at church. The question you've turned over in your head a million times over the years. You want to know what happened after I left your house that day, don't you?"

He looks down at his hands clasped together. He closes his eyes, as if praying for strength or courage. When he looks at me again, I see my pain meshed with his, a tangled glob of regret and mistakes we both wish we could take back, and of consequences we can't reverse.

His voice is a whisper. "Please, if it's not too much trouble, yes, I would like to know."

"Okay. I'll tell you what happened."

38

KENNER, LOUISIANA, 1988

I WAS HIDING in my bedroom, jamming to Whitney Houston on my Walkman, when my little brother Michael knocked on the door. He was eleven going on twenty. Michael and I hung out in my room a lot. She wouldn't hit me if he was with me.

Michael and Daddy were the only two people in the world who loved me, and maybe Anton, but I didn't think so. Not after what he said. *The jerk!* Maybe she'd stop hitting me once I told her the news. Anything would be better than being hit with pots and pans, shoes, the belt, or the switch. Listening to music was my escape. I could pretend I didn't live in that house, on that street where all the houses looked the same and everyone went to the same church on Sunday. Where everyone gossiped.

Michael walked over to my dresser and picked up the latest issue of *Teen Beat* Magazine, then sat on the edge of my bed and thumbed through it. Kirk Cameron from the TV show *Growing Pains* was on the cover. I untucked my legs from my sitting position and told him to move over.

"Can you keep a secret, Michael?"

"Sure. What is it?" He continued to thumb through the magazine.

"I'm going to have a baby."

His head popped up, and his eyes went big. "You're lying. No way."

"Yes. I'm serious."

He frowned and put away the magazine. "How do you know for sure? Your belly doesn't even look big."

"I just know, okay. I—"

"Mia, open up." It was Daddy knocking at the door.

"Shhh," I told my brother. "Don't say anything."

Daddy walked in with a brown paper bag and a big grin on his face. His clothes were greasy from working at the garage. Daddy was the best mechanic in town and owned his own shop. I scooted off the bed and grabbed the paper bag from him. I squealed when I opened it and found the best bread pudding in Louisiana from the bakery across town. All the kids went there after school because they had the best beignets, bread pudding, and Petit Fours.

Michael and I started eating like two greedy little pigs. We didn't even offer Daddy any. He just stood there, laughing at us.

"So, what are you kids up to?" Daddy asked.

"Mia's going to have a baby," Michael blurted out.

Silence descended on the room. The bread pudding didn't taste so great anymore. I stopped eating and slowly looked up at Daddy's face. Michael ran out of the room, slamming the door behind him. I was going to kill him.

Daddy slowly walked over and stopped in front of me. He knelt down to my eye level. I'd never seen him look so serious and sad.

"Is it true Mia? Are you pregnant?"

I couldn't look at him. It hurt too much. I disappointed him. I looked out my bedroom window and noticed the setting sun. The last rays of daylight burst through my window, like it was casting light on my secret, no longer a secret. Everyone would know I brought shame to my family. They would probably kick me out of school. I started crying and couldn't stop.

"I'm sorry, Daddy. I didn't mean to get in trouble. Anton said it was going to be okay and it wouldn't hurt, but he lied. He said he loved me and wouldn't let anything bad happen to me. When I told him this afternoon, he didn't want anything to do with me. He acted like he didn't even care. I was so stupid. I believed everything he told me. It was just that one time. I don't understand… and…"

Daddy's arms wrapped around me, and I held on tight. My tears drenched his shirt.

"Anton Devereaux did this to you?" he asked.

His voice sounded strange, like it didn't belong to him. I let go of him and still couldn't look at him in the eye. "It was my fault, too. I let him."

"Why, Mia?"

"Because I loved him, and he said he loved me, too, and he would wait for me even after he went off to college."

"This is bad," Daddy said. A deep frown creased his brow. "I'm going to have a word with Anton's parents. He has to take responsibility for this."

I tugged at his arm. "No. You can't. Don't you say one word to him, Daddy."

"What did you say to me?"

"Anton said he didn't want his family name dragged through the mud. You know how the Deverauxes are. They're all hoity-toity, and they could make real trouble for us."

"I'm not afraid of Thornhill Devereaux and his clan," Daddy said. He was mad. I could tell by the way that big vein in his neck kept pulsating. "His son got my daughter pregnant, and they're going to hear about it. They're going to have to deal with it, too."

Fresh tears streamed down my face. I was in full-blown hysteria. Daddy's rough hands wiped away my tears. "Go wash up before your mother sees you."

I opened the bedroom door and ran smack into my mother. I slowly backed away from her and bumped into Daddy. My legs felt like overcooked spaghetti. I glanced at Daddy, and he didn't look so good, either. Mama's face had the same expression it always did when she saw me—all wrinkled like one of the California Raisins, except she never smiled. She wore her nurse's uniform, the white dress with white stockings and white shoes. Her nametag was still pinned to her dress. Betty Lansing, RN.

Some people in the neighborhood claimed Mama was pretty. I never saw it. All I saw was how mean she was. I'm glad I don't look like her. I took after Daddy, who was always kind.

"What's going on? What did you do now, Mia?"

Daddy and I said nothing.

"Girl, don't try my patience. I asked you a question," she said, glaring at me.

I felt frozen in time. My brain wasn't working well. I didn't know what to say.

Daddy spoke first. "Betty, we need to talk. It's important, but I don't think we should do it tonight."

Mama came all the way into the room. "No, we're gonna talk about it right here, right now. What trouble did Mia get into?"

Mama stood close to me and turned my face toward her. "I won't ask you again. What did you do?"

I started bawling all over again, my heart beating erratically. I felt sick. I held my stomach so I wouldn't throw up. "I'm… going… I'm… pregnant."

Mama looked at Daddy and then back at me.

"Anton Devereaux did this," Daddy said.

Mama didn't speak, which was strange, because she was

always yelling and carrying on about something or the other. Because I was looking down, I didn't see her raise her hand. I almost fell when she slapped me hard across the face. It hurt. Daddy caught me before I hit the floor.

"Betty, stop it."

Mama acted like Daddy didn't even speak. "So, now you're the town tramp who got knocked up? You couldn't keep your legs closed after all the talking I did. All the warnings I gave you. I always knew you were no good from the day you were born."

"I'm not a tramp, Mama," I whispered. "I don't sleep around."

I didn't know why, but it was important for me to tell her I wasn't slutty. Anton was the first boy I had ever been with. Mama never thought anything good about me, anyway. It didn't matter that I made straight A's in school and was well-behaved.

Maybe I shouldn't have said anything because she got angry. Her eyes bugged out of her face, and she pushed me down on the bed. Then she started hitting me in the face and stomach.

"Stop it! Daddy, make her stop."

Daddy pulled her off me, and I rolled to a corner of the bed and curled up with my back to her so she wouldn't hit me. Mama was almost wheezing.

"I want this no-good filth out of my house."

"Stop it. You don't mean that," Daddy said.

Mama put her hand on her hips and let out a big sigh. "Okay."

Daddy and I looked at her like she'd lost her mind. She was never this agreeable.

"Richard, I need to speak with my daughter. Alone."

Daddy's eyes darted all over the room. Then they landed on me.

"Are you sure I can't stick around?" he asked Mama.

Mama just cut her eyes at him. When he wouldn't leave, she

shoved him out the door. "Don't make me place that phone call, Richard."

Daddy looked at me with sad puppy eyes. He did what Mama said and left the room. I looked up at Mama, and she was almost smiling. She started looking around the room. I sat up straight on the bed and followed her movements with my eyes. She went into the closet and started looking through my clothes. I've never seen her do that before. She pulled out a wooden hanger, strode to the bed, and whacked me across the face.

I screamed in agony and grabbed my face. It felt like someone poured boiling hot water on me. She hit me again in the stomach. I fell to the ground and yelled at her. "Stop it! Stop it!"

Mama stopped for a second. I got up and made a run for the door, but she was too quick for me. She pushed me back, and I stumbled. I took refuge in the bed again.

"You think you can defy me? I will kill you."

Mama looked like a wild animal, out of control. I snatched a pillow and placed it around my stomach. She tried to wrestle the pillow from me. I was getting tired, but if I let go, she would kill me and the baby.

"Let go of the pillow."

"No." I left the bed and backed into the corner near the window. If I went for the closet, she would drag me out. I was better off standing. At least I could fight her.

"Mia Caroline Lansing, get over here," she said.

I touched my cheek. The spot where she hit me with the hanger. It felt like a hundred bees stung me, and I started crying again. I knew she would come get me from the corner and grab me by my hair. That was why I cut it whenever it grew past my shoulders. I had to keep the short version in a bun so she wouldn't notice the blunt edges.

I was sick of her. I wouldn't be scared anymore because it

made Mama feel important but made me feel lower than dirt. I would survive, just to get even with her. I would go off to college and study something important.

One day I would have a family of my own, and I wouldn't be mean to my kids. I would love them and comfort them when they were sad or scared. But most importantly, I would marry a man who was strong and not afraid of anyone or anything, a man who would protect our children. Not like Daddy, who ran away like a coward.

"I'm not leaving this corner. You're not going to hit me anymore," I yell.

"Shut up! Who asked you to speak?"

"Nobody. I'm tired."

"You're tired? You haven't seen tired yet." She dragged me from the spot near the window and hit me again. I wrestled the hanger from her. She punched me with her fists. I pushed her hard, and she fell to the ground, stunned. I didn't feel at all sorry. She grabbed me by the ankles, and I lost my balance, falling hard on the wooden floor next to her. I cushioned the fall with my hands. Mama jumped on top of me, and we started wrestling each other like WWF contenders in WrestleMania.

"I hate you!" I screamed. "You're not my mother; you're a monster."

Her body stiffened, and then she rolled off me. She appeared dazed by my outburst. I got up from the floor and so did she. We were both breathing heavily, but she recovered first.

"What did you say to me? You looking to have all your teeth knocked out?"

"No, ma'am. But I'm done with you hurting me. Done with you making me feel ashamed to be part of this family. Done with you hurting me every day of my life. What did I do to you that was so bad? Why can't you love me because I'm your daughter?"

She was at a loss for words. She just stared at me like she couldn't comprehend what I was asking.

"This won't work," she said calmly. "You think because you let Anton Devereaux knock you up, you're grown? You think you can disrespect me?"

"No. I'm telling you how I feel."

"You should know by now your feelings don't mean diddly-squat to me. I want you gone. Tonight."

I knew Mama hated me, but I didn't think she meant it. Maybe if I asked nicely, she would change her mind.

"Where will I go? What if something bad happens to me?"

"I don't care. Now I can be finally rid of you."

I didn't want to cry. I didn't want to seem weak in front of her. Still, I was so sad and scared, and my tears knew it too, so they just kept falling, soaking my favorite hot-pink t-shirt.

"That's not true. I've never been in trouble before this."

Mama placed her hands on her hips and bit her bottom lip, the way she did when she made up her mind about an issue.

She said, "What kind of example would I be setting for Michael if I allowed his slutty sister to remain in this house? You ignored all the morals I tried to instill in you. I can still save Michael. Pack your clothes and get out of here. You have five minutes."

I dragged my luggage through the hallway to the kitchen. Mama wouldn't let me through the front door in case the neighbors saw me. Daddy leaned up against the kitchen counter. Michael clung to him. I've never seen Daddy cry before. He squeezed a small envelope into my hands and whispered that I should hide it. He told me he didn't want me to go, but Mama wouldn't listen to reason. Daddy said I should forgive her. *Never!* Michael sobbed and begged me not to leave. In that moment I knew if I was to survive in the world, I had to forget they existed.

39

JASON TOOK THE Waltham exit off the Mass Turnpike. He'd be in the office shortly for a quick meeting to sign off on some paperwork for the IPO, and then he'd head home again. Jason expected Tom Bilko to come by the house later, hopefully with good news.

He kept his PI busy, trying to find out more about the police investigation and pursuing all leads. The police eliminated Isabella Rossi as a suspect in her husband's murder. Her alibi was rock solid. She had driven to Melrose the night before to visit an aunt. Her EZ Pass record showed the time and date. Also, cameras caught her going through the toll within the timeframe the coroner estimated to be Alessandro's time of death.

Jason hadn't shared with Tom what Isabella Rossi told him about Shelby answering a call from Alessandro's burner phone. That troubled Jason. It made him suspicious in a way he didn't like. He couldn't ignore the signs any longer. Shelby and Alessandro's relationship was much more than she let on. So what was he going to do about it?

His phone vibrated. He glanced quickly at the caller ID to decide whether he should answer. It was a Texas area code, a number he didn't recognize. Jason ignored the call. The phone vibrated several times more, and he made the split-second decision to answer. He pressed the button with the phone receiver icon on the steering wheel, which allowed him to put the call on speaker.

"Cooper," he answered gingerly.

"Bro. It's been a long time."

Jason should be angry, but he wasn't. To say he expected the call would be stretching the truth, but he recognized the tactic. First, Bob warned him that Nicholas Maza contacted him about buying Orphion shares and said his connection to Jason would be bad for business. Then Bob strong-armed Jason, telling him it would be best to resign. Now this.

The voice was unmistakably Nicholas's, although they were college kids when they first met and hadn't seen or heard from each other since that fateful night outside Austin.

"Nicholas. We've both grown a few gray hairs since we last spoke. It's been decades."

"Who's counting?" Nicholas asked dismissively. "I could never forget my old buddy. Never."

"We're buddies now? No recriminations about the past?"

"Water under the Rio Grande, amigo. And a colossal waste of time."

Jason wondered whether this call was a setup or an opportunity to turn the tables on Bob.

Nicholas Maza took over from his father as the leader of what had become one of the largest drug distribution enterprises in the country. According to Bob, Nicholas was now in real estate. Maybe he was, and maybe that was a front for whatever Nicholas was into these days. The moment in time when Jason's path crossed with the Mazas had almost gotten him killed.

"What do you want, Nicholas?"

"Just looking up an old friend. You did good, Jason. Taking a big company like Orphion public. *Felicitaciones*. I mean that."

Jason turned into Orphion's massive parking lot and pulled

into a space reserved for executive team members. Nicholas didn't call him to discuss old times. Jason was certain Bob Engels had sent Nicholas, but what did Bob promise Nicholas in exchange for setting up Jason? The shares that Nicholas wanted to buy once the road show began?

"Gracias. Now why don't you tell me why you're really calling?"

"So suspicious, Jason."

"You of all people should appreciate that, given the nature of your business."

Silence. He had offended Nicholas, but Jason didn't care.

"You're on edge, Jason. Understandable," Nicholas said. "You have a lot going on, the wife being in jail, a murder charge hanging over her head. Pressure from the board with this IPO."

"What is your mission, Nicholas? I know Bob Engels sent you after me. What is his goal with this staged reunion?"

Nicholas's answer surprised him. "We should meet. Today."

SINCE IT WAS Nicholas's idea to meet, Jason wanted the meeting to take place on his turf. It was potentially a risky move, but unless Nicholas was being followed, which Jason doubted, no one would think to look for him at a suburban café thirty miles from Boston. Nicholas was an older version of the college kid Jason remembered—the one who was always on, heavy with the charm and a head of thick wavy hair, hardly a gray strand in sight, and amused brown eyes, as if life was one big party.

"Why are we here, Nicholas?" Jason asked.

Nicholas leaned back in his seat and studied Jason. "Some people want to take you down, bro."

"Bob Engels. You can say it out loud. How do you and Bob know each other?"

"He called me."

"He did? That's interesting. Bob said you called him." Jason eased back into his seat and relaxed his posture. He removed his scarf and gloves, placing them on the seat next to him. Nicholas took a sip of his drink, cupping the mug with both hands. He placed the mug down on the table.

"Think about it," Nicholas said, leaning in closer. "Why would I call Bob Engels? I don't know the man."

"You're right. It doesn't make sense. So what brought you to Boston?"

"I wanted to see you."

"Why?"

"I owe you."

Jason cocked his head. "How do you figure?"

Nicholas studied the coffee rolling around his mug as he swirled it. "Come on, Jason. When this Bob Engels guy called me, I knew he was bad news for you."

"What exactly did Bob say to you? Did you confirm we knew each other and how?"

"I told him the truth, that we were classmates at the University of Texas, Austin. Bob was quite talkative. He said you were bad for Orphion and although he respected your talent, he feels your past association with me could ruin the IPO. Then he went on to suggest you may not be the right guy to take the company into the future."

"You're here to rescue me? I'm touched, Nicholas. What did Bob promise you in exchange for helping him ruin my good name?"

Nicholas placed the coffee mug on the table and steepled his hands. He looked up at Jason. "A piece of Orphion, of course."

"The road show," Jason said. "He would position you to snap up substantial shares of company stock. Bob was willing to sell out to take me down."

"I smelled a rat when he called me," Nicholas said. "So I had him checked out."

"What did you find out?"

"The holier-than-though routine is just that." A shadow descended over Nicholas's face.

"Meaning what?" Jason asked.

"Cover-ups, payoffs, lies, and death. He wouldn't be stupid enough to get his hands dirty, but guilty is guilty."

Jason needed a moment to digest what he'd heard. Nicholas accused Bob of corruption and possibly murder. Bob was CEO of ABX Pharmaceuticals, a massive global drug company that in recent years had major success with its bone cancer drug. Just before Bob supposedly retired from ABX, a huge merger took place with Alderon, a major Swiss pharma company. What did Nicholas know that Jason didn't?

"Care to be more specific about the corruption allegations?" he asked Nicholas.

"All in good time, amigo, all in good time."

If Nicholas had information that could derail Bob's plan to toss him out of Orphion, Jason needed that leverage soon. If the time ever came where Jason had to quit Orphion, he would do so on a timetable that suited him.

"How did you come by this information?" Jason asked Nicholas.

"I have my ways. When the powerful former CEO of a major Fortune 500 company calls me up, you bet I get suspicious. And when that former CEO asks me about someone who saved my ass, I get doubly suspicious."

Jason couldn't resist the carrot being dangled in front of him. There was always the possibility that Nicholas could double-cross him. But Nicholas owed him. Big time.

40

AUSTIN, TEXAS 1988

JASON THREW HIS backpack over his broad shoulders and made use of his long limbs, sprinting up the steps of the Perry-Castanela Library. He had goofed off the past couple of weeks with partying and recreation. It was time to get back to business. Jason Cooper was a twenty-year-old junior and finance major at the University of Texas, Austin.

Turns out he had a knack for the field and breezed through his courses. His career plans were right on track. He already had an internship at a major energy company under his belt and a few Wall Street firms had shown interest. But what he really wanted was to start his own company.

Jason found an empty section of the library and settled down for what would be a marathon study session. Jason had barely cracked open the textbook when someone plopped down in the seat next to him. The guy grinned at Jason through a maze of thick black hair and amused brown eyes.

"Hey man, what gives? Can't you see I'm studying?" The interruption annoyed Jason to no end.

"This won't take long, bro."

"I'm not your bro. What do you want?"

Nicholas Maza was too cocky for Jason's taste. They were in the same major, so he saw a lot more of Nicholas than he would like, mostly because Nicholas always needed Jason to explain the lectures to him. Too bad charm wasn't a major because Nicholas would be in the Ph.D. program by now.

"Word is you're a kick-ass finance dude. Got all the professors talking about you."

"So?" Jason hoped Nicholas could detect the hostility rolling off him like an energy field.

Nicholas edged closer to Jason and whispered, "So, I know someone who could use your skills."

"What are you talking about?"

Nicholas pulled a piece of paper from his pocket and handed it to Jason. "Call me later. He would pay you serious dough for your advice. This finance stuff is a cakewalk for you. Why not fatten your bank account by doing what you're good at?" Nicholas stood. "Gotta go. Call me, bro. I'll be waiting."

Curiosity got the better of Jason, and he called Nicholas. Just a phone call. If he didn't like what Nicholas had to say, Jason could always decline the offer. Two days later, however, Jason was in Nicholas's car heading two hours outside of the city to a gated mansion. A week after that, Jason was on the payroll of Sebastien Maza, advising him on how to hide money, launder it, and funnel it into legitimate businesses.

Nicholas hadn't been joking about fattening his bank account. Jason learned the drug trade was extremely lucrative, and once you earned the trust of those in charge, you had it made. He didn't question why he was doing it or what consequences would follow. Jason wasn't hard up for cash per se; his parents made a good living, and he and his sister Robin had a great childhood. However, the money he made would put him well on his way to starting his own business after graduation.

But consequences followed. One night during the spring semester, Jason, Nicholas, and Daniel, another Maza employee, were sitting at a table at the Last Call night club. Just a few guys hanging out, enjoying the club vibe. Daniel excused himself from the group with no explanation. In Daniel's absence, two tough-looking dudes approached the table. Both had tattoos on their necks. The shorter of the two wore an eye patch. Both had on suits.

"You friends with Daniel?" the taller one asked. Jason and Nicholas looked at each other.

Nicholas asked, "Who wants to know?"

The one with the patch took a seat across from them. "Daniel owes us money. And since he left, I figure you two need to pay up."

Talk about random run-ins, Jason thought. This was absurd. The best approach was to reason with these thugs.

"Look, man, we don't have any beef with you. Whatever Daniel is into has nothing to do with us. We're just two college kids hanging out, taking a break from school."

Nicholas backed up Jason. "That's the truth, man."

"College kids, huh?" the taller one asked. "Where you go to college?"

Jason figured the university had a huge campus and as long as he didn't give his name, he would be safe. "UT Austin."

"Both of you?"

"Yes."

Jason noticed the usually charming, cocky Nicholas sat perfectly still and avoided looking the thugs in the eyes.

The one with the patch placed a gun on the table.

These guys aren't kidding around, Jason thought. Nicholas's face went blank.

"Well," said the one with the patch, "I'm Rico, and this here," he said, gesturing to his buddy, "is Felix. Since you two pimply faced wusses were nice enough to answer our questions, we'll give you a little time."

"Time for what?" Jason asked.

"Time to come up with our money."

"Huh?" a dumfounded Jason asked.

Felix spoke up. "What Rico's saying is, you two ain't leaving here until we get our money." For emphasis, Rico placed his hand over the gun.

Jason and Nicholas exchanged desperate glances. "But we don't know you, and we don't owe you any money."

"Don't matter. Daniel skipped out of here, so now his debt is your debt."

Jason guzzled down his drink.

Rico got up from the table and took his gun with him. "I'll let you fellas think about how you're gonna get us our money. We'll be back in twenty minutes."

After the thugs left, a desperate Nicholas asked Jason, "What are we going to do?"

"I don't know, man. Your father's connections got us into this club, no questions asked. Maybe we can ask the club manager to get those guys to back off."

"My dad doesn't know I'm here," Nicholas explained. "He'll kick my ass if he finds out."

"Are you kidding me?" Jason was fuming and didn't bother pretending otherwise. "We can't just sit here waiting for them to come back and shoot us."

"I don't know who these guys are any more than you do," Nicholas said. "Looks like Daniel has some side racket going. He's dead, man. My dad won't like this."

Jason could see Rico on a pay phone with someone and looking in their direction. Fear clawed at him. "Let's hit the dance floor."

"What?"

"Let's hit the dance floor. Ask some girls to dance. I need to think."

"Nah. I'm okay. You go," Nicholas said and remained at the table.

Jason secured a dance partner in no time. The DJ spun a remix of Jody Watley's "Some Kind of Lover." His dance partner was a little chatty, which didn't bode well for his ability to think and come up with a solution, but he had to if he wanted to get out of that club alive. Two thoughts occurred to him. He could ask the bartender to call them a cab and make an escape when Rico and Felix weren't watching, or he could try reasoning with them again.

Jason thanked his dance partner when the song ended and headed back to the table. To his chagrin, the two extortionists were there, talking to a terrified Nicholas.

"You're back," Felix said. "We were just asking your buddy for our money."

"We need more time," Jason said, sitting down. "We're just college kids." Jason reached for his wallet, and Rico reached for his gun.

"I'm just getting my wallet," Jason said.

"Hurry up," Rico barked.

Jason took out his UT Austin student ID and asked Nicolas to do the same.

Another idea occurred to Jason. It might help him—not so much Nicholas—but he was sweating, scared, and desperate to get back to campus and forget this evening ever happened. Luckily, tomorrow was Friday, and he had no classes scheduled. He handed Rico his Connecticut driver's license, too.

"I'm just here for school, man. Connecticut is home. We're not friends with Daniel. He just came over and sat with us. Isn't that right, Nicholas?"

"Yeah, that's right."

Rico stroked his chin. He returned the IDs. "We'll be back."

He and Felix left.

"We gotta get out of here now," Jason said to Nicholas.

"How? They'll see us."

Jason said, "I'll ask the bartender to call us a cab. Let's separate and use the crowd to our advantage. They'll be expecting to see the two of us together. See you outside in twenty minutes."

Jason cajoled and pushed his way through the thick crowd of club-goers. The cigarette smoke in the air burned his lungs, but he figured it was a small price to pay to stay alive. So far, he hadn't seen either of the two tough guys. He breathed a sigh of relief when he made it to the bar. It was a busy night, so it was difficult getting the bartender's attention. Jason finally did, and like he predicted, the cab would be there in twenty minutes. He had to find a spot and wait out the time.

Nineteen minutes passed by, and he spotted Nicholas heading toward the door. He joined him. The out of nowhere, Felix and Rico magically appeared like two genies. "Going somewhere?" Rico asked.

"We just want to get some fresh air," Jason said. "It's smoky in here, and I have asthma."

"How about I shoot you to send a message to Daniel?" Rico said to Nicholas.

A petrified Nicholas begged. "Please, man, I got no beef with you. My dad would be grateful if you would just let us go."

Jason elbowed Nicholas. That was a dumb idea, using his father. If these guys were from a rival drug ring, they could kill both Jason and Nicholas on the spot.

"Don't listen to him," Jason piped up. "He's scared shitless and doesn't know what he's saying. Look, man, we're two kids trying to make something of ourselves. We just had the bad luck to run into Daniel here. I hope you find him and can get your money back, but this isn't our fight."

"I still want to shoot him," Rico said.

They are some trigger-happy jerks, Jason thought.

Felix leaned in closer, staring Nicholas up and down. "Say, ain't you Sebastien Maza's kid?"

This is not good.

Nicholas didn't answer.

"I asked you a question, boy."

"Yes."

Rico smiled. "The boss is going to love this. Y'all are coming with us."

Jason panicked. He might have been naïve to get mixed up with Nicholas and his family, but Jason knew with certainty that if he left the club, they were both dead. He had to think on his feet.

"Wouldn't it be better if his father owed your boss?" he asked Rico.

"What are you talking about, college boy?"

Jason took a long breath. "I'm saying if you let us go, your boss has leverage over Mr. Maza. He's going to have to play ball with your boss. You know, out of respect for letting us go."

Jason didn't know what the heck he was saying and didn't know who Felix and Rico's boss was. Jason could start a drug war for all he knew, but that was their problem, not his.

Both men considered the offer. "Get the hell out of here," Rico said. "And if I see either one of you wimps around here again, I won't be so understanding."

They didn't need to be told twice. Luckily, the cab was still waiting, and they told the driver to step on it. After that, Jason wrote a letter to Sebastien Maza and asked Nicholas to deliver it. He was done. For weeks afterward, he lived in fear that Maza would send someone after him. You didn't just quit a crime lord. But Nicholas must have told his father Jason saved his life, because Jason's fears were unfounded. As for Nicholas, they agreed to never speak about that night to anyone, under any circumstances.

41

MY CELLMATE WENT off to the prison library, and I'm grateful to be alone to stew in my misery. I'm referring to the special misery of celebrating this holiday season behind bars, away from my babies, my husband, my friends, my home. Christmas has always been a big deal in our home. I went all out, including driving to a special Christmas tree farm an hour away from home to find the perfect tree.

Decorating was a family affair. Hot chocolate and homemade cookies (lots of homemade cookies) would follow. I welcomed the challenge of finding spots the kids didn't know about to hide presents. I began cooking on Christmas Eve and wouldn't stop until Christmas day.

I lived for the feeling that the house would burst at the seams from laughter, cheer, and the belief that the world wasn't such a bad place, that people were inherently good. What a difference a year makes, as the saying goes. I want no visitors, especially not Jason or Vivian. I won't be able to stand it.

I've received a holiday card. I guess it's not the same as having visitors, but close. I sit on the lower bunk and remove the card from inside the envelope. It's blue with gold lettering and snowflakes on the front. Inside shouts *Season's Greetings*, and there are multiple notes and signatures all over. It's from my staff at work. For a moment, I clutch at this piece of my former life and shut my eyes tight. It's an unexpected yet pleasant surprise. There are people outside of my family who believe in my innocence.

I read every note and signature, some multiple times. "Next year will be better," Chris Snowden, my research assistant, writes. "I know this holiday sucks. We expect you at next year's office Christmas party," Greg Larson, a bioinformatics specialist; "Still the best boss ever, Merry Christmas," my administrative assistant Inez Diaz. "You promised to take me to the conference. Will hold you to it," my postdoctoral fellow Emma Chan. I read her note two more times. I promised to take her to a genomics and bioinformatics conference in Salzburg, Austria. Emma is bright and dedicated. One day, she'll run her own research lab.

I scan the contents of the card one more time, but as I'm about to close it, I have a flash of memory. The Fairmont Hotel back in October. I was the keynote speaker at a bioinformatics conference. Emma attended, along with a few scientists and staff from GeneMedicine. I placed little importance on what she told me then. I now realize it was a costly mistake.

"I need to talk to you about something," she had said.

"Oh. We can discuss it at lunch."

"That's okay. I'd rather talk to you without a crowd."

"Is everything okay?" I asked.

"Yes."

My antenna was on high alert. What could Emma possibly have to tell me that needed my undivided attention?

"Okay. What is it?"

She nodded toward seating near the reception area, and I followed. After we sat down, I waited for her to speak.

"I ran into someone at a networking event a couple of weeks ago, and they were asking about you. I didn't make a big deal about it at the time. He knew so much about you, I thought you were friends. Then I Googled him."

"Who?"

"Dr. Mehmet Koczak."

That piece of information gobsmacked me. "What did he want?"

"He asked if you were still at GeneMedicine and talked about how much he admired your work."

"I suspect he's trying to make a comeback and rebuild his reputation. I'm sure you got all the gory details about what happened from your Google search?"

"I did. Was he really selling proprietary data for a fee?"

"Unfortunately, yes. Strange that he would lead you to believe we were friends."

"I take it you weren't?"

"No. He wasn't a fan when I joined GeneMedicine, and I didn't have the stomach for his brand of sexism. We were constantly butting heads."

"So you don't hate him?"

"Hate? No. I wish him well and hope he never does anything that stupid again, but I don't waste emotions worrying about it."

"Well, I just wanted you to know."

The card falls from my trembling fingers as I realize the answer was right there all along. His accent and formal speech, seemingly endless supply of personal information about me, the insistence that I should pay for my sins, and the threat to my children's lives to force me to cooperate. Mehmet Koczak has been planning to destroy me all along as payback for blowing the whistle on his game of corporate espionage.

42

I CHECKED OUT Mehmet Koczak," Tom Bilko said.

"And?"

"You won't like what I uncovered."

Jason and Tom were in Jason's home office. The kids were at school, and Vivian had returned to Chicago to handle some business.

"What did you find out?" Jason sat in his swivel leather chair near his desk. Tom sat on the sofa across the room.

Tom pulled a dossier from his bag and handed Jason the file. He took a few minutes to read through quickly.

"This can't be right," Jason said.

"I'm afraid it is. Koczak re-entered the U.S. from Turkey under a different name by way of Canada. That's why we couldn't find out anything when we first started digging.

"We assumed he would come back to the States using the name we knew him by. He came back two years ago. Got a job as an instructor at a community college and lives in Cambridge."

Jason was elated. He swiveled around the chair several times, like a kid on a teacup ride. "Are you telling me this nightmare could be over soon?"

"I spoke to Emma Chan," Tom said. "Koczak gave her his new alias, but she recognized his face. She confirmed her conversation with Shelby at the Fairmont. I think the guy was putting his revenge scheme in place and used Emma to get information. Good thing she was smart enough to mention it."

"We need proof," Jason said.

"Working on it," Tom said. "Fingers and toes crossed Koczak is our guy so Mrs. Cooper can come home to you and the kids."

"That would be wonderful, Tom. Anything else?"

"You might be interested to know that your wife's assistant, Inez Diaz, made a call to Alessandro Rossi the day he was killed."

43

TWO DAYS AFTER her brother blew up her entire high school existence, by blurting out her secret feelings for Ty during that doomed family dinner, Abbie was still too humiliated to face Ty. She avoided him like a popular senior avoided being seen with an uncool freshman.

Apparently, the incident had embarrassed Ty also because he didn't text her like he usually did. He wasn't in the dining hall having lunch, and she hadn't seen him all day.

"Should we tell her?" Anastasia asked. The girls sat at their usual lunchtime spot in the dining hall.

"Tell me what?" Abbie had tuned out her friends, content to pick at her food and drown in an ever-expanding pool of jealousy and misery. Ty clearly preferred Kerri, and there was nothing anyone could say or do to change that.

The girls looked at each other and decided silently amongst each other. It was going to be Frances who would deliver whatever news they wanted to tell Abbie.

"Look, Abbie, it sucks what your brother did, but maybe it's for the best."

"Really, Frances? How is that? What twisted logic do you have to explain the fact that my life is over? I may as well show up to school wearing a ginormous paper bag over my head."

"You don't have to. I know you're hurting right now, but the best way to get over Ty is to pay attention to someone who's actually in love with you."

"Frances is right," Callie said. "It's time to move on, Abbie. And I think what we have to say will help you do that."

Didn't they understand? Nothing and no one was going to help her move on. She would love Ty forever, and she had to accept that he would never feel the same way about her. Abbie imagined the flashing neon "Loser" sign on her forehead growing by the minute.

"I'm not interested in moving on to anyone else. This is exactly why I didn't want him to know how I felt. It would change things between us, our friendship would suffer. I hate this. I miss my mom so much. She would know what to do."

The sobs escaped Abbie as a small whimper at first and then a full-blown, body-racking ugly cry, right there in the dining hall. She put her head down on the table, not caring if her hair ended up in her food.

Abbie felt someone stroking her arm and another her hair. She guessed her girls were rallying.

"It's okay, Abbie, Callie said. "It won't hurt like this forever."

"I'm going to punch Ty in the face the next time I see him," Frances promised. "And this will make your decision to banish him forever easier. He asked Kerri Wheeler to the Platinum Ball. Now you can officially toss him to the curb."

If Frances was trying to make her feel better, it had the opposite effect. Fresh waves of pain and misery washed over Abbie in enough quantities to drown an elephant. She couldn't recall a time in her life she was so sad, not even when Grandpa Erasmus, her father's father, died. Curious stares from fellow students came their way.

"What are you all looking at?" Frances yelled.

"You had to tell her that now?" Anastasia asked Frances.

"It's better to rip off the Band-Aid than have her die a slow, painful death before our eyes," Frances countered. "This way she can start planning her revenge, and I know just where to start."

Abbie lifted her head, sure she looked as hideous as she felt. Callie handed her a napkin. Abbie wiped her tear-stained face and then blew her nose, which, by the looks she was getting from her friends, was gross.

"We need to get you to the ladies' room. Your eyes are redder than a hot chili pepper," Frances said.

Before the girls could head for the bathroom, someone approached their table.

"Are you all right, Abigail?"

It was Mr. Newman, one of the guidance counselors. Frances, Anastasia, and virtually every girl at St. Matthew's thought he was the hottest guy on staff. Mr. Newman was polite, a little nerdy, but great with students whom he preferred call him Lee. Abbie never did.

Abbie raked her fingers through her hair and hoped it didn't look too messy. "I'm fine, Mr. Newman. Thanks for asking."

"Good. Can you come by and see me in my office soon?"

Abbie promised she would.

A VISIT TO the student lounge was just what Abbie needed. An in-between-classes hub of relaxation and socialization, the lounge was a blend of leather sofas, multicolored arm chairs, bright open space, and large windows.

Her cell phone lit up, a text message.

(Ty) I'm sorry.

A burning sensation formed at the back of her throat. She stared at the words as if they would tell her how to respond. *Ignore the text.* No sooner had she dumped her phone in her backpack,

Ty walked into the student lounge. He waved to a couple of classmates, who nodded back at him. Abbie quickly unzipped her bag, grabbed a textbook, and sat on the sofa. By the time Ty approached her, she was pretending to be engrossed in her French textbook.

He flopped down next to her. "Why aren't you answering my texts?"

Abbie stayed silent. She grabbed a hot-pink highlighter from her backpack, pulled off the cap, which she kept in her mouth, and began highlighting random paragraphs for which she already knew the English translation. She was afraid her voice would betray her tumultuous feelings if she spoke.

"I'm not going anywhere, Cooper," Ty announced. "Talk to me."

More silence.

Ty placed his backpack on the floor. He reached over and removed the highlighter cap from her mouth. She didn't protest.

Abbie absent-mindedly twirled the edges of her scarf. She asked, "What do you want me to say, Tyler?"

"Tyler?" he asked, frowning, as if the use of his full name offended him. "So that's how it is?"

"I'm great at taking hints," Abbie said.

"What is that supposed to mean?"

Ty wouldn't look at her after Miles dropped the bombshell. He just sat there at the dinner table like he wanted to die. Then he went off the grid for days. Not so much as a text or phone call to see if she was still alive.

As if that wasn't bad enough, he asked Kerri to the Platinum Ball. After days of the silent treatment, he just popped up next to Abbie, acting like nothing happened. He claimed he and Kerri only hung out, and it was nothing serious. What a crock. The Platinum Ball was the social event of the year. No senior guy would ask a girl he wasn't serious about.

"You lied. Don't pretend that I'm the one who wrecked our friendship."

"You're flipping out, Cooper. How did I wreck our friendship?"

"Are you seriously going to do this?" Her voice went up a notch, and several students were doing a terrible job of pretending they weren't listening. One of them was Kerri's minion, Lindsay Easterbrook.

Abbie lowered her voice to a whisper. "Don't make me out to be the one who's losing it. It's insulting."

"I didn't mean it like that. Something is obviously bothering you. Tell me what I did, and I'll fix it. I've been trying to, but you wouldn't answer any of my texts."

"You sent me *a* text a few minutes ago saying you were sorry and then you just showed up here."

"I sent you like twenty text messages after that dinner at your house. You couldn't bother to answer even one. That was seriously messed up, Cooper, just plain rude. I expected better from you."

"I didn't get any text messages from you," she said indignantly. "Maybe you got me confused with Kerri."

"That was uncalled for," Ty snapped. "It's not like you. And for the record, I could never get you confused with any other girl."

"You took our friendship for granted," Abbie said. Her chest ached from carrying around this hurt for so long. "I asked you straight out if Kerri was your girlfriend, and you denied it. You said it was nothing to make a big deal about. Then you asked her to the Platinum Ball. That's a big deal. You didn't have to lie. You could have just said she was your girlfriend. Everybody at school knows it, but you lied. I guess I'm not really your best friend anymore. Thanks for the newsflash, Ty."

Her words hung in the air, awkward and convicting. She had put everything on the line. There was nothing else left. Abbie took a moment and allowed her thoughts to create some distance between them. Why would he claim he sent her text messages when she received none of them? What did he hope to gain by lying about that? She understood he might have been trying to spare her feelings by denying Kerri was his girlfriend, but why claim he sent her a bunch of text messages she never got?

Then she realized her mistake. During one of her temper tantrums and I-hate-Ty diatribes, she'd blocked him from her phone so she couldn't receive messages from him, and she forgot to reverse the block until this morning because she missed him, not that Abbie would ever admit it. It was her own stupid fault she didn't get his messages and, of course, she had to go thinking the worst. She screwed up. But she wasn't about to fess up.

"I would never take you for granted, Cooper. I'm sorry if I made you feel that way. I'm sorry if I hurt you. I would never do that on purpose. And just so you know, I didn't ask Kerri to the Ball. She asked me. I wasn't planning on going at all, and I guess I couldn't come up with a good excuse to say no when she asked." He looked at Abbie, his eyes pleading for understanding. "You believe me, don't you?"

That big, fat, neon loser sign flashed on her forehead again. She reamed him out for something he didn't do. If she were Ty, she wouldn't want to be friends with her anymore.

"Sure. I believe you," she murmured. "Obviously I didn't get your messages. Maybe my phone is screwy. I shouldn't have jumped to conclusions. So why don't you tell me what you said in those messages?"

"I will. But not here."

They met up at the chapel. Abbie paced up and down the aisle, her arms folded.

"Well?" she said.

Ty floundered, searching for the right words. Abbie figured

her pacing intensified his nervousness.

"Look, Cooper, I admit it was a little weird when your brother said what he said. You didn't deny it, but you acted like you wanted to get out of there and never speak to me again."

"Forget what my brother said. Forget everything about that night. It was just my kid brother trying to act grown up. He thinks you're cool, and we should date. That's all."

Abbie felt like a total Judas for throwing her little brother under the bus, but she couldn't tell Ty the truth. Not then. Maybe never.

"What about the notebook?" Ty asked.

"What notebook?"

"Miles said you would write my name in your notebook. What's that about?"

"Oh… no big deal. Sometimes I write my to-do list in my notebook instead of my phone. I must have written your name to remind me to ask you something."

Seriously? That neon loser sign is flashing again. You should just leave it on your forehead permanently.

"And that's it?"

"Yeah," she said, her eyes downcast.

He joined her in the aisle, standing so close to her she could count the freckles on his nose. "I'm not clueless, you know."

"What do you mean?"

"Cooper, I've never met anyone like you before. You get me. I like how we can sit together and say nothing at all. You don't need to be running your mouth all the time. I like that you always look amazing, but you're not obsessed with clothes and makeup, or trying to be sexy. I like that you're not full of drama or desperate for attention."

"Where are you going with this?" Abbie knew she wouldn't like the answer, but she had to ask.

"I'm saying I don't want you to change. You're my safe place.

I hope you feel the same way about me. I don't want to screw things up between us."

He doesn't see you as girlfriend material. You're permanently in the friend zone. Boom!

Abbie wished the ground would open up and swallow her. If she'd held out any hope that they would end up together, that he would be her first kiss, he just took a machete to her dreams. It hurt to breathe. The pain pressed down on her lungs like a boulder. Until this point in her life, everything had gone her way. Abbie never knew what it was like to want something she couldn't have. How was she supposed to go on being his friend while she was dying inside?

"Sure thing, Ty," she said, her voice wobbling. "I don't want things to get complicated, either. But next time you feel like flirting with me, don't." She walked away from him to collect her bag from one of the pews.

"What do you mean?"

She turned around. "You were flirting with me at my house the night of the dinner. Before we went downstairs, and my brother said what he did. You almost kissed me. And what was that crack about finding a wife who would give you lots of babies?"

"Oh," he said guiltily.

"That's all you have to say?" Abbie didn't wait for an answer. She just picked up her bag and left the chapel.

44

I PICK UP the story where we left off last time. Every Tuesday without fail, Anton shows up, like an addict anxious for another hit. He's a regular now. The guards even nod at him when he comes into the visitor's room. It's always the same. We pray. He asks questions. Sometimes I answer. Sometimes I don't.

Anton wants to know what happened next. I like the control it gives me, being the only one alive who can provide the details he craves, the only one who can finally remove that constant thorn he's been carrying around for decades—the not knowing, the wondering, the guilt, the shame. For most of my teenage years and into adulthood, I could only think of him as the boy who ruined my life.

"After my mother kicked me out," I begin, "I made it to New Orleans with some of the guilt money Daddy gave me. When the money ran out, I lived in abandoned buildings, ate out of dumpsters, and tried not to gag on my own filth. When I started showing, I ended up at a shelter for runaway teens. Ironic, because despite my crazy mother, I didn't run away from home."

He tugs at his shirt collar and whispers, "I'm sorry. I'm so sorry."

"I don't know what happened to the baby," I say. I struggle to push down the volcano of emotions threatening to erupt and bury me. "I know his whereabouts is the only thing that matters to you. That's why you come."

Anton whips his handkerchief out of his shirt pocket and turns away from me. He dabs the corners of his eyes. When he looks at me again, something fleeting passes between us—a silent recognition and acceptance of our respective suffering. In his eyes, I see reflected the self-absorbed, ridiculously handsome eighteen-year-old boy who had meant the world to me. The boy who callously told me he wanted no part of the pregnancy. "I need a kid like I need a jackhammer drilling through my skull," he had told me when I announced the news.

Anton had planned to attend college that fall and enter law school afterward. He wouldn't allow a little thing like getting his underage girlfriend pregnant to derail his plans, especially a girl from the wrong side of the tracks as far as his parents were concerned.

He attended law school and graduated top of his class. After he lost both his parents within a year of each other, he had to take stock. It led him to the ministry and now, at forty-three, he's been saving souls for the better part of fifteen years.

"You gave the baby up for adoption?" he asks, his voice shaky. "What did you name him?"

What I did was cruel. If I live to be a hundred, the shame will never leave me. When they placed him in my arms at the hospital, I glanced at him for a few seconds. Then I made my decision. I couldn't—wouldn't—allow myself to bond with him. I never named him. I didn't ask how much he weighed at birth or whether he was healthy or had any complications. If I was going to make it in the world, I had to leave him behind. So I did. I left him in the hospital alone and unloved. Just like his mother was.

"I didn't give him a name, Anton. I didn't know how I was going to raise him. In my teenage mind, leaving him at the hospital was the best solution. They would have to take care of him and find him a family. I couldn't stay in a shelter with a baby. On the streets with me, his chances—"

I stop to catch my breath and rein in my pain. "He was better off without me," I finish.

"You just left him?" Anton is incredulous.

I nod.

"So, you have no idea where he might have ended up?"

"None."

"Did you ever feel anything for him, wonder where he was after you had gone on with your life?"

"You don't get to judge me, Anton. If I remember correctly, you were especially cruel the day I told you I was pregnant. You went so far as to ask whether the baby was yours when you knew full well I was a virgin when we got together, and hadn't been with anyone else."

I glare at him, long buried memories rising to the surface. "All you cared about was your precious family reputation and standing. Oh no, we couldn't let it get out that you got a young girl pregnant. You dismissed me like I was trash. Then I went home, and my mother beat the hell out of me. She kicked me out of the house that very day. She didn't care where I went. I was fifteen years old."

Anton can't look me in the eyes. His body tenses, and he just stares at the wall, while profusely apologizing.

After I catch my breath and calm down, I lay it all on the line, the burning, dreadful truth I couldn't admit to myself for years.

"I didn't have the luxury of giving in to my feelings, Anton. As despicable as it was, leaving our son was the most loving thing I could have done.

"Having him live on the streets, an uncertain and dangerous life, with a kid mother who couldn't provide for him would have been worse. Leaving him was the only shot at a life I could give him. Why can't you understand that?"

Anton turns and looks at me with dull eyes. "You turned out okay," he says. "Thank God for that."

"By a miracle. When I walked out of that hospital in New Orleans, I went back to the shelter. I couldn't stay there much longer. I told them the baby was stillborn. While I was there, a donor named Rita March walked in. She took a liking to me. That chance encounter changed my life."

I close my eyes and take a moment to calm myself once more, then continue with the story. "Rita became my foster mother, and within a few months, she and her family moved to North Carolina, taking me with them. Rita and her husband Daniel raised me alongside their daughter, Vivian.

"When college rolled around, I got into Duke on a partial scholarship, and Rita footed the rest of the bill. After Duke, I went off to graduate school at Johns Hopkins. The rest, you probably know."

"Wow," Anton says, shaking his head. "That's an incredible story."

"I can't help you. I don't know if he made it or not. You're chasing a ghost."

"Let's bow our heads in prayer and ask for forgiveness for our sins," Anton says.

When the prayer is over, I want to tell him what I've been holding back, what I suspect is the primary reason he wants to know what happened to the child we conceived. People change. But do they really? How much of the old self is still present?

"You're a liar," I say to him.

"What did I lie about?" he asks, like a known troublemaker who's not sure which of his misdeeds he's being busted for.

"Easing your conscience and asking for forgiveness aren't the real reasons you wanted to know how things played out, Anton. There's more. Like filling a void in your life. You want to find our son because you and your wife can't have children."

Anton stares off into space, as if in a trance. Visiting hours are almost over. Chairs scrape against the ugly concrete floors as visitors leave. The guards escort inmates back to their cells.

"Look at me," I command.

He won't at first. When he does, the words coming out of his mouth don't sound like they're his, as if something alien has taken over his voice box.

"You're right. Jade is the same age as you, forty. We tried every procedure there is. Nothing worked. I thought if I could find our son, maybe I might have a chance at fatherhood, even if it is to an adult son. Does that make me a horrible person?"

"Who am I to judge?"

After Anton leaves, I return to my cell and weep for the infant I was too scared to love, for the family I lost because of one mistake. I weep because I will never know what became of him, because I was too much of a coward to try and find him.

I tried once, but gave up, convincing myself he would hate me and want no part of me, that I had no right to disrupt his life, after I deserted him as a helpless newborn. Better to leave well enough alone. I hold on to that rationalization as if my life depends on it.

45

DR. SINGER SAID, "Your call surprised me."

"Why is that?" Mia asked.

"Things ended on a sour note last session. You didn't want me as your therapist anymore."

"I changed my mind."

"Oh?"

Mia figured she should give Singer another go. What was the point of starting all over again? All the work she put into researching Singer would have been for nothing. She needed to keep a cool head whenever she met with him, however.

The weather wasn't helping her mood. Rain. Wet snow. A watery mess, and she almost had an accident on Route 85 on her way here.

"It's obvious I need help," she said. "I'm not too proud to recognize that's the case."

Singer crossed his legs. They both sat in their usual spots. "I'm proud of you for coming to that conclusion. It's not always an easy thing to ask for help."

"Yeah… well… what choice do I have?"

"Did you check out the methods we discussed last session?"

"I started up with yoga again. It helps to calm me down, but sleep is still an issue, and the old woman…" Her voice trailed off.

"She still appears?" Singer asked.

"Yes. It's getting to be a real drag. I'm sick of hearing what a saint Shelby Cooper is. If the old woman would get out of my head and stay out, I think this sleep thing could work out."

Singer contemplated her statement for a moment. "Can you pinpoint exactly when the old woman started appearing and what was happening in your life during that time?"

Mia looked straight ahead. She wasn't about to divulge that. It was none of his business, anyway.

"Just before I started seeing you."

"Did it get worse when the Cooper case hit the media?"

"What are you asking me, Dr. Singer?"

"I'm trying to pinpoint your triggers. We've spent a lot of time in your sessions talking about Shelby Cooper."

Mia's blood boiled. Her hatred of Shelby Cooper threatened to spill out and form a raging river of venom. "She's a liar, a deceptive woman who got where she is by manipulating people into believing she's something she's not. She's a heartless witch. Does it surprise you that somebody like that is capable of murder? Maybe the guy found out her secrets and threatened to tell. She offed him to silence him."

"The police don't yet have a motive. How did you come by this theory?"

"It just makes sense," Mia said, her confidence growing by the minute.

"Do you know something about this case?" Singer asked.

Mia sat up straight. "Why would you ask me that?"

"It's just a question. I want to make sure you're not compromising your treatment by getting too caught up in this situation."

"Thanks for the concern," Mia said sarcastically. "But I'm fine."

"Do you have any hobbies?" he asked.

Yes. Watching Shelby Cooper rot in a jail cell is one of my favorites. Having my minion terrorize her bratty teenage daughter is another. Let's see. Oh, and leaking evidence to the cops to make sure she spends the rest of her miserable life behind bars takes the cake.

"Don't need a hobby," Mia mumbled.

Mia only half listened for the rest of the session. The highlight for her was Dr. Singer finally wrote her a prescription sleep aid. When it was over, she couldn't wait to get out of there.

Mia was about to pull out of the driveway when she realized she forgot the prescription. She got out of the car and went down the steps to Dr. Singer's basement office. She opened the door.

But Dr. Singer didn't hear her. His back was to her. She planned to pick up the prescription off the desk, wave it to him so he understood why she came back, and quietly exit. As she got closer into the room, she heard him clearly. He was in the middle of a conversation that made her fume.

"Yes, Mia Lansing. What do you think of the notes I sent over? Aha. Yes. I came to the same conclusion. She could be dangerous. Absolutely. What about the Cooper case? No doubt in my mind she knows something about it. I realized that this afternoon. The authorities will have to get involved. Yes. Well, thanks for the consult, Aaron."

Singer turned around, surprised to discover her presence. With lightning speed, Mia picked up the letter opener on top of the desk drawer and stabbed Dr. Singer deep in the neck. Blood spouted, and he dropped to his knees, his eyes wide with shock. She grabbed the prescription and turned to run, but she had to make sure he couldn't go running off at the mouth. Mia felt for a pulse after he hit the floor. Nothing. She knocked over a few objects, ransacked the place as much as she could, and then got the heck out of there before trouble came looking for her.

46

A ROBBERY GONE WRONG, the news reports said. Good. It meant no one would become suspicious. The woman who called herself Mia had stayed up all night. Her only sustenance was a bag of potato chips and water. She felt no guilt about Singer. He planned to rat her out to the cops. He'd left her no choice.

Mia needed to speed up her timetable, however. Everything had gone according to plan so far, but she didn't anticipate the Singer complication. Was she losing her edge? That nervous idiot she hired to help her carry out her plan said Abbie wasn't afraid of him. Her mother being in jail made her brazen. Mia would up the ante herself. Make the little brat want to crap her pants. And she knew where to start.

Mia pulled up a chair to her makeshift workstation in her tiny apartment and went through her tools. It was time to ratchet up the pain on Shelby Cooper.

You're getting desperate now, aren't you? Desperate people make mistakes. That's how they get caught.

"Shut up, old woman. Leave me alone!" Mia pounded her head with her fists, shaking her head in rapid motion from left to right.

You can't get rid of me that easily.

The old woman took a seat on the sofa. She pulled her hair back in a bun, and she was wearing white. She always appeared in white.

"Don't make me shoot you," Mia threatened.

Go ahead. You'll be wasting your time. How long do you think you can keep this up?

"I'm warning you. Stay out of my business."

How could you? How could you do this to her?

"She's a selfish witch. A liar who destroys everything she touches. She's gotten away with too much for too long."

You don't know what you're talking about. You never did.

"Well, now, she's paying for her crimes, isn't she? Shelby Cooper is going to rot in that jail cell."

You're such a stupid girl.

"Shut up! Shut up. I'm not stupid. I know exactly what I'm doing," Mia yelled.

But the old woman had disappeared.

47

ABBIE SAT ACROSS from Lee Newman in his small office off the central hallway of the main school building. A neat stack of papers sat on the left side of the desk, next to a personal printer. The computer sat on another small desk off to his right, and behind him was a large file cabinet.

"Thank you for coming in to see me, Abigail," Mr. Newman said. "I'm glad you did."

"You can call me Abbie. Everyone else does. What's this about, Mr. Newman?"

He sat behind the desk, a grave expression circling his face. "I wanted to make sure you're okay and nobody is giving you a hard time. This is a difficult period for you and your family, and I want you to know you can talk to me and it will go no further than this office. You have people who care about you among the administration and staff."

"Thanks, Mr. Newman, but you don't need to worry about me. My mother will come home soon. I know it."

"That's a great attitude to have."

"There's no other attitude to have. She will come home," Abbie insisted.

Her lips trembled, but she refused to break down in front of Mr. Newman like she did at lunch the other day. She was a mess lately, crying the minute anyone mentioned her mother.

He said, "It's okay, Abbie. You can cry if you want to; it's perfectly fine."

"I'm not a crybaby, Mr. Newman. I'm just dealing with something else. It's stupid, really, but I'll handle it."

"Something other than your mother's situation?"

"Yes."

"Care to talk about it? I'm a good listener."

"That's okay, I'm good."

He leaned forward. "Abbie, you're only fifteen. You're not supposed to have all the answers. You're not supposed to understand all that you're feeling or why certain things happen. It's okay to be angry because you feel helpless, like you don't understand why things are unfolding the way they are."

That was exactly how Abbie felt. Nothing made sense anymore. Her life was spinning out of control, and she didn't know how to put everything back in order. Maybe Mr. Newman truly understood.

"Coopers don't whine about their problems," she informed him. "They wrestle with each one until it's solved. Kind of like a math equation."

When he smiled, he didn't seem that much older than she was. Abbie hadn't noticed before, but he had dimples, the kind that made her want to poke her fingers in them to see how deep they would go. Mr. Newman should smile more often. His brown eyes were big and bright, like stars that light up the night sky.

"What's so funny?" She asked him.

"You're brave," he said. "But you don't have to carry the burden alone. We have resources here at school if you need it. The staff is committed to making sure you stay on track. If anything changes, I want to know about it."

"Why? There are over four hundred kids at this school. Why

so much attention on little old me?"

She was being a brat, but she didn't want anyone treating her like a charity case.

"I would do the same for any student in your situation," he said. "You're an exemplary student and a wonderful young lady. Your teachers have nothing but praise for you. I want you to make it out of this situation intact. And I'd like to see you go about the rest of the school year without disruption or distraction."

Well, the distraction ship had sailed. Abbie spent more and more of her time daydreaming in class about Ty. One minute she'd be imagining the two of them, grown up and getting married and living happily ever after; the next moment, she'd be fantasizing about using his face as target practice, and she wasn't even on the school's archery team.

"I'm doing fine, Mr. Newman. I have to. Otherwise, my dad will tell my mom and they'll make a big deal about it. The last thing I need is them getting all over me about my grades."

"You're lucky to have parents who care so much, Abbie. It's a gift."

"I'm sure you had great parents, too. Look how well you turned out."

"Listen, I'm glad we had time to chat," he said, and stood. "I feel better knowing that you're doing okay. Call me anytime."

48

JASON SKIDDED INTO a parking space at Shoppers World, a retail park in Framingham, twenty minutes from Castleview. A steady deluge of rain and the large piles of melting snow from the previous storm added to the slushy mess. He popped his umbrella after he exited the car and rushed into Starbucks for the meeting he hoped would provide answers.

Jason found an empty table and waited. It was a Wednesday afternoon in early December. Patrons sprinkled throughout the café, placed their orders while others worked on their laptops, taking advantage of the free Wi-Fi. The aroma of rich, full-bodied coffee wafted in the air.

The conversation with Tom Bilko in Jason's study two days ago still rattled around in his mind. *Inez Diaz called Alessandro Rossi the very day he died.* It seemed like the tragedy of Rossi's murder occurred in some by-gone era. Less than a month had passed. Less than a month since Shelby landed in jail, but it might as well have been decades.

Inez approached the table, soaking wet, which did nothing to diminish her striking looks. Her long, dark hair stuck to her scalp, and her beige coat had patches of rain splattered all over. Jason rose and offered to take her coat.

"Thanks for coming," Jason said. "Have a seat. Can I get you a latte or a scone, anything?"

"No, Mr. Cooper, I don't need anything, but I your call surprised me. After the police searched Dr. Cooper's office and interviewed everybody, I didn't think there'd be anything left to ask."

"There's always something, Inez. How are they treating you at GeneMedicine? Anybody giving you a hard time?"

"Are you asking me if I still have a job?" Inez said.

Jason smiled. "You got me."

"Don't worry about me. I still have my job. There are plenty of other scientists at the company who need help. It's not the same as working for Dr. Cooper, though. She was more than a boss. I consider her my friend."

"And she you," Jason said. "I'm glad you're doing okay. If anything changes, if you need anything at all, please call. Promise me you will."

"I promise."

"Now, do you mind telling me why you called Alessandro Rossi just before he was killed?"

Inez retreated farther into her seat and leveled an incredulous stare at Jason. "I don't know what you're talking about."

Jason didn't mean to come off accusatory, but he was a desperate man. The longer it took to find the real killer, the easier it would be for the prosecution to settle on Shelby as the culprit. The easier it would become to take the case to trial if the police found no other viable suspects. Koczcak's return to the country under an assumed name was a hot lead. Jason hoped Tom Bilko would find the evidence to back up a motive. He needed ironclad proof so he could spring Shelby from jail.

"I have it from a trusted source that someone placed a call from your office to Alessandro Rossi on the day he died," Jason explained.

"Your source is wrong, Mr. Cooper. I'm sorry, but I never

heard of Alessandro Rossi until the news broke that he was killed and Dr. Cooper was accused of doing it."

Jason berated himself for grasping at straws, but he had to try. Then a thought occurred to him. "What if someone wanted him to think that you were calling on Shelby's behalf?"

"Why would they do that?"

"Because they were setting him up to be killed."

Inez shivered. "How about I get you a hot drink?" Jason offered.

"Yes, please."

Jason returned to the table with medium-sized mocha lattes for them both. Inez grabbed hers with trembling hands and tried to take a sip.

"I don't understand how someone could make it look like I made that call," she said.

"The killer could have cloned your office number so Alessandro Rossi would pick up on his end."

"But Dr. Cooper only saw him for physical therapy, and that's been over for several months now. Wait a minute," Inez said, tapping her latte container. "I almost forgot. He was at GeneMedicine recently."

The unexpected tidbit jolted Jason. "When was this?" he asked as casually as he could.

"A couple of days before the murder," Inez said. "I was heading out to grab some lunch, and I saw Dr. Cooper with a man who looked like Mr. Rossi. They were leaving a meeting."

"Are you sure?"

"Yes. I thought it was some random business meeting she forgot to mention because it wasn't on her calendar. He seemed depressed. He looked up at me briefly. I remember his deep-blue eyes. His hair was on the long side. When the news broke, I checked the visitor's log. I wanted to see if it was the same guy, but when I checked, the name I found was a Sam Weston."

"An alias."

"Why would she sign him in under an alias instead of his real name?"

Jason didn't answer, but it occurred to him it was time to face his wife. Time to face what he had suspected for some time.

49

WHEN JASON ARRIVES in the visitor's room, before he takes a seat, before he utters a single word, I know things will be different. His eyes are bloodshot. He's unshaven, his outfit haphazardly thrown together. My husband takes pride in his appearance, and he's always impeccably groomed.

"You know, don't you?" I ask as he pulls out a chair.

He swallows hard and then gives me a deep, long stare. He looks away, as if trying to gain control over his thoughts, his emotions, and speech.

"Were you ever going to tell me?" he asks, finally.

"I don't know."

"That's all you have to say? Even after he died, you continued to keep it a secret?"

"I had to consider the consequences, Jason."

He shakes his head in disbelief. "That's not good enough, Shelby."

"I was ashamed, Jason. When I broke it off, I selfishly believed no good would come from me admitting what I had done."

"So it's true? You were having an affair with Alessandro Rossi?"

I don't answer right away. I can't. His glassy stare is carving my insides up into little pieces. I look down at my empty hands resting in my lap. A blanket of silence continues to cover us. Tears snake down my face.

"How did you find out?" I can barely get the words out. Perhaps they don't matter.

"How could you do this?" he asks. "Carrying on like a common tramp with a married man. A man I faced for months while you recovered from your injuries. Were the two of you mocking me behind my back? Stupid Jason, he's clueless."

"It wasn't like that at all, Jason. I never intended to hurt you so badly."

"Don't tell me it just happened," he hisses. "It's a stupid cliché."

I wipe the tears with the back of my hands. Shame pools in my stomach. I owe him an explanation that makes sense, although nothing about this situation does.

"At first, I was angry about your affair with Stephanie Hunt, devastated. That pain caused me to lose focus the day of the accident. On a subconscious level, I blamed you. If you hadn't cheated, if I hadn't gone riding that day and didn't get distracted by thoughts of you and Stephanie in bed together, then maybe…"

"So this was about payback, Shelby?"

"I don't know. Maybe. I don't think so. He was broken too."

"How long did it last?"

"A few months."

"All the while I was begging you to forgive me, to give us another chance, you were sleeping with him?"

I wince at his words. "No, Jason," I say weakly. "When I started to get better, we grew close. He was struggling in his marriage, partially because his wife was violent toward him and their children. We were both a mess."

"Do you know what I've been through while you've been in this place? Do you understand our children are destroyed because of the choices you made?"

"That's not fair, Jason. I had no way of knowing Mehmet

Koczak would commit murder to get his revenge. Alessandro is dead because of me. Gone from his family, used as collateral damage. That's an awful thing to live with."

Jason clenches his jaw, the way he does when he's trying to restrain himself. "If this gets out, law enforcement will have a motive in this case. They'll say you killed Alessandro to keep him from revealing the affair. Did you?"

A sudden coldness hits me at my core. My husband of sixteen plus years just asked me if I killed a man in cold blood. My brain goes on pause for a while, unable to form words. What is the appropriate answer to such a damning question?

"You can't be serious. How could you ask me if I did something so horrific, Jason?"

"So that's a firm no?" he asks.

"You're angry, and you have every right to be, but that was a low blow."

He sighs heavily. "You're right, I'm sorry."

"I know words can't fix what's broken, but I would take it all back if I could."

He pulls away from the table and stands up. "I have to go."

"Please don't. I have something important to tell you." The desperation in my voice gets his attention.

He sits once more. "What is it?" he asks, his tone cold and detached.

"Koczak didn't just kill Alessandro to get even with me. He stalked me for weeks leading up to the murder."

Jason leans in, hands steepled together. "What are you talking about?"

I explain all of it. The harassing phone calls, the photo of Abbie, the threats on the kids' lives, the GPS tracker on my car, the picture with my head cut off, the note I received in jail with two coffins labeled with the kids' names, and how I helped

Alessandro plan his exit from the U.S. and provided the resources to help him do so.

Jason tips his head from side to side. Then he says, "That's why you're in jail? Because you were trying to protect our children?" His voice is a whisper, audible only to the two of us.

"I did what I had to. Don't you feel guilty. I couldn't risk Koczak carrying out his threat of murdering our children. He killed Alessandro as proof of what he was capable of. I had to take him seriously. That's what he was betting on. If I was scared enough, I wouldn't tell you, and his plan would fall into place."

Stunned silence hangs in the air like an unwelcome stench. I plead with him to say something. Anything.

"I don't know what to say. I'm trying to grasp this, Shelby, and it's not easy."

Jason reaches across the table and covers my hands with his. He squeezes. He glances at the guards. The move is met with granite-hard stares. No touching allowed. They didn't make a big deal about it, nor did they make any sudden moves. A good thing, because I don't think my husband can take any more shocks to his system.

50

JASON RECLINED IN the leather chair as he drained his second glass of scotch. His study had become his sanctuary since the beginning of the family crisis. Tom Bilko was certainly earning every penny of the hefty fees Jason paid him, as the urgency to find Mehmet Koczak reached a fever pitch. As for Shelby's affair with Alessandro Rossi, did her sacrifice cancel out her betrayal? He didn't know. Jason shoved the question deep down. He would deal with his emotions later.

A knock on the door startled him. He placed the empty glass on a side table and stood to go answer.

"Who is it?" he asked.

"It's Vivian." Her muffled voice came through.

He ushered her in, and she took a seat. "What's going on?" she asked.

"What do you mean?" Jason remained standing.

"You reek of alcohol, and you look terrible. Something has got you upset, and I don't mean the fact that Shelby is in jail, although that is enough to make us all go off the deep end."

Jason didn't think about it. It just came out. "Shelby had an affair with Alessandro Rossi."

Vivian's mouth hung open. Then she shook her head in denial. "Who told you that ridiculous lie?"

"You didn't know?"

"You ask me that as if it really happened."

"It did. I heard it from her own lips," Jason said.

"Shelby never said a word to me, and you know we tell each other everything."

"The relationship must have been intense, huh?" Jason said. "She kept it a secret, even from you."

"Jason, please sit," Vivian said, patting a spot on the sofa next to her.

"Look at me," she commanded. "I love you and Shelby. I'm truly sorry you're going through this, but please don't do anything rash. Promise me you're going to bring her home and the two of you are going to fight for your marriage."

"I still don't understand why she did it," Jason murmured. "We were working through our issues and finding our way back to each other when she started up with this man."

"Only Shelby knows why," Vivian reasoned. "But I do know you're the love of her life. It would devastate her if she lost you."

"It doesn't make any damn sense," Jason whined. "It was the way she did it."

"What do you mean?"

"So calculating and deliberate. There were no signs that she was tempted or unhappy in our marriage."

"You feel robbed of the chance to convince her it was a bad idea?" Vivian deduced.

"Exactly. She says it wasn't revenge, but maybe it's my fault."

"There's no easy answer that makes the pain go away, Jason."

"I know. I can't help but feel like a hypocrite for getting angry about it, though."

Vivian touched his cheek with her palm. "It's going to be okay. It won't always hurt this much."

"I don't know what it means for us once this nightmare is

over. I can't focus on that right now. We must find the killer first. Do you know that psychopath was stalking her before the murder?"

Vivian's face twisted into a questioning frown. "What are you talking about?"

"The killer was harassing Shelby before he put a bullet in Alessandro Rossi and framed her for it." Jason provided an abbreviated version of the story he got from Shelby.

"That's just sick, Jason. Poor Shelby."

"The good news is, we might be closing in on him."

"The killer?"

"Yes. You won't believe this, but Mehmet Koczak might be behind it."

Vivian repeated the name, trying to make a connection. "The guy Shelby busted for selling out GeneMedicine?"

"That's the one."

"Are you serious? How did you find out?"

Jason recounted the story Shelby told him and Tom Bilko's evidence regarding Koczak's re-entry into the U.S.

Vivian stroked Jason's arm. He knew he wasn't imagining that or the unmistakable look in her eyes. *I'm not that drunk.*

"It's a lot to take in," he said, removing his arm from her reach. "But I can't go to the cops without proof. It's the only way to save Shelby."

Jason stood and paced up and down the study, wearing a hole into the plush rug. Vivian took several steps and placed her hands on both his shoulders.

"You're in a lot of pain, Jason," she said. "I wish there was something I could do to ease it, even if it's temporary. I would do anything for you. I hope you know that."

When did this become about me?

"I'm going to check on the kids," he told her and left her alone in the study.

51

JASON STOOD OUTSIDE the bedroom door and knocked twice. It was a spur-of-the-moment idea, inviting Vivian to dinner, just the two of them. It would give him an opportunity to have a serious, uninterrupted conversation with her about the other night. He didn't want to ruin their friendship over a potential misunderstanding, so he planned to clear the air regarding the boundaries between them.

He knocked three more times. Only silence followed. Jason pushed open the door and stepped into the bedroom Vivian occupied when she came to visit. He wasn't sure why he entered, but some invisible force beckoned him. It was a spacious room, and Vivian had decorated it with some of her favorite artwork and photos. She added a bookshelf and a rocking chair with an ottoman.

Nothing seemed out of the ordinary until he heard a distinct sound, a classical piece he recognized but couldn't name right away. Jason followed the sound, which came from the bed, which was empty except for a few decorative pillows. The ringing persisted. It sounded as though it came from the pillows. Strange. He lifted an ivory throw pillow and found nothing, but the sound grew louder.

Jason removed the pillows one by one until he found a cell phone. He picked it up and hit the answer button. A panicked male voice came through.

"I've been trying to reach you all day. We need to talk. It's urgent. Meet me in the abandoned lot behind Henry's Steak House at 10:00 p.m. tonight. Please. It's of the utmost importance."

The caller hung up. Jason stared at the phone. His mind raced. Dinner plans were now off the table. He deleted the call from the incoming log and returned the phone to its spot under the throw pillows. He reached for the door and looked both ways before leaving the room and closing the door behind him.

52

JASON ARRIVED AT the location the panicked caller mentioned. If he had to guess, he would say the caller was Mehmet Koczak. But why would Koczak call Vivian? That question had Jason in knots. Was Koczak threatening her, too? Was Vivian afraid of him?

Five minutes before the appointed time, he parked in the far corner of the parking lot, away from the lamppost, and shut off his headlights. Seconds ticked by. He started sweating and shut off the heat. It was a clear, brutally cold night in early January, and Jason had made sure he was bundled up. He anticipated having to exit the car.

At exactly ten, a dark SUV entered the parking lot. The driver killed the headlights as soon as the vehicle came to a stop. Jason flashed his headlights. Nothing. He flashed them again and waited. The door of the SUV swung open. This was it. Anticipation and caution bubbled up in equal measure. Jason couldn't say for sure who he would be dealing with. If it was Koczak, he had to be extra careful. The man was a murdering psychopath.

The figure got closer. A man wearing a heavy coat, scarf, and knit cap. The man cupped his hands and blew into them, an attempt to keep his hands warm against the brutal cold. Timing was crucial. Jason needed him close enough to catch him if the man decided to run. The man came into full view. *Mehmet Koczak.*

Jason clutched the door handle. When Koczak approached the window, he slammed the door open, smashing into Koczak's knees. The man squealed in agony and crumpled to the ground. Jason exited the car with lightning speed, shut the door, and knelt down beside him.

"Don't move," Jason commanded.

Koczak writhed in pain. His glasses were a few feet from where he fell. Jason ripped off the knit cap.

"Who are you?" Koczak croaked.

"Jason Cooper. Shelby Cooper's husband." Koczak attempted to get up under Jason's watchful eye. "Don't try to run."

Koczak managed to stand and staggered when he tried to walk. Jason took the opportunity to pat him down. "What are you doing here? And don't lie to me."

"I have to go. This was a mistake," Koczak said.

"No, it wasn't," Jason insisted. "You're going to tell me what I need to know."

Jason grabbed him by the collar of his coat and slammed him up against the car. Koczak winced. "You're crazy. You won't get away with this."

"Start talking," Jason said. "I won't ask you again. You're going to tell me why you asked Vivian to meet you here, and you're going to confess to the police that you killed Alessandro Rossi and framed my wife for it."

"I don't know what you're talking about."

Jason kneed him in the groin. Koczak fell to his knees in agony, then keeled over, hitting the cold cement with resignation. Jason stood over him, his fury barely contained.

"Let's try this again. Why did you call Vivian and tell her to meet you here? You said it was urgent, of the utmost importance."

Koczak struggled to sit up. Jason didn't offer to help. "It's freezing," he said, his teeth chattering. "Need to get to my car."

"You can sit in my car. If you try anything funny, you'll be eating out of a tube for a while," Jason threatened.

Koczak nodded miserably. Jason helped him up, and Koczak went to retrieve his glasses.

"Talk," Jason ordered, once Koczak was in the front passenger seat and closed the door.

"Could you put the heat on, please?"

Jason glared at him, then obliged.

"Thank you."

Jason had run into Mehmet Koczak a couple of times when he visited Shelby at GeneMedicine and never liked him. Shelby's stories about how Koczak tried to belittle her work because of her gender and her race made Jason's blood boil.

"I'm waiting for answers. Tell me now or else…"

"I don't know anyone named Vivian," Koczak said. "Perhaps I dialed incorrectly in my haste. It was a simple error."

An idea occurred to Jason. He reached into his pocket and pulled out his phone. He scrolled through some photos and found the right one.

He placed the phone in front of Koczak's face. "This is Vivian. She's the one you called."

Koczak frowned in confusion. "She's black."

Jason wanted to punch him in the face, but resisted the urge. Instead he said, "Your powers of observation are astonishing."

"I meant no offense, only to say that the woman I thought I was calling, Mia Lansing, is white, with blonde hair, green eyes, and freckles on her face and chest. She's very beautiful, but evil rules her." Koczak shivered. "I never intended to call this Vivian person."

A stunned Jason stared at Koczak so intently Koczak put his hands up in a defensive gesture, clearly afraid Jason would strike him again. Betty Lansing said her daughter Mia was dead.

Even more improbable, Betty Lansing was a black woman of light brown complexion. Was it possible that two women with the same name crossed his path? Vivian said Mia Lansing was Shelby's high school friend. Was this green-eyed blonde also a friend of Mia's? Did she assume her name to honor her memory? Not likely. Not if she's in cahoots with Koczak.

Jason grabbed Koczak by the collar. "Tell me everything you know about Mia and what she has to do with my wife being in jail. This is your one chance to set things right. Start from the beginning."

Koczak turned to him. "Please, I have a wife and children. If anything happens to me, they'll be in dire straits."

"I have a wife and kids, too. They *are* in dire straits because you took their mother from them."

Koczak rocked back and forth, hugging his body. Jason was getting impatient.

"Start from the beginning. And leave nothing out."

"I didn't want to do it, but she insisted," Koczak began.

"Who?"

"Mia. She said Shelby had to pay for what she did, that she destroyed Mia's family with lies."

"Go on."

"She offered me the opportunity to get my career back on track if I would help her."

"Help her how?"

Koczak swallowed hard. "Get rid of Shelby. Mia said she wanted Shelby to suffer. So she asked me to start stalking her, gave me information I could use."

"Where was she getting this information from?"

"I don't know. She said she knew everything there was to know about Shelby. At first, I thought I wasn't causing any harm. I could make a few calls, scare Shelby, and that would be the end of it. I would collect my reward and never cross paths with Mia again."

"But that wasn't the end, was it?" Jason couldn't keep the bitterness out of his voice.

"No." Koczak scratched his head. "When she introduced phase two, I realized I was in too deep."

"Phase two was to kill Alessandro?"

"Yes. Mia made it clear I would be severely punished, and my family executed if I didn't go along with her plan. She said she knew how to make it look like Shelby murdered Alessandro Rossi."

"What did she mean by that?"

"I don't know. She planned to call Mr. Rossi and pretend to be Shelby's assistant. She was setting the trap. I don't know the details."

Jason now shivered despite the heat cranked all the way up. His head spun. What kind of person would do something so heinous? Why did this Mia person hate Shelby so much? What was Shelby's history with the woman? Obviously, Mia was not her real name. Jason was sure of it. Those kinds of coincidences just didn't happen in his world.

He spent another hour in the car with Koczak, extracting details about the setup and anything that could help him catch "Mia Lansing." Koczak said she approached him one day after a lecture. She had read about Shelby blowing the whistle on him selling company secrets.

Mia said she had a way Koczak could get even with Shelby and gain back his reputation. She would pay him handsomely for his cooperation. But Mia was tight-lipped about her personal life. All she would say was that she grew up in Maryland, and that she and her sister lost their father tragically. It was just the two girls and their mother until they moved away for college. Mia never said how she knew Shelby.

Jason kicked Koczak out of his car and told him not to plan on taking a vacation any time soon. As he drove home, Jason couldn't help but think that the fake Mia Lansing might have attended Johns Hopkins with Shelby. What happened between the two women that was so bad it drove fake Mia to commit murder and pin the crime on his wife?

53

JASON STOOD OUTSIDE Vivian's room and knocked. She ushered him in and asked him to sit. He hadn't planned what to say, but the matter couldn't wait.

"I prefer to stand," he said.

"You're scaring me, Jason. What's going on? Bad news about Shelby?"

"Why would you think that?" he asked.

"The look on your face. It's tragic."

"This whole thing has been a tragedy. Too many casualties."

"Meaning what exactly?"

"Vivian, did Mehmet Koczak threaten you?"

"I… I… why would you ask me that?"

"It's important, Vivian. I won't get angry with you, but I need you to be truthful. Did Koczak threaten to do you harm if you didn't keep your mouth shut about what he had planned for Shelby?"

Vivian sat in the rocking chair. Jason knelt in front of her and lifted her chin so he could look her directly in the eyes.

"Were you afraid for your life and kept quiet about what Koczak was doing? Did Mia Lansing threaten you?"

Vivian almost fell out of the chair.

"I need the truth, Vivian," Jason pressed. "Koczak is going

down for his part in framing Shelby while the cops pursue the mastermind, this Mia Lansing. Shelby will be home any day now."

"Can I trust you?" she asked, finally. "I mean really trust you not to abandon me?"

"Have I ever abandoned you, Vivian, or betrayed you?"

"No, you haven't," she admitted.

"So tell me what's going. Let's end this nightmare."

"You're right, Jason." Vivian left the rocking chair and paced the room. "Koczak contacted me. We had met once before when I came to town. Shelby and I were having drinks at a hotel bar. The Intercontinental if I remember correctly.

Anyway, Koczak was there, and Shelby introduced me as the closest thing she has to a sister. He was cordial enough and then went about his business. I thought that was the end of it until Shelby ratted him out for corporate espionage."

"What happened next?" Jason asked.

Vivian stopped pacing and leaned up against the dresser. "A couple of months before Shelby's arrest, Koczak reached out to me. It caught me off guard. He said he knew of my reputation in the art world, and some wealthy art-collector friend of his wanted to meet me. I assumed he was still in Turkey where he supposedly went after they kicked him out of GeneMedicine.

Vivian resumed her pacing. She said, "Then things turned ugly. He started asking deeply personal questions about Shelby. I got suspicious and told him I was done talking to him. He said it would give him great pleasure to kill Shelby for ruining his life, and the only way I could save her was by telling him what he wanted to know."

Jason swore. He approached Vivian, grabbed her by the shoulders, and shook her. "So you just sold out Shelby to a killer?" His voice was almost hoarse with emotion.

She looked up at him defiantly. "He had a hit list, Jason,

his own sick, twisted idea of vengeance. If I got in the way of his plans for Shelby, he warned me the kids would be first. Miles and Abbie. Then he said he would take you out afterward, and then me. When he murdered Alessandro Rossi, he called me to brag about his handiwork, and to remind me we would all meet the same fate if I didn't keep my mouth shut."

Jason dropped his hands from Vivian's shoulders. They hung limp at his sides. He took a few shaky steps and plopped down on the bed. He didn't trust his legs to support him. Koczak's plan was well orchestrated. He had both Shelby and Vivian in his evil clutches and used Jason's kids as leverage to carry out his vendetta.

Jason understood Vivian was afraid, but the two of them had been close once. Why didn't she trust him? Why did she allow Shelby and the kids to suffer so much? What wasn't she telling him?

Vivian walked over to an armchair to retrieve her purse. She rifled through it, then removed a photo and handed it to Jason. He took the photo from her, and recognition flooded his brain. Shelby described this very photo to him when she confessed Koczak was stalking her for weeks leading up to the murder. Jason remembered the day the picture was taken at Gillette Stadium. The Patriots played the Carolina Panthers. Vivian and Shelby felt guilty for rooting for the Panthers because they grew up in North Carolina.

Jason shook his head. Doubt and confusion took root. "Kozcak said he doesn't know you. He didn't recognize you when I showed him your photo."

Vivian scoffed. "The man is a killer and obviously a good actor. Do you think he's going to tell you the truth?" she asked, folding her arms. "Look, I'm not proud of what I did, Jason, keeping this from you and Shelby. I thought cooperating with Koczak was the only way to stop things from escalating."

"You could have said something, Vivian. Warned me, dropped a hint."

"I figured it was the only way to keep us alive until you could spring Shelby from jail. I didn't think she would be in jail this long, Jason, almost two months. And Koczak didn't let up with the threats, even after she was arrested. I had to keep you guys safe. It's what Shelby asked me to do, to look out for you and the kids."

Vivian joined Jason at the edge of the bed. "I know you're disappointed in me. I didn't know any other way to deal with the situation. I would do anything for you guys, the only family I have, even if it meant helping a psychopath. You're alive, and the kids and Shelby. It may sound cruel, Jason, but that's the most important thing to me. The rest," she said and shrugged her shoulders, "will work itself out. Shelby will come home because she's innocent."

"You could have let me know you were in trouble," Jason insisted, his voice tight.

Vivian wiped her tears and looked up at him with new grit and determination. "I did what I had to do. I was honest with you about why I did it. If you can't deal with the truth, I'll leave your house right now. I can't stay here if you're going to pass judgment on me."

54

SHELBY WOULD BE home soon, but Jason needed to be careful with the information he unofficially extracted from Koczak. He wanted verification. He didn't want to give Shelby hope and have that hope savagely ripped from her if the police and District Attorney's office declined to pursue those leads.

Jason had returned to the master bedroom in anticipation of his wife's return. He peeled off his shirt and tossed it on the empty vintage armchair, not bothering to place it in the laundry basket. His phone buzzed from the bed, where he placed it earlier. It was Tom Bilko calling. Jason picked up immediately.

"Did you find anything?" he asked.

"No. I have bad news, Jason," Tom said. "Mehmet Koczak is dead."

He flopped down on the bed. The realization of what this could mean for Shelby's release crashed in on him, choking him. "What happened?"

"Not sure. State police went by to interview him earlier this evening, and when they got to his apartment, he was already dead."

"How?"

"Bullet to the head. Same as Alessandro Rossi."

Jason said nothing. He was incapable of forming a coherent thought.

"Jason, are you there?" Tom Bilko's anxious voice came down the line. "I'm terribly sorry, man. I thought we had this one in the bag. But at least we know he was involved. His conversation with you is more information than we had before. Now that he's gone, Shelby can get out on bail until they catch this Mia Lansing chick."

"We'll talk in the morning," Jason said, and then hung up.

55

KOCZAK'S FIRSTHAND ACCOUNT would have been powerful," Alan Rose says. "But I want you to focus on the good news. He gave us a name. Now, we hunt for this Mia Lansing and bring her in. We deliver a solid suspect."

I'm only half listening to Alan, who sits across from me in the tiny attorney-client meeting room. Jason finally broke down and told me Koczak confessed his involvement in framing me, but wound up dead. When Jason delivered the news, it was as if all the air in my body escaped and there was nothing left except a limp, shriveled up carcass.

"Shelby, this news makes our case that much stronger and the district attorney's case more difficult to prove," Alan says, pulling me out of my thoughts. "We have more than reasonable doubt. Koczak partnered with Mia Lansing, who gave him the opportunity to make his revenge fantasy a reality. The fact that she's a cold-blooded killer benefits us, no disrespect to the deceased Mr. Rossi."

"All this great information that could free me is coming from my husband, not exactly an impartial third party," I say.

"I'm going to file the paperwork to have all the charges dropped," Alan announces. "You're going to be out of here soon."

I sit up straighter in my chair. "Do you really think you can get the charges dropped? There's no one to corroborate Jason's story about his encounter with Koczak."

"Why don't you let me worry about that? And don't forget that Koczak also threatened Vivian. Her statement will carry weight as well."

Excitement builds in my veins. Little drips at first, and then a dam breaks wide open. "There's documented evidence that Koczak had reason for a vendetta against me. A simple Google search will pull up kinds of articles on the whole mess. I can point you to the right people at GeneMedicine who can explain how his scheme cost the company millions."

"Now you're thinking." Alan smiles. He has this one all buttoned up, he seems to be saying. There's only one problem with all this good news. Neither Jason nor Alan knows that I'm the real Mia Lansing.

A LETTER ARRIVED today. It's from my brother Michael, who warned me it was coming. The ladies from Cell Block D28 and E30 are at arts and crafts. While they string beads together and draw, I sit isolated with the letter on the table before me. I pick it up. Whatever it says won't change anything. But I'm dead wrong.

Dear Mia,

You must think it's strange hearing from your daddy after all these years. If you're reading this letter, it means I'm dead or close to it. If you're reading this letter, I know you made it. Thank God. Baby girl, I messed up bad. I was supposed to protect you, but I was too scared. Too scared the truth would come out if I went against your mother and stopped her from hurting you.

I'm sorry I was weak, and you had to pay for it. But I can't undo what I did—letting you walk out of the house at fifteen, alone, pregnant, scared, and confused. Every day for weeks I tried to find you, to bring you home, to tell you it was a mistake. And every day I went home empty-handed. Your daddy ceased to exist the day you walked out of that kitchen. Every night I dreamt you would walk through the door and your smiling face would make me so happy. I would have your bread pudding from LaFayette Bakery waiting for you. I was willing to take whatever your Mama was going to throw at me, but I came to that point too late. Maybe it was God's way of taking you away from a Mama who was as mean as Satan and a daddy who betrayed you because he couldn't stand up for you.

Years ago, when you were little, I did something terrible. Your mother knows what I did. And ever since that day, your daddy has been a prisoner to the secret and your mama the warden. I don't want you to blame her cause I messed up. I always taught you and your brother to respect her and never talk bad about her, but I think you're grown enough to hear the truth now.

When you were about eight years old, and your brother Michael was three, I had a secret lady friend. I know it wasn't right, and I won't make excuses. This lady also had a husband who wasn't very nice to her. We met when she came to my garage to fix her car. Anyway, we got to chatting, and before you know it, she would come by the shop almost every day.

One night, her husband showed up unexpectedly, acting crazy. When he found us, he came after me and we got to tussling. The guy went for my throat. In self-defense, I shoved him hard.

I must have pushed too hard because he lost his balance and hit his head on the dresser. The blow killed him instantly. My lady friend told me she would say he was drunk and fell, and I was never there. Since nobody knew about us, it was easy enough to cover up. But my conscience wouldn't let it lie. I had to tell your mother. And ever since, your daddy had to do what she said.

I'm so ashamed, baby girl. I wish I was the kind of father you deserved. One who was strong and would protect his little girl no matter what her Mama said or did. If you're married, I hope you chose wisely so my grandbabies can have a better daddy than you did.

I ask your forgiveness, baby girl. That's the only thing that matters to me now.

I love you.
Your Daddy

I focus on the ladies on the bench next to me. I can't see what they're drawing, but my eyes lock in on their movements because if I don't distract myself, I will break wide open in front of them. The tears are circling, so I stare harder. The burning in my chest intensifies as I clutch the letter with such force that my fingernails dig into the palm of my hand, leaving marks. My cellmate Elsa looks up from her task.

"What you staring at, college girl?" she asks.

I don't answer. I'm incapable of pulling off the simplest of speech. The other women turn their attention to me.

"Look out, she's gonna blow," one of them says.

And I do.

56

THREE DAYS AFTER state police discovered Mehmet Koczak's body, Jason arrived in the busy lobby of Boston's Four Seasons Hotel. Guests were checking in and out, while bellhops hauled overburdened luggage carts to and from the cars that pulled up to the front of the hotel.

He spotted Nicholas right away, seated in a cluster of chairs with a small table at its center, across from the front desk. Nicholas caught sight of Jason and gestured for him to come over.

Nicholas's expression was inscrutable, his hands firmly on a black leather folder on his lap.

"Is that it? The information that's going to help me take down Bob Engels for good?" Jason asked.

"Use this wisely." Nicholas handed Jason the folder. "What's in here—let's just say Bob Engels is not a nice man."

Jason pondered that remark for long seconds. Whatever was in that file could destroy lives. But, he reasoned, if he wanted to checkmate Bob Engels, he needed a little vacation from his conscience. Besides, everything had changed. Jason wasn't one to walk away when the going got tough, and it had been tough for the past couple of months. But somewhere between Shelby's arrest, the pain and suffering it brought to the family, and Bob's attempts to throw him out of Orphion, Jason had reached his limit.

"I already knew that," Jason told Nicholas.

"I'm just saying, you have a family to consider."

"It's that bad?" Jason asked.

Nicholas said nothing. Jason opened the file and started reading. The first page summarized the findings. He looked up at Nicholas. Nicholas just nodded, as if he understood, and told him to keep reading. He did. By the time Jason reached the third page, he closed the file and loosened his tie.

"Tell me again why you went through so much trouble to get me this information? And don't say it's because you owe me. There's more to the story."

Nicholas looked away. When he focused on Jason again, there was pain in his eyes.

He said, "My parents grew up in Chiapas, Mexico. To say the poverty rate was high is an understatement. I'll spare you the details of how they made it out and came to the United States. My father got an opportunity to make some money, so he took it."

What he means, Jason thought, *is that his father entered the drug trade.*

"He worked hard and learned as much as he could, and soon he was calling the shots in his own enterprise."

"What does this have to do with the reason you handed me this file?" Jason asked.

"I'm getting to that. I don't condone what my father did. He destroyed many lives because of the way he earned a living. That's why I worked hard to make the family business legitimate. It wasn't easy, but I succeeded.

"Now, along comes Bob Engels, and others like him. They get preachy about illegal drugs. But Bob's business operated on the same principle as a drug cartel. Profit first. Eliminate your enemies. Show no mercy."

Jason breathed in and out and tried to control his spinning

thoughts. Did he really want to know *all* the grisly details of what was in that file? Nicholas wanted revenge. To stick it to the hypocrites, and what bigger hypocrite was there than Bob Engels?

"Is that how you really see things? That Bob Engels should pay for his greed, and I should be the one to bring him down instead of you?"

"I owe you," Nicholas said.

"You keep saying that. How long have you been waiting for an opportunity to call it even?"

"Does it matter?"

"I guess it doesn't," Jason conceded.

"Don't forget, Bob came to me, not the other way around. We're both successful in business because we have good instincts."

"So you're really legit, or is real estate just a front?"

"Ah, amigo, you've always been blunt," Nicholas said with a chuckle. "Real estate is one of my many business ventures. I pay corporate taxes and hire Harvard MBAs. And sometimes, my senora gets asked to be on the board of some charity or fancy museum."

Jason couldn't help it. He chuckled, too. Nicholas had given him an unexpected gift. He marveled at the irony. The most shameful thing he had ever done in his life, getting involved with Nicholas and his family business, had circled back decades later to hand him a vindication he never thought he would need.

57

WHEN JASON'S PHONE rang and he saw it was Alan Rose, he picked up right away, even though he was on a major highway with a tollbooth straight up ahead. Alan didn't bother with his customary greeting.

"The district attorney's office is taking the case before a grand jury," Alan said. "A recording of Shelby threatening to kill Alessandro Rossi has surfaced. As if that wasn't bad enough, video footage of the garage where she parked her car has also surfaced.

"It shows Shelby leaving and returning from the garage the day of the murder. The defense is not allowed at a grand jury hearing. A grand jury indictment will speed up the trial date."

Jason remained silent. He drove past the tollbooth and braked hard. Then he backed up and dug for change in the cup holder. He should have listened to Shelby, who was always nagging him to get an EZ Pass. He kept putting it off and then just forgot after a while.

"Jason, are you there?" Alan asked.

"Yes. Give me a second."

He paid the toll and sped off. "How long before the DA's office makes the announcement?"

"A few days."

"I see," Jason said. "Have you told Shelby?"

"No. I'm on my way to visit her."

"Don't say anything to her yet. Give me a few hours. I promise I'll circle back with you."

After Jason hung up, he broke the speed limit and kept his fingers crossed the police wouldn't pull him over. His family had enough legal woes to last a lifetime, which is exactly what would happen if Shelby didn't get out of Bayport.

He pulled into a parking space at Orphion headquarters. His hand shook as he picked up the file Nicholas gave him off the front passenger seat. Jason read every page. He then opened the car windows to let in some fresh air. The cold blast hit him full force. Enough, he mumbled, and closed the windows with the push of a button, killed the engine, and exited the car.

Jason headed to the copy machine on the third floor, where he was less likely to run into anyone. His assistant taught him that trick. He removed the papers from the folder, fed the entire stack into the machine, and watched it suck the document in, page by page.

"Hey, Jason. I didn't know you were coming in today."

It was Susan, his head of investor relations.

"Plans change."

Susan stepped closer to him. "Are you okay, Jason? Why are you copying documents? You have an admin for that."

He couldn't afford to act guilty or nervous in front of Susan. "I do, but sometimes you need to do things yourself. I don't mind."

Susan's expression was one of confusion, but Jason couldn't worry about that. The next sentence out of her mouth floored him, however.

She leaned in and whispered. "Did you hear about the meeting? Is that why you came in?"

Play it cool. Don't get rattled.

"Which one are you referring to? I spend a lot of time in meetings."

"Come on, Jason. Don't play coy. Charlie is in with the full board in a hush-hush, impromptu meeting. Since you're the CFO, I figured you got wind of the meeting and wanted to be here when they get out."

"You got me," he said to Susan with a forced smile.

Jason excused himself and took the elevator to the twentieth floor that housed the executive offices, including his own. He knew exactly which conference room the meeting was in. He didn't knock, just barged in, uninvited. Everyone turned around, startled, and speechless. Charlie couldn't hide his shock. His mouth fell open. Bob crossed his arms and sneered. The remaining seven board members sat stone-faced.

Jason tucked the folder under his arm. He apologized for interrupting the meeting, even though he was anything but sorry. Angry? Yes. Betrayed? Absolutely.

"What's going on, Jason? We're in the middle of an important meeting. Board members only," Bob said.

As if he could forget. Chairman of the Board also went with the CEO title, a role Jason had looked forward to when he took over from Charlie.

"I know this is a board-members-only gathering, but I have something to say that might be of interest to the board and may affect the outcome of this meeting."

Papers shuffled. People murmured. "Can't this wait, Jason?" Charlie asked. "It's quite unusual to interrupt a board meeting this way."

Good old Charlie. He knew how to insult you without making it look like he was.

"No, it cannot wait, Charlie." Jason took an empty seat next to Charlie's admin, Sarah Roberts, and poured himself a glass of water from the pitcher on the table.

Clyde Simmons, the longest serving board member, nodded

in Charlie's direction. Charlie's lips formed a grim line. He cleared his throat.

"Jason, perhaps it's a good thing you're here after all. We—"

"It's all right, Charlie. I know why you convened this meeting in secret. I guess you're rewarding my loyalty and dedication to Orphion with treachery."

Jason let that statement sink in. He took in the expression of every single person in the room. Charlie had the decency to lower his head slightly. Clyde Simmons looked like he wanted to say something but thought better of it. Sarah pretended to write in her notebook.

"I'll be moving on from Orphion, effective end of business today," Jason told the gathering. "You'll have my official resignation letter, of course."

Turning to Charlie, he said, "I'm sure you'll want to get on a call with Wyndham PR soon. If you don't mind, I'd like to read and approve the press release announcing my departure before it hits the business press."

A hush fell over the room. Charlie's mouth dropped open. Clyde reached for a pitcher of water. Sarah got to it first and poured. The other members stared at the wall.

Charlie recovered first. "Jason, you're invaluable to Orphion, and no one can deny you've been an incredible asset—"

Jason interrupted Charlie for the second time since crashing the meeting. "No need for platitudes, Charlie. I understand my current domestic situation doesn't reflect well for the company. My family needs me more than I need Orphion.

"You were right, Bob," Jason said, turning to him. "Family is everything to me, and I won't compromise them for anyone or anything, not even the IPO of a lifetime. They need one hundred percent of my attention."

"You're doing the right thing, Jason," Bob said. "We always

knew you would do what was right for the company. You're a man of integrity, and the company was lucky to have you at the helm of its finances."

"Thank you, Bob. I'm glad you feel that way, which is why I couldn't in good conscience leave Orphion without revealing what I know."

Bob's smirk disappeared. Charlie leaned in; his palms flat on the table. All eyes were trained on Jason.

"What is this, Jason?" Clyde asked. "Some kind of shakedown?"

"No need for insults, Clyde. We're among friends, aren't we?"

Clyde held up his hands in surrender.

Jason wanted the farce over with, so he jumped right in. "My pending exit is the least of Orphion's problems. The information in here," he said waving the file, "could be nothing less than catastrophic for the company if it gets out."

Jason wasn't one for theatrics, but the idea of outing Bob in the presence of the entire board made him want to break out the champagne.

The board members all looked and each other, and then shook their shoulders as if to say, *I have no idea what he's talking about.*

"If you have something to say, then say it," Clyde said.

"I have documented evidence in this file that Bob Engels, while CEO of ABX Pharmaceuticals, was aware of rampant corruption in his organization and did nothing to stop it."

"I would be very careful if I were you," Bob said. "You just hurled a serious accusation at me. There will be serious consequences."

Jason ignored him. "Specifically, falsifying data for the company's Alzheimer's drug and hiding the real data from federal regulators. There were dozens of confirmed deaths from the failed clinical trials. Bob was complicit, if not fully involved in the coverup.

"The lead scientist conducting the trials threatened to go to the authorities. Before he had the chance, a cleaning crew discovered his dead body in his lab. An apparent suicide, investigators said. Yet, Dr. Charles Lipkin had everything to live for. He looked forward to the birth of his first child."

Bob pointed a finger at Jason. "This is an outrage. How dare you? Who do you think you are barging in here with your ridiculous fantasies? Do you know who I am?"

"Yes," Jason said. "A lying, murdering hypocrite."

"Jason," Charlie said, his voice low. "You better explain yourself. Quickly."

"I'll do better than that." Jason opened the file, pulled out a single sheet, and reached over to hand it to Charlie. "Thomas Cardwell of the U.S. Attorney's Office Eastern District will tell you everything you need to know."

Jason then turned to Bob, whose face had lost all color. Charlie passed the sheet to Clyde Simmons, who took off his glasses and threw them on the table after he read the document. One by one, the board members read what their colleague had done. One by one, they shook their heads, incredulous.

"I turned over all the evidence I had to Tom Cardwell this morning," Jason told Bob. "The file I'm holding is my original copy. Trying to obtain it won't do you any good." It was a trick. Jason didn't want Bob coming after him because of the file. The man was capable of horrible things. He was the U.S Attorney's problem now.

Jason pulled his chair away from the table and then stood. "I'll let you gentlemen continue with your meeting."

58

WE'VE SUFFERED A setback," Alan says.

I was expecting him to tell me he posted my bail, and I can get out of here. Koczak is dead, and he confessed he helped the real killer frame me, although I'm still not clear on why a woman I've never met would do this.

"What are you talking about? They can't keep me here, not with the main suspect running loose and her accomplice confessing."

"The district attorney is taking the case to a grand jury. Next week."

"That's bullshit, Alan!" I screech, slamming my hands on the table. "They can't do that. They should be looking for that psychotic woman. Why aren't they?" I demand.

"The police received an anonymous tip that you were having an affair with Alessandro Rossi, and your motive for killing him was to stop him from exposing the affair to your powerful husband, who would take your children from you."

Alan's smile is brittle. He won't look at me. At the moment, he's a friend, not my lawyer. A friend I betrayed. He warned me from the beginning he didn't want to get blindsided, that it could make the work to prove my innocence more difficult.

"I'm sorry. I don't know what else to say. For the record,

Jason would never take the kids from me. He threatened to do that once, but he didn't mean it." I'm babbling and need to stop.

"That's not all," Alan says wearily. "There's a recorded phone conversation of you threatening to kill Rossi if he exposed the affair. The district attorney has that recording and will play it for the grand jury. I'll have to wait until afterward to listen for myself."

I remain silent as I hear the sound of my freedom being flushed down a very large toilet.

Alan continues. "In all my years of practice, I've never had a strange case like this, a client who sabotaged their own case."

I'm thinking about how I can get admitted for a mental health evaluation and treatment. I should tell them I'm suicidal. They'll pump me full of drugs. Once in a drug-induced haze, I won't feel a thing.

"Shelby, are you listening?" Alan asks.

I can barely breathe. *Is this how it ends? Oh God, please don't let it end this way.*

"It doesn't look good, does it?" I say.

"It's disappointing, but far from over. There is one thing that really worries me, though."

"What is it? What else could go wrong?" I gripe.

"The district attorney and his team claim they have, in their possession, videotape of you leaving the parking garage at GeneMedcine and returning, all within the timeframe of the murder. The coroner says Alessandro Rossi was killed between 11:00 a.m. and 3:00 p.m. on November 14. Either all of your colleagues lied when they backed up your alibi or you have a twin running around town committing murder."

"I swear on my children's life, I did not leave the garage that day until it was time to go home. Maybe this psycho found someone who looked like me to drive the car and return it, but it wasn't me. You have all the documentation that proves I was in the office between those hours."

"I know. The tape hasn't been authenticated, and I can argue they were doctored. All the killer had to do was superimpose your head on someone else's body, someone with the same build as you. It's diabolical, but that's what we're dealing with.

"I'll also challenge the chain of custody on all the prosecution's evidence: the tapes, the recorded phone conversation, etcetera. The burden of proof is still on the prosecution, not us."

Panic stabs me like a hundred sharp needles. My family's suffering is about to increase tenfold. My husband will be publicly humiliated. It's one thing to confess to an affair in private, and quite another to have it out in the open, to be judged by people who don't know you.

"I fully expect to win this case, Shelby," Alan says. "The voice recording hasn't been verified. The person hasn't identified him/herself or explained how he/she got the audio recording of a private cell phone conversation. That casts doubt about the credibility of this witness. I can get that tossed out easily. Jason can corroborate your testimony about the stalking. I'm not worried yet. Concerned, yes, but not worried. A grand jury will see this for the shaky circumstantial case it is. We will win."

I'm only half-listening to Alan because I'm mentally making funeral plans. What dress should I wear? Something dark or pastel? A nice Chanel suit should do it. May as well go out in style.

I'll ask Anton to help me pick the right scriptures. Wouldn't it be funny if he performed the funeral service? I'd like to think we've come to terms with our history. He even mentioned that he started a search for our son.

What would even be funnier is if our son showed up at my funeral. "Here lies my no-good mother who threw me away," he would say. "Glad I never got to know that witch. I was better off without her."

59

PLEASE, MR. NEWMAN," Abbie pleaded. "I don't have anyone else I can ask."

She hoped her desperation was enough to compel Mr. Newman to help her. The guidance counselor who had been a lifeline for her at school was Abbie's last resort. The past couple of days had been hell on earth. Just when it looked like mom was coming home, everything blew up. Now the DA's office wanted her mother to stand trial for murder because of so-called new evidence that recently came to light.

The LAN line at home rang non-stop. TV crews camped out at the end of their driveway and shouted mean questions at her dad. Dad resigned from his job before everything went nuts. Abbie suspected he knew what was coming and wanted to protect her and Miles.

When Abbie thought about her mother possibly spending the rest of her life in prison, it was just too much to bear. She had to see her mom. Help her shore up the courage to keep fighting until she was free.

"You're asking me to go against the wishes of both your parents. Not to mention if the headmaster finds out, he could fire me," Mr. Newman reminded her.

Why did he have to be so logical all the time, so straitlaced? "You gotta live a little, Mr. Newman. You think all the people who changed the world played by the rules? They didn't. Martin Luther King, Jr., Nelson Mandela, Shakespeare, Sir Isaac Newton, Confucius, Ben Franklin… I could do this all day."

"Okay, okay," he said, holding up his hand and grinning. "I get it. But can I ask you a question?"

"You can ask me anything."

"Why are you so determined to see your mother after both she and your dad made it clear they didn't want you or your brother in the jail environment?"

Abbie swallowed. "You don't understand. I feel lost without my mother, like there's a huge hole in my heart and only seeing her can fill it."

Mr. Newman stiffened. The pen he was holding looked like it could snap at any minute. Then he said, "I do understand what it's like to want something so badly you're willing to bend the rules to get it."

"So, you'll help me?" Abbie asked, hope sprouting from her.

"I'll think about it. We would have to do this on a day I'm out of the office."

"Just name the date and time, and I'll be there," Abbie said eagerly. "I even looked up the visiting rules online."

"I'm not making any promises. But you know they'll need proof of parental consent."

"Already thought of that. Saw it on the prison website. The consent form has to be presented when we go in. All I need is my dad's signature."

"How do you intend to get it?" Mr. Newman asked, his gaze curious.

"I'll download the forms from the prison website. After that, the less you know, the better. I can't explain how I work my voodoo."

He shook his head. "There's nothing I can do to talk you out of it, is there?"

"Nope. And don't worry, I won't tell anyone."

"Not even the Rainbow Posse?" He smiled that adorable, dimpled smile.

"You know about that?"

"I pay attention."

"Well, I can't risk this getting out for the reasons you mentioned. So, no, not even my girlfriends."

60

TWO HOURS WILL be plenty of time for us to get there and back," Abbie said. "I'll call my dad on the way and let him know I'm going with you to the art supply store, so he won't get suspicious."

"Are you sure you want to do this?" Ty asked. "Your parents could get really mad at you and ground you forever."

"I wouldn't do it if there was another way. They've left me no choice."

"You've never disobeyed them before. Not on anything major."

"I've never had to. It's like I told Mr. Newman, sometimes you have to break the rules to get things done, and it's not like I'm doing anything bad. I just want to see my mother. Don't you think I deserve that?"

"You deserve everything your heart desires, Cooper. Everything."

"Thanks, Ty. I appreciate you saying that."

Abbie and Ty sat in the chapel finalizing the details of the great escape from school to Bayport Women's Correctional Institution in Framingham, a fifteen-minute drive from Castleview. Abbie knew she could trust Ty implicitly and he would help her, no matter what.

They planned to take a cab to downtown Framingham. Abbie would enter Creative Juice art supply store from the front entrance on Concord Street but exit in the back on Howard Street. Mr. Newman would be waiting to drive her to the women's prison. The cab would return with Ty after thirty minutes with Sarah Giles, a classmate who was the same height and build as Abbie. They didn't look alike, but that was okay. The idea was to make it look like Abbie and Ty went to the store and left together with their purchases.

"Are you sure you can handle it? Seeing your mom like that, I mean?" Ty asked.

"I can't think about that. I'm not the first kid visiting a parent in jail, as horrible as it sounds."

"What about Mr. Newman? He could get in serious trouble. And your dad could go postal on him."

"My problem. I'll handle it."

"Mr. Newman must really care about you to go out on a limb like that."

"I know. It's strange."

"Strange how?" Ty asked.

"He was always nice to me, but ever since Mom's been in jail, he's been going above and beyond."

"Really?"

"Yeah. He said he understands why I need to do this," Abbie explained.

"Wow. That's deep."

"Yeah. I feel like I can talk to him about anything."

"Tell Mr. Newman you already have a best friend and confidante," Ty says.

Abbie chuckled. "Jealous much?"

"Maybe. I don't want any other guy moving in on my number-one girl, even if it's good old Mr. Newman."

61

A PRISON GUARD IS banging on the bars of my cell with his baton. I find the intrusion rude and inhumane. "Hey Cooper, you got visitors," he yells.

He caught me during my daily afternoon ritual of self-pity, self-loathing, and rage. I'm not expecting visitors, which makes his intrusion more infuriating.

"Who is it?"

"Do I look like your social secretary? Move it!"

I get up from the bottom bunk and follow him to the visitor's room.

It can't be true, but my vision still works fine. I step into the visitor's room, my back to the wall. I see my daughter, head bowed, staring at her hands. Her guidance counselor, Mr. Newman, sits next to her.

She's frightened, but I recognize her game face. They haven't yet spotted me, and for a split second, I consider going back to my cell, ashamed and humiliated, but mostly worried about what it would do to Abbie.

I run my fingers through my hair and then place my hands over my face to take care of any stray tears that may have appeared. She will fall apart if she suspects I'm not coping well. I'm not sure how she convinced her counselor to bring her here, but that's my

Abbie: resourceful, determined, unstoppable. I take a deep, aching breath and walk toward them.

"Abbie, sweetheart, what are you doing here?"

"Mom!" She stands, arms outstretched, then drops them to her sides.

"I had to see you," Abbie says, barely able to breathe as she takes a seat. "I had to see… see for myself how you were doing. We miss you, Mom. We just want you to come home."

"I know, sweetheart, that's what I want, too. And I will. It's just taking a little while. Look out for your brother and obey your father. Can you do that for me?"

Abbie nodded.

"How is Miles?" I ask.

"He's sad all the time, and just wants you home, like we all do. He hangs out in his room too much, so I check on him often. Dad is threatening to take us to a child psychologist."

"Your dad is worried about the both of you."

"Nothing's wrong with us, Mom. We don't need therapy; we just want our mother home."

"Hang on just a little longer. Have faith that things will turn around. Don't ever give up hope, no matter what's being said or how bad things look."

I turn my attention to Mr. Newman. "I suspect Abbie was very persuasive, convincing you to bring her here. You have my gratitude. I won't say a word to Mr. Cooper or the headmaster."

"Thank you, Mrs. Cooper. I was glad to help. Abbie has been doing remarkably well, considering…"

Mr. Newman tried to find a nice way of saying Abbie was doing well, considering the possibility that I could spend the rest of my life in prison. I let him off the hook.

"You can say it. I'm an accused killer. It's my reality for now."

Mr. Newman looked away, nervous and unsure of what to

say. Abbie says to him, "It's okay, Mr. Newman. Mom doesn't bite. She might bark a little, but no one takes it seriously."

"Sweetheart, promise me you won't come back to visit," I plead.

"But Mom, I need to see you."

"You don't belong here, Abbie. It's not a good environment for kids. I love you and your brother more than my own life. I may be behind bars, but I'm still your mother. My priority is the well-being of you and your brother. The two of you need to go on about the business of being kids. Even Mr. Newman would agree with me."

"Your mother is right, Abbie," Mr. Newman concurred.

My daughter remains determined, however. "How can we do that when you're in here? Nothing is going to be normal until you're out of this place."

"Try. Promise me, Abbie. Don't spend your days worrying about me. I'm too stubborn to be in here much longer. Now, can you please get back to school before your father finds out you tricked him?"

62

ABBIE COULDN'T LET Mr. Newman see her do the ugly cry, so she covered her face. They had barely made it out of Bayport when she let it rip. She believed she was strong, ready to face anything. Turns out she was fooling herself. Mr. Newman pulled over on a side street in a residential area so she could get it out of her system.

"It's okay, Abbie," he said, trying to soothe her. "What you experienced today was life-altering. You have every right to feel crushed. We can sit here all day long if you'd like."

He pressed something soft into her hands. Tissue. She turned away from him while she wiped her tears.

Abbie bunched the wet tissue in her right hand and turned to him. "When my mother gets out of Bayport, we'll have you over for dinner. Mom will cook you an amazing seven-course meal. That will be her way of thanking you for what you did for me."

"You're a good kid, Abbie. It was no trouble at all. Your mother doesn't need to thank me."

"It doesn't matter what you say. She's from the south, and she's going to cook you a big old southern-style dinner, whether you like it or not."

"Your mother is from the south?" Mr. Newman asked, snapping to attention. "I never knew that. I pegged her for a solid

New Englander."

"Don't let her fool you," Abbie said. "She's Louisiana born and bred. Kenner, Louisiana. She lost her family when she was young."

"What a coincidence," Mr. Newman said. But he was sad when he said so, Abbie observed. He stared straight ahead without blinking, as if he was in some far-off place that only existed in his head. "My birth mother is from Louisiana, too. Kenner."

"Get out of here," Abbie said. "Looks like we have some things in common, Mr. Newman. Does your mom still live there? Do you go home to visit her?"

His eyes twitched. "I don't know if she still lives there or not. I don't know the woman who gave birth to me. That's different from being a mom."

"Oh," Abbie said, leaning back into the seat. She tried to hide her surprise, but didn't quite succeed. "I'm sorry, Mr. Newman. I didn't know you were adopted. But you turned out great. It's your mom's, I mean the woman who gave birth to you, it's her loss."

Mr. Newman never talked about his personal life. He kept it all professional. The kids at school knew all about the teachers, guidance counselors and administrators, where they vacationed, who was getting divorced, who was hooking up, who had financial troubles, stuff like that. Not even the headmaster Dr. Kellogg was immune from the rumor mill. But Abbie never once heard any gossip about Mr. Newman.

"It's okay, Abbie. I shouldn't have said anything. You're a student. I must respect my professional boundaries. I shouldn't have brought up my personal issues. It's inappropriate and won't happen again."

Abbie glared at him. "Are you serious? I invited you into my private nightmare, and you entered willingly. You saw my mom in jail. She won't let anyone see her besides my dad and her lawyer.

You got the up close and personal treatment.

"Mr. Newman, we crossed the professional line the day I came to ask for your help. You're an honorary member of the Cooper clan now. That means I get to be all up in your business. Just ask my mom, she'll tell you."

He studied her for a moment. Then he said, "You're one of a kind, Abbie Cooper. The world needs more people like you. You spread light wherever you go. Don't ever lose that glow."

Abbie folded her arms. "Flattery won't work. You know all about my family, so now I get to hear about yours."

"Okay, Ms. Bossy," he said, his voice low. "There's not much to my story. My biological mother abandoned me the day I was born in a hospital in New Orleans. She was a teenager. That's all I know about her.

"Anyway, I ended up a ward of the state and bounced around from foster parent to foster parent for years. When I was fourteen, I decided I had enough and ran away. I hitched a bus to Baltimore and ended up at a home for boys. One day, I was out on the streets and tried to rob a man who was in town on business. That encounter changed my life."

Abbie was at a loss for words. She needed a minute to gather her thoughts. She had no idea Mr. Newman had a tough upbringing. He was so polished and sophisticated, like he was born to royalty.

"I didn't know," was all she could say.

"Nobody does. I don't make a habit of broadcasting my private business. But you have strong powers of persuasion. You got me to crack. That's a huge deal, you know."

"It's a special gift," Abbie said, nudging him. "So the man you robbed, he adopted you?"

"Tried to rob," he corrected her with amusement. "Yes. Jake Newman had a soft spot for troubled youth because of his brother

Joel. He sat me down and talked to me, and the next thing I knew, I was on a plane to Boston."

"Where did you grow up?"

"Dover. Jake and his wife Lydia formally adopted me a year after he dragged me off the streets of Baltimore."

"Dover, huh? So you grew up a rich kid," Abbie teased.

"I couldn't have made that up, even in my dreams."

"What about your birth mother?" Abbie asked. "Are you ever going to try to find her? Do you know her name or anything about her?"

"I don't see why I should bother. She obviously didn't want me, so why would I waste my time trying to find her?"

"It will give you closure. Isn't that what all the adults say? Besides, you said she was a teenager. Maybe she couldn't take care of you. I'm a teenager. I can't imagine having a baby at my age. I have trouble keeping track of my phone charger."

Mr. Newman cracked his knuckles. Abbie had never seen him do that before, not that she spent much time with him.

"Perhaps you're right," he said, not looking at her. "Maybe Mia Lansing didn't have a choice. It sounded like she had no family, and giving me up was the only way she could survive. I'm glad she did, though. Look where I ended up."

"You're exactly right, Mr. Newman. Everything happens for a reason."

63

WHO ARE YOU?" Jason asked the stranger at the front door. The man was black, well built, and appeared to be in his thirties, Jason's best guess.

"I'm Michael Lansing," the stranger said.

Jason gaped at him. *Lansing.* According to Koczak, Mia Lansing was white. "I don't know anyone by that name. Are you sure you have the right house?"

"Yes, sir. I'm Michael Lansing, Mia's brother. She's in a heap of trouble. That's why I'm here."

"Okay. Who are you, and what do you want? Start talking, or I'll have you arrested for trespassing." Jason had limited patience for whatever this game was.

The stranger looked upward at the overcast sky, then back at Jason. He then shivered. "I'm here for Shelby, your wife. She's my sister."

Jason stumbled backward, as if the pronouncement had landed a physical blow. He had no choice but to invite the man in. This stranger might have information to share. Solve the mystery of the connection between Betty Lansing, a black woman who said her daughter Mia was dead, the psychopath who was destroying their lives named Mia, and now this Michael Lansing who says Shelby is his sister but called her Mia at first.

"Why don't you start from the beginning, Michael?" Jason said. The coffee table in the center of the living room created some distance between him and his unexpected guest. "How do you know my wife?"

Michael looked annoyed, like Jason was a simpleton to whom he had to keep explaining the same thing repeatedly.

"I read about the murder, and that my sister was arrested and sent to jail until the trial. Sorry for the imposition, but I had to come."

"But my wife doesn't have a brother." Nothing Michael said so far made sense to Jason, other than Shelby's arrest.

"Sir, I'm telling you the truth. Your wife, the woman you know as Shelby Durant, is my sister, Mia Lansing."

It had to be a joke. Jason couldn't even entertain the idea that what this man was saying could be true—that his wife had an alias, the same name used by the killer who framed her.

"Why do you say my wife's name is Mia Lansing? What proof do you have?"

Michael shifted his gaze to the wedding photo across the fireplace. "I don't know where to begin," he said, then refocused on Jason. "Mama used to say Mia was too hard-headed for her own good and it would get her in trouble one day.

"I told her over and over again that she should tell you the truth and that her babies had a right to know where their Mama came from, who their family was. But Mia wouldn't listen."

Whenever Jason brought up Shelby's childhood, she always changed the subject. There were no childhood photos of her around their home. She told him the story of her parents' death in a fire, and he took the story at face value. He believed she had every right to be reluctant to discuss such a tragic tale. So it made sense she only talked about her brief stint in a home for teens and how Vivian's mother, Rita March, saved her.

"Go on," Jason encouraged.

"We're from Kenner, Louisiana, as you know. When Mia was fifteen, Mama threw her out of the house for getting pregnant. Mia and Mama didn't get along much because Mama could be meaner than a charging rhino, and Daddy didn't know what to do about it.

"Anyway, things changed after Mia left. Nobody knew where she went. Daddy was beside himself with grief and guilt. Mama carried on like nothing happened. We thought Mia might have ended up dead somewhere."

Jason shuddered. The thermostat was up to a comfortable seventy-three degrees, but neither that nor his cashmere sweater stopped the cold, numbing feeling snaking its way through his body. *If Shelby is the real Mia Lansing, who then is the imposter who killed Alessandro Rossi?* A barrage of unanswered questions swirled around his head.

What did Vivian know about this? Why did she tell Jason that Shelby had a high school friend named Mia Lansing? Vivian had to have known Shelby *was* Mia Lansing. So why send Jason on a wild goose chase? And what about Betty Lansing, who said her daughter was dead? Jason took it literally. Apparently, Betty Lansing meant it figuratively.

Michael took Jason's silence as a sign that he should continue with the story. Even if Jason wanted to stop him, he couldn't.

"Three years went by and no news. We didn't know if we should hold a memorial for Mia even if there was no body or if we should just assume she was okay. Then one day, by the grace of Almighty God, a month after Mia would have turned eighteen, a call came into the house. Mama answered.

"A woman named Shelby Durant asked to speak to me. Mama didn't even recognize her own daughter's voice. When I got on the phone, she told me to act normal, that it was Mia, but she had legally changed her name. She said she was living in North Carolina with a nice family and that she was okay. Said she was going to attend Duke University on a scholarship. That was the happiest day of my life. My sister was alive."

Michael stopped to catch his breath. Jason asked him if he wanted something to eat. They headed to the kitchen, where Jason made them sandwiches. He had sent Abbie upstairs to watch a movie with her brother when Michael arrived. Jason instructed her they were not to come downstairs until he said it was okay.

Jason and his brother-in-law ate in silence. Jason's gut told him everything he'd heard so far was the truth. Besides, he detected a slight family resemblance between Michael and Shelby.

Michael started up again. Jason wondered how long his brother-in-law had been waiting to unburden himself.

"I don't know what happened to my sister after she left home, but she's not the same girl I grew up with. Mia never lied, ever," Michael said. "I'm not judging her. I'm sure she had good reasons for not being straight with you about who she was, and our family.

"Our daddy is dying of kidney disease. I think he's holding on so he can see his baby girl one last time before he goes home to be with the Lord."

"I'm sorry to hear that," Jason said. He was on information overload, all his mental energy drained. He would confront Shelby about her lies later and find out what became of the child she bore. Staying in today was a good idea. He would get lost in whatever movies were available on Netflix. A good revenge caper sounded good.

Jason wanted revenge on the phony Mia Lansing so badly he could taste it. For now, he would march himself upstairs, grab his kids, and introduce them to their uncle.

64

AFTER BREAKFAST THE next morning, Jason gathered everyone in the living room for a reality and sanity check. He had to be honest about what they were in for if the grand jury indicted Shelby on murder charges. They would know in a couple of days. Michael looked up at the wedding portrait above the fireplace, the same way he had when he first arrived.

"Your sister never sent you a wedding photo?" Jason asked.

"No, sir. I only have a couple of pictures of Abbie and Miles when they were still babies. I'm glad my sister met you, though."

Michael moved closer to the fireplace, as if something drew his attention. "Well, will you look at that," he said, picking up the pair of crystal swans. "These are beautiful," he said, turning them over in his hands.

"They were an anniversary gift from me to your sister."

"Swans, huh? Don't they—"

"Mate for life."

"I see," Michael said, flashing a mouthful of teeth. "Well, that's pretty special if you ask me."

He was about to put the swans back when one of them dropped on the floor directly beneath the fireplace and shattered.

A mortified Michael apologized profusely and busied himself with picking up the pieces. Then a strange look clouded his face.

"What in the heck is this?" He held up a tiny, black square object found next to the eye of one of the swans on the floor.

Jason drew closer to see what he was talking about. Miles and Abbie gathered around, too. Jason took the object from Michael—a listening device, a tiny, square wireless transmitter. It looked like somebody drilled around the eye of the Swan to make a small hole, inserted the device, and replaced the eye.

"That's pretty clever," Abbie said. "Who would think to put a device in there?"

Jason didn't answer. He had the place swept for bugs before he installed security cameras on the property and hired armed guards. The woman calling herself Mia Lansing had breached the fortress he had created around the house. He suspected she used Vivian to do it. After all, Koczak was working with Mia. It wasn't a stretch to believe that they both had Vivian under their thumb.

"Seems to me whoever did this has been to your house before and knows the importance of those swans," Michael observed. "It's like they're mocking you and my sister by putting that device in there. They don't think you have the good sense God gave you to figure out that's how they know all of your business."

All thoughts of the meeting he had planned to prep the family for what was coming next flew out of Jason's head. He broke up the meeting, then removed his cell phone from his pocket and called Tom Bilko.

65

WHEN IS AUNT Vivian coming back?" Abbie found her dad in his study, working on some documents. He removed his reading glasses.

"In a couple of days. Why?"

"She borrowed my spare charger. I can't find my regular one, and my phone's about to die."

"Why don't you just got to her room and get it," her dad said. "I doubt she took it to Chicago with her."

"Okay, I'll go get it."

"And Dad?"

"Yes?"

"We love you. Please don't leave us. I know Mom cheating on you hurt a lot. It will for a long time, but you can't divorce her."

Her dad didn't respond.

Abbie opened the door to Aunt Vivian's bedroom. She looked on top of the dresser, an obvious place, but the charger wasn't there. Next, she checked the nightstand near the bed, opened the drawer, and found nothing.

Abbie remembered her mom looking for her iPad under the bed one day before everything fell apart, so she took a cue from her mother and got down on her knees. She would see the charger immediately if it had ended up under the bed somehow.

Abbie was about to move on when she spotted something that looked like a bottle of pills. It must have rolled under the bed without Aunt Vivian knowing. The bottle was a little too far in, so she lay flat on her stomach, extended her arms, and touched enough of the bottle to grab it and pull it toward her.

The prescription was written out to Mia Lansing for a drug called Risperdal. *What the heck? Aunt Vivian is friends with a psychopath?*

She tore out of there and went to her room, booted up her laptop, and Googled the drug. What came back had her staring open-mouthed at the screen and then back at the pill bottle and the screen again. Risperdal was an antipsychotic drug used to treat schizophrenia and bipolar disorder.

Abbie raced down the long flight of stairs and burst through the door of her father's study. Slightly out of breath, she held up the pill bottle and said, "Dad, you have to see this."

Her dad eyed her curiously, then took the bottle from her. He read the label, then looked up at Abbie. "Where did you find this?"

Abbie explained how she came to have the prescription in her possession. Her father held the bottle between his thumb and index finger and shook it absently, a faraway look in his eyes.

"Dad, stop doing that," Abbie chastised. The sound of the pills rattling inside the container made her on edge.

Her dad said, "Don't tell anyone about this, especially Vivian."

"What are you going to do?" Abbie asked.

"Not sure. But I'll get to the bottom of it."

66

IT WAS MID-AFTERNOON when Vivian informed Jason she was leaving for the Natick Mall, fifteen minutes from Castleview, to do some serious shopping, but would be back by dinnertime. When Jason suggested she borrow his car, Vivian adamantly refused, saying it would be easier to call an Uber to pick her up from the house and bring her back when she was done shopping because she didn't feel like driving.

Anyway, she reasoned, Jason needed to be mobile in case something popped up with Shelby's case. Jason had asked Tom Bilko to find out where the Uber was really going, and Jason would follow.

Vivian never made it to the mall. Instead, she ended up in an apartment complex, a stone's throw away from Bayport, where Shelby was being held. Jason was convinced that Vivian knew more than she was saying, and today, he would find out for certain.

Jason pulled in at the back of an empty carwash to avoid detection and placed a call to Tom. "Did she leave yet, or is she still in the apartment?"

"She's still in there. How do you want to play this? It could go on all night."

"No," Jason said. "She'll come out. She has to come back to Castleview from her 'shopping spree.' Let's wait a bit longer."

VIVIAN PICKED UP her special bag from the couch and walked to the bathroom. She placed the bag on the covered toilet seat. She needed to get out of Castleview. It was so depressing in that house. The constant wailing and moaning about Shelby were enough to bring anyone down. It sickened her how they all pretended Shelby was a saint. But Vivian knew better; yes, she did. She looked into the mirror and spoke to her copper-toned reflection.

"What do an Academy Award-winning makeup artist and Vivian March have in common? They're both freaking geniuses."

She served up a cruel laugh as she reached for the bag and pulled out the clever disguise that had allowed her to straddle two different worlds, grabbing them both by the tail and bending them to her will. It was fun. Vivian had felt powerful and invincible. Soon it would all be over. But she had one last loose end to tie up, and she would have to hurry to make it back to Castleview by dinnertime.

Vivian pulled the prosthetic over her head and down over her face. Flawless. After all, her friend Elaine customized it to fit the contours of her face and neck properly. She teased out her blonde hair until she was satisfied it was perfect.

She had already put in her contact lenses during the Uber ride. *Sheer genius.* Vivian laughed again at how gullible the Coopers were, not that she blamed them for not catching on. Her brand of genius was beyond their grasp.

Shelby shouldn't have taken what didn't belong to her. Vivian thanked her lucky stars that she was a patient woman and had bided her time. All her careful planning had paid off beyond her wildest dreams. The Coopers were no match for her. They thought they were so shrewd, with their investigators, high-priced lawyer, and tactical maneuvering that amounted to nothing because Vivian was always several steps ahead.

"Too late, Coopers. I already won," she said to her reflection.

Now they would never find out the truth. In a couple of days, she would clean out this apartment, turn in the keys to the management, and take up permanent residence at 643 Meadow Lane until she could convince Jason to send that brat Abbie to a real boarding school far away. None of this local student at a boarding school in town nonsense.

Vivian had already picked out a couple of schools in Switzerland and one in London. At least she was giving the brat choices. She would tolerate Miles until he became a problem, and then she would get rid of him, too.

67

IS SHE STILL in there?" Jason asked Tom impatiently.

"No sign of her yet, but she could have also gone out the back door. Not much going on here except this blonde woman looked at me like she knew me and smirked."

"You pick this very moment to tell me some chick was checking you out?"

"No, Jason. I'm saying there's something not right about her."

"She came from the building?" Jason asked.

"Yeah. I need to find out what unit she came from."

"I'll be right there," Jason said.

They were careful to put everything back, just as they had found it. Jason and Tom Bilko found out things they couldn't believe. A police scanner, the number to the newsroom of one of the local news channels on a yellow sticky note in the living room, several medications on the dresser in the bedroom.

"Hey, Jason, come check this out." Tom sat at a desk in the living room with a laptop. "Look at all these pictures," he said, pointing to the screen.

Jason looked over Tom's shoulder. Multiple photos of the family appeared, but they all had one thing in common: Shelby was photoshopped out of all of them and replaced with a photo of Vivian.

"This chick has it bad for you," Tom said. "But I don't understand what she has to do with that blonde woman who walked past me earlier."

"I do," Jason said. "And I'm going to do something about it."

"Are you going to tell me what it is?"

"Not yet. Right now, it's just a theory, but if I'm right, Shelby will be home in a matter of days."

68

WHAT IS IT?" Vivian asked anxiously. "Is there news about Shelby's case? Please tell me. We could use good news around here for a change."

Jason closed the door of his study. The kids were at school, and he shut the ringer off on his cell phone.

"I have bad news, Vivian."

"I can't take any more bad news, Jason. It was hard enough dealing with the grand jury coming back with an indictment. The trial is our only hope that the expensive lawyer you hired is going to get Shelby acquitted."

"That won't happen." He stood directly in front of Vivian, who leaned against the desk. "Shelby won't be coming home. Not to this house. Not for a very long time."

Vivian shook her head. "I don't understand. You're not making any sense. The trial hasn't even begun, and there's still a chance exonerating evidence could surface. We have to remain positive, Jason."

"I wish I could, Vivian, but the facts are the facts."

"What facts?"

"Shelby won't go to trial. They'll remove her from the pre-trial unit, the jail she's been at all this time, and move her into the prison population."

Vivian couldn't control the hiccups that were so big they shook her entire body. Jason produced a bottle of water from the mini refrigerator he kept in his study for late night calls to other markets.

"This is how it is," Jason said. "Shelby and I agreed to spare the children the pain of a trial. The DA's office has compelling evidence against her and getting an acquittal was slim. You know the Koczak confession didn't work out. Once the tape and the garage video surfaced, her fate was sealed.

"Alan is brokering a plea deal with the DA's office as we speak. Shelby will admit to killing Alessandro Rossi in exchange for serving twenty years to life with the possibility of parole in fifteen. It was better than life in prison with no parole."

"No, Jason. No," Vivian cried. "Isn't there anything we can do to secure a better outcome?"

"No. I've tried everything. I need to focus on the children now. That's what Shelby wants."

"Have you told them?" Vivian asked.

"Not yet. They'll be hit with a double dose of bad news, though."

"What do you mean?"

Jason reached for his briefcase on the floor next to the desk. He pulled out a stack of papers and handed them to Vivian. "I asked my attorney to file the original."

Vivian skimmed the top page quickly and looked at him. "Are you serious? You're doing this to her now? She's losing everything in one fell swoop. This is cruel, Jason."

"It's better to do everything at once and start over fresh."

Vivian handed the paper back to Jason. "I can't believe it's ending this way."

"It was her idea. The divorce. We probably would have headed down that road even if she had gotten out of Bayport. I don't see how our marriage could have survived her lying to me since the day I met her about who she really was and the child she never told me about. Then the affair—I just couldn't. We were too far gone. There was no way we could come back from all of that."

Vivian appeared puzzled. "I thought she told you about the baby. I couldn't see any reason not to."

"I only found out recently. But that's beside the point. I'm all the children have now, and they are my number-one priority."

Vivian reached out and hugged him. "They have me too, Jason. Never forget that."

"I need all the help I can get. It would be best if they had someone they love and trust to help them with the transition."

"I wish this had turned out differently," Vivian said through her sniffles. "I wish I could write an alternate ending to the story."

"Life isn't fiction. We can't erase the page and start all over again."

"So somebody got away with murder, and she sacrificed her life for her kids," Vivian said.

"If there is one thing I can say about Shelby, is that she does motherhood proud. No other woman will ever come close to being the kind of mother she was to our kids."

69

THE BEDROOM DOOR is slightly ajar, and I peek in. Vivian sits on the bed, yoga style, thumbing through a magazine. She stops for a moment and extends her left palm to admire the massive diamond on her ring finger.

I can't stand it any longer. The cruel, diabolical lengths she went through to steal my life and exact her own twisted version of vengeance is something I will never forgive. She did all this while pretending to be my sister. Because that's what I thought Vivian and I were: sisters.

I open the door wider and walk in. "Hello, Vivian."

My voice startles her. She jerks upright. "Shelby. Oh, my goodness. What are you doing here?"

"We need to talk, don't we?" I shut the door behind me and approach the bed, but remain standing.

"You look—"

"Good for someone who's supposed to be doing twenty-five to life?"

"Welcome home. It's good to see you. What happened? Did Jason bribe someone to get you out? We have so much catching up to do, and the children will be so happy."

For as much as she claims she's happy to see me, my so-called best friend has yet to make a move to embrace me. Vivian sits nailed to the spot in the middle of the bed where I found her thumbing through a bridal magazine and admiring the ring my husband bought her.

"Jason didn't bribe anyone because I did nothing wrong. See, our legal system works."

"How did you get here? Are you feeling okay after your prison ordeal? I can't imagine what it must have been like."

"Pure agony," I say calmly. "The worst part was not being able to see my children, but you already knew that."

"Of course. They missed you terribly. It was tough on them, especially Miles."

"Then why did you torture them so? Why did you almost destroy them, Vivian?"

I inch closer to the bed, and Vivian tucks her ring finger under her thigh. "Is that an engagement ring? Who proposed to you?"

Like a robot come to life, the real Vivian emerges. "I'm sorry, Shelby. Things have changed. I'm with Jason now. We're going to be married this summer."

I snatch the magazine from her and turn the pages. "Are you, now? Did you know that polygamy is illegal in Massachusetts?"

"What do you mean?" Vivian removes her ring hand from under her thigh, declaring war in what I'm certain will be our final encounter. She wants me to see the ring, to convince me my marriage is over.

"Jason can't marry you if he's still married to me, now can he?" I explain.

Vivian sits up straighter, with shoulders pushed back. She's determined to have her way.

"This is hard, Shelby. With everything you've been through, to come home and find out that your husband is engaged to your best friend, well, you'll get used to it."

"There's nothing to get used to Vivian, dear. Jason isn't going anywhere."

She stretches and lets out a big sigh. "It's over Shelby. I won."

"You sound so sure of yourself. Tell me, what exactly did you win?"

"The man who should have been mine in the first place, the life you stole from me."

I look at her like the demented human being she is. "Hmm, I don't recall taking anything from you, Vivian. I don't recall taking *anything* from you."

"Don't pretend to be innocent. You took my father from me the day you claimed he tried to rape you. He was never the same after my mother threw him out. You destroyed our family, after everything we did for you. You were a street rat, a nothing and nobody when my mother took you in, and this was the way you thanked her, by lying."

"Your father was an alcoholic who tried to rape me during one of his drunken episodes," I say calmly. "Rita walked in on the incident and asked him to leave. She was a brave woman, a woman of principle and integrity. It couldn't have been easy for her to do that. The marriage was hanging on by a thread, anyway. For Rita, that was the last straw."

Vivian sneers at me, her eyes raging pools of malice. "You're a liar and a poser. Pretending to be some wholesome girl that Jason fell for when in fact, you were nothing but a two-bit tramp who got knocked up as a teenager and then abandoned her own kid.

"Then you had the nerve to wear white on your wedding day. That was *my* dress," she says, pointing at me. "But you convinced my mother to give it to you instead. You destroyed that beautiful dress. They had to cut it down to fit your inelegant, miniscule frame."

Her delusions about her father I understand, but not the

dress. Rita March got married in a gorgeous, Grace Kelly-inspired wedding gown. When Jason proposed, Rita decided right away that I would wear the dress, and she wouldn't hear anything else to the contrary. Vivian didn't seem to care, but it was all an act.

"I won't argue with you about a wedding dress. Maybe Rita gave it to me because she knew I would cherish it, and I would feel honored to wear it, which I was. You didn't appreciate her much with your rebellious behavior and ungrateful attitude. You can't blame me for that, Vivian."

"You were so desperate for love and attention. Always sucking up to her, doing whatever she said, like a lapdog. You were pathetic," she says scornfully.

She slides off the bed and stands, looming over me. She's a good seven inches taller than I am, and she's looking down at me, wagging her finger in my face.

"You deserved what you got, and too bad they didn't keep you locked up. But you're not going to steal my happiness from me this time."

"You don't know how to be happy, Vivian; that's the sad thing about you. You had two loving parents who gave you everything, and it wasn't enough. Didn't matter what you had accomplished or what you had acquired. You're just a big black hole that sucks up everything in its path but never gets filled."

She shoves me, and I stumble backward. I shove her harder, and she lands on the bed. I point a finger at her. "I've suffered enough. I'm going to tell you what really went down, and when I'm done, you're going to pack your stuff and get out of my home and my life. I don't give a damn where you go."

She recoils as if I've just slapped her.

"Rita gave me the dress because she wanted her daughter to wear it on her wedding day. She considered me her daughter because she was the mother I never had, and every day, I let her know how grateful I was. I respected her and loved her. She gave me the dress, Vivian, because in her heart, I was her real daughter."

"It doesn't matter, anyway. When I marry Jason, I will be wearing a fabulous couture Marchesa wedding gown. And you'll have to watch me walk down the aisle with the love of your life. It's going to be epic. Can't wait to tell you all about the honeymoon."

I ignore her childish statement. "You're right, Vivian. I guess it doesn't matter, because Rita March was your aunt, not your mother. Her sister Delores was your biological mother. As you know, she died in childbirth. What you didn't know was that child was you. See, you were a killer straight out of the womb."

I let that sink in for a moment. Vivian looks ghostly. "You're a damn liar. I hate you!"

"Yes, I think you've made that quite clear. It was all for naught, Vivian. You never had a shot at Jason."

"I have a ring that says otherwise."

"Jason never got a divorce. The papers were real, but his lawyer never filed them. He never intended to leave me for you. It was all a hoax."

70

LIAR! LIAR, LIAR," Vivian screams.

"Vivian, calm down," I say.

She throws the heavy bridal magazine I placed on the bed at me, and I dodge. It lands on the floor.

"Everything was going fine until you got careless. The whole setup, murdering Alessandro to get rid of me, terrorizing my daughter, the GPS tracker on my car, the recording devices all over the house, Mehmet Koczak. It worked beautifully until that bottle of medication rolled under the bed. It was a prescription for Mia Lansing, remember?"

Recognition dawns on her. She's like a trapped rabbit, but I haven't sprung the biggest trap on her yet. "From then on, it was a matter of keeping tabs on your movements. The investigator Jason hired found the apartment you rented, your command central, the disguise you used to get around. Honestly, Vivian, a green-eyed blonde? They also found the notebook of that poor murdered psychiatrist, Dr. Singer."

I wander around the room as I tell the story. It's time to tighten the screws. "It was my idea to have Jason propose to you. We needed you relaxed and comfortable. Purchasing the ring added authenticity to the plan. We had to make it convincing. Boy, did we have a good laugh about that."

"Stop it, stop it. You think you know everything? You don't." A diabolical smile plays at the corners of her mouth. "Do you know how much your Brazilian lover begged me to spare his life right before I put a bullet in his head? I almost felt bad shooting him because he was so pretty.

"He told me about his daughters and how much they needed him, even said he loved you. That's when I pulled the trigger. I had to put the poor bastard out of his misery, didn't I? It was easy enough to lure him to that park in Cambridge by calling and pretending to be your assistant."

Like a deer caught in the headlights of an oncoming car, I listen to her lay out exactly how she planned and executed the murders and how the frame worked. She had planned it for two years. For two years she watched me, learned my routine and habits.

Though we were close, we led separate lives in separate states. She had to make special trips to do her reconnaissance. And in her absence, like Jason, she hired an investigator to keep tabs on me. Vivian even flew to Turkey to track down Koczak and brought him back to the U.S. He owed her. That's how she got his cooperation.

As for the manufactured evidence, me leaving the garage, it was all a trick of technology. She hired someone of my height and build to leave and return from the garage. Later, she digitally superimposed my head on the body of the person she hired and leaked the tape to the police when it suited her.

"You can leave now, so Jason and I can go about the business of planning our future."

That comment snaps me out of my pity party. "The only future that's waiting for you is a prison cell."

"That's what you think. I got away with three murders, including Mehmet Koczak," she brags. "What makes you think I won't walk away with the man you stole from me?"

"Because you're not as clever as you think, Vivian. You're so full of yourself you can't analyze a situation and know when something is off."

"What the hell does that mean?"

Gone was the smug, condescending attitude of a few moments ago.

I point at the ceiling. "Look up."

"Why?"

"Just look up. Look at the smoke detector."

She does, but confusion is clear on her face.

"It's a listening device. It recorded our entire conversation."

Vivian grabs a chair. She places it in the middle of the room. Her intention is obvious. "No use in dismantling it. The police were listening, and they have everything they need."

She lunges at me and misses. "Just give yourself up, Vivian. It's over."

"I'm never going to serve one day in prison."

"Still cocky after you've been caught?" I ask.

That diabolical smile appears again. "You see, Shelby, I suffer from bipolar disorder and paranoid delusions. I received the diagnosis in my early twenties, so I've been suffering for years. "There is a world-renowned psychotherapist in Chicago who diagnosed and treated me.

"Even Doctor Singer, the shrink I was seeing here, has notes that tell the sad, sad story of what my life is like, living with these disorders. It's terrible," she says, shaking her head. "Just terrible. I can't be held accountable for my actions. I'm not competent to stand trial."

Vivian pushes past me and opens the bedroom door. I follow. Something inside me breaks. It can't end like this. She has to pay. I grab her sweater, but she's stronger than me and keeps going.

She's in the hallway now. Next, she'll head for the stairs and make a run for it.

"Vivian, listen to me, turn yourself in. The police are less than a block away."

She turns around and punches me in the face. It hurts, but I must push through the pain. It's a long hallway, but soon she'll reach the stairs. I grab her again as she reaches the top of the stairs. It's a tug of war, and I'm pulling with all my might, but she's as strong as an ox and has thirty pounds and seven inches on me.

Vivian pushes me off, but I'm like a pit bull. I refuse to give up. My main objective now is to slow her down, so I trip her by sticking my leg out. She falls flat on her butt, and I grab one of her legs and try to pull her away from the stairs, back toward the bedroom.

She kicks me in the chest with her free leg. I fall backward and end up on the floor, too. She jumps up and dashes for the stairs again. I get up. I have to stop her. Vivian takes the first step in descending the long staircase, and I'm right next to her. There's barely enough space for both of us walking side by side.

"They'll find you. There's nowhere you can hide. It's better to turn yourself in now. Have some sense for once."

Vivian doesn't say a word. Instead, she lets go of the banister, extends her arms, and launches herself off the step. As if in slow motion, she free falls down the long flight of stairs. My reflexes aren't fast enough to grab her. In the split second it takes me to realize her intention, I'm too late.

She lands at the bottom of the stairs with a loud crash. Then an eerie silence descends over the house. On wobbly feet, I make it to the bottom of the stairs. Her dead eyes are open, looking straight at me, while blood pools from the back of her skull.

EPILOGUE

THE LOST SON

ONE MONTH AFTER my release from jail, I was hit with another bombshell. Since my release, I've been vacillating between the sheer joy of coming home to my family, a free woman, an innocent woman, and the melancholy of Vivian's shocking betrayal and tragic death. Tonight, I come face-to-face with the child I abandoned in a New Orleans hospital twenty-five years ago.

When Abbie came to me and told me she believed her guidance counselor, Mr. Newman, was the son I abandoned all those years ago, I almost passed out. No exaggeration. My son grew up thirty minutes from Castleview, a town I've called home for the past decade plus.

Since Abbie promised Lee I would cook him a big old southern style dinner as a thank you for bringing her to see me while I was in jail, the perfect opportunity had presented itself. Although I can't help but feel as if I'm about to ambush the man, but if I don't take this opportunity, I may not get another.

Lee sits across from me in Jason's study, the best place to give us total privacy. I've practiced dozens of times what I would say to him, but my well-prepared speech has dissolved into a pool of nervousness and dread. My knees tremble as he studies me.

"I know you're wondering why I asked to see you in private," I say. "The truth is, Lee, I don't know where to begin."

"The beginning is usually a good place," he says. "As I've already told you, all of this was unnecessary, the dinner, the big fuss. Abigail needed my help, and I was glad to offer it."

"I'll never forget your kindness. But that's not what this is about."

"What is it then? Why have you asked me to meet in private, Mrs. Cooper?"

There's an empty feeling in the pit of my stomach. I never thought this would be easy, but by his tone and body language, he's in no hurry to get better acquainted. When Abbie dropped the bombshell, I asked her not to say anything to Lee.

I contemplated reaching out to his adoptive parents, but squashed the idea. Then I turned to online research to learn all I could about him but shut it down. I felt guilty, as though I were spying on him after what I had done. If I was going to confront my past, it also meant facing whatever consequences would follow.

"It's about me and you, Lee. Abbie tells me you were adopted?"

"I was."

"Did you ever have any desire to search for your birth mother?"

"Mrs. Cooper, I mean no disrespect, but I was invited to have a nice meal at the home of one of my students and her family as a thank you for doing her a solid. Now I'm being interrogated about my personal life. I think it's time I leave."

He stands. "Please, Lee. Sit. I'm sorry, I meant no offense. It's just that this is very difficult for me and I'm not doing a good job of handling it."

"Handling what?" he asks, as he re-takes a seat.

"The reason I asked about your birth mother is because I know who she is."

Panic swells up inside of me. This may have been a terrible idea. A terrible idea with an outcome I can't control.

"What's your agenda, Mrs. Cooper? Why am I here?"

I take in a slow, deep breath. "Lee, my birth name is Mia Lansing. I believe you're the son I gave up twenty-five years ago in New Orleans."

My mouth goes dry. Lee stares at me blankly. I hold my breath, waiting for a reaction.

"You? You are the woman who threw me away as a newborn in a hospital and went on with her life as though I was an inconvenience that needed handling?" His eyes are cold and unfriendly, his face reveals no emotion.

"Lee, I was a child, not a woman. A child who had been tossed out to the world, alone, abused by a sick, emotionally stunted mother who beat on her every day. In my teenage mind, a hospital was the best place. There were nurses and doctors who would care for you. I couldn't, living on the streets."

"So you decided now was the time to ease your guilty conscience? Come clean, once you found out Abigail and I are close?"

I swallow hard. His words land a powerful punch, and I can't escape the pain. Sitting here, facing him in the flesh, as an adult, it's hard to take in.

"What I did still haunts me to this day," I whisper.

"But not enough to try to find me after you went on with your life; you grew up, went off to college and graduate school, married a millionaire, started a family.

"What you did haunted you so much that at no time in the past several years did you bother to find out what happened to the child you just abandoned. What kind of mother does that?"

It doesn't matter what I say. None of my rationalizations, excuses, or explanations will make any difference to him. I give it a shot, anyway.

"I thought if you were okay, I had no right to disrupt your life. I looked for you before I married Jason. I got nowhere."

It almost killed me to admit to Anton that I didn't give our son a name before I left the hospital. I told the nurse I would fill out the birth certificate with the relevant information before I was discharged, but I never did. Besides, years later, there was a flood at that hospital that destroyed old records. That's the main reason it was so difficult to make any progress when I tried tracking Lee down.

"So that made it, okay?" he asks. "Your conscience was cleared, and that was that."

"Please try to understand, Lee. I swear to you, I did what I did because it was the only option I had. There was nobody to advise or counsel me. I had no resources. I couldn't go back to my parents. My mother beat me the day I told her I was pregnant. That would not have been a good situation for either one of us."

"What about my biological father? How does he fit in?"

I almost forgot about Anton. I haven't said a word to him about Lee being the son we conceived. "Like my parents, he abandoned me. Said he had no interest in having a kid and he pretended it never happened. Then he went off to college that fall."

It sounds like shifting blame, but it's the truth. Lee just shakes his head as if he can't believe this incredulous story.

"Wow. My biological parents, you guys are something else. You both did me a favor, though. I had a rough beginning but turns out I had great parents waiting for me. I don't need you and it turns out I never did.

"As for my biological father, I don't want to know his name or anything about him. My real dad is Jake Newman, and my mother is Lydia Newman. I have two sisters, Sarah, and Amanda. If you're looking for forgiveness, you've come to the wrong place."

Tears circle my eyes, but I won't cry in front of him. I flash back to the day Mama kicked me out of the house, the hate in her eyes, the rage. I don't know what I was expecting, meeting with Lee, but somehow, his rejection hurts as badly as my mother's did, as Anton's did.

"I'm sorry, Lee. I wish things had worked out differently. I can't go back and change the past, but I hope perhaps one day, in the not so distant future, we could take small steps toward getting to know each other."

I'm shooting in the dark, hoping for a shot at redemption. It doesn't come.

Lee stands and smooths out his sweater. "There's no need for us to ever see each other again, Mrs. Cooper. Please stay clear of me and I will do the same for you. As for Abigail, I will continue to be a support system for her at school. My relationship with her is not a stepping stone to get to me. It won't work so don't try. Thank you for the dinner. Goodbye, Mrs. Cooper."

EPILOGUE

THE PRODIGAL DAUGHTER

I'M STANDING AT the door of my childhood home like an anxious prodigal daughter. Michael doesn't know I planned to visit. Mama and I have unfinished business. When I arrived at Louis Armstrong International Airport three hours ago, I headed straight to the cemetery. It was the reason I've come back to Louisiana for the first time in a quarter century.

I told Daddy how sorry I was I didn't make it in time to say goodbye, sorry that he didn't get to meet his grandchildren. Guilt-ridden that I refused to come back while he was still alive, heartbroken that I denied my children part of their heritage.

He needed to know that I'd forgiven him for allowing Mama to hurt me, and I never stopped loving him. I sang our favorite song, Mahalia Jackson's "Summertime/Motherless Child". I have a feeling he heard me, and he's smiling up in heaven.

I knock on the door and wait. I'm dressed as I would have been if I had attended Daddy's funeral: a black Chanel suit, black heels, and a triple strand pearl necklace with matching earrings.

A senior citizen answers the door and blinks at me. She leans on a cane for support. Her face, once as familiar to me as my own because of its perpetual gaze of contempt, now looks at me with a blanket of weariness. She's thinner than I remember, but still physically fit at sixty-four. There's a sprinkling of age spots on her hands.

"May I help you?" she asks, her voice cautious.

My limbs tingle, and my breath hitches. How do I answer that loaded question?

"Mama, it's me. Mia."

She blinks again and fingers a necklace. It was a mistake to come. I want my feet to move but they won't, as if my brain is delaying the signal.

"Mia?" she asks, as if she's not sure she heard me right.

"I just came from the cemetery. I thought I would come by to see how Michael was doing before I head back to the airport."

As far as lame excuses go, this one takes first place. Michael lives on his own twenty minutes away, although he may very well be here since the family is grieving.

"Come in," she says and opens the door wider.

We sit in the living room. Neither one of us knows what to say. I scan the room. She made some changes since I left. It appears bigger and lighter with its blue and white sofa and chairs. Photos, plants, and a couple of lamps create a welcoming atmosphere, although I can't say for sure if I'm welcome at all.

There's a photograph of Michael in a cap and gown, surrounded by our parents. Mama is smiling in the photograph. Michael was always her pride and joy. There are no pictures of me of course, not a trace of evidence I ever existed in this home once upon a time.

"Would you like some tea?" she asks.

"No, thank you."

"It took your daddy dying for you to come home, Mia?"

I'm stunned by the question. I smooth out my skirt with

nervous strokes. I weigh the pros and cons of my response. How dare she put this on me?

"It's hard to come back to a place where you're not wanted," I say. "A place where you never felt safe."

She lowers her gaze. "I suppose now that your daddy's gone, you're looking for answers." Then she looks directly at me and says, "I was a different woman back then. I didn't know how to deal with my grief."

I force myself to ask the next logical question. Mama is about to justify why she treated me like some disease she was hell-bent on eradicating, but I figured she's waited forty years to unburden herself.

"What were you grieving about?"

"When you were born, you didn't come alone."

"I don't know what you mean by that."

"Just listen. I have to get this out. Your daddy is gone now and ain't no use holding on to the past."

She looks up at the ceiling as if praying for strength. To see Mama unsure of herself is puzzling.

"You came out first, and then your sister did. She was the prettiest little thing you ever saw. The Lord blessed me with twin daughters. But then he turned on me. Maybe punishment for something I did. He took Maddie away. It wasn't fair. You lived, and Maddie didn't make it. I blamed you. It had to be your fault because you survived."

I place my hands in my lap, weighed down by the complexity of my emotions; I'm one half of a duo who came into this world. I had a sister nobody ever talked about. Knowing my mother, she probably forbade Daddy from speaking about it.

"Every time I looked at you, it was a reminder of losing Maddie. And your daddy, he just thought you were the moon and the stars. It was as if he didn't care that we had lost her. He just moved on, and focused all his attention on you."

"Grief is a complex emotion. Perhaps focusing on me helped him to cope with the loss. Daddy was a humble, grateful man. I imagine he was thankful he didn't lose us both. He at least had one child to call his own. But you decided I didn't deserve to live, that I should have died with my twin."

Her glassy stare was all the confirmation I needed.

"I just didn't know how to deal with my grief. I'm not saying it was right, but I couldn't see past… I just couldn't—"

"Find it in your heart to love me," I finish for her.

"Your mama knows you'll never forgive her, but I thought you deserved to hear my side of the story."

It's still all about her after all these years. I will never reveal to her what Daddy told me in the letter, how she used a tragic accident to terrorize him in his own home.

"I forgave you, Mama. When it stopped hurting so badly, that's when I knew I had moved past the pain. I had a lot of time to think in that jail cell. That's what gave me the courage to come here and demand closure. You owed me that much. My own mother discarded me. It used to be my identity, but not anymore."

Her face is expressionless as she shifts her gaze to a rocking chair in the corner. She's alone now that Daddy's gone. Michael will be around, but he has his own life to live.

"I should go," I say. "I don't want to miss my flight back home."

Mama looks at me. "Michael told me you changed your name, but you'll always be Mia to me."

I nod, and then stand to leave. Mama wants to ask me something but isn't sure how. It's almost a whisper when it comes out. "How did you make it after… well, you look like you did well."

"Where will I go? What if something bad happens to me?"

"I don't care. Now I can finally be rid of you."

The painful flash of memory pierces my heart. She didn't care what happened to me on the night she threw me out of the house, alone and frightened. I was Abbie's age. So why the questions now? Guilt? Regret?

"It's in the past. I prefer not to dwell in that space."

"I understand," she whispers, but she's not done with me yet. "Did you have the baby?"

I don't know why it's important to her. When Abbie told me that her guidance counselor, Mr. Newman, was the child I gave up all those years ago, I couldn't believe it. I tried to establish some kind of relationship with him, but he made it clear he wanted no part of me. I don't blame him.

"Yes, ma'am, I had the baby. Some good folks adopted him; he had a happy upbringing. He works at my daughter's school. They're close, but I don't think that closeness will ever extend to me. It's my loss. That's life," I say, shrugging.

"Well, that's good," Mama says.

I pick up my handbag from the sofa and sling it over my shoulder. I'm about to walk out of this house again, not knowing if it will be the last time.

"Goodbye, Mama. I wanted to know why, and now I do."

I hop in the rental car and make my way to the airport. As I take the exit for the JetBlue Airways departure terminal, a sobering thought occurs to me. I lost both my parents twenty-five years ago, but when they abandoned me, I gained something priceless: The life that was meant for me.

AWARD-WINNING FEARLESS SERIES

Abbie Cooper takes center stage in this multi award-winning series that kicks off two years after *Fool Me Twice*. Buckle your seat belts for a rollercoaster ride of deception, obsession, revenge, and murder most foul.

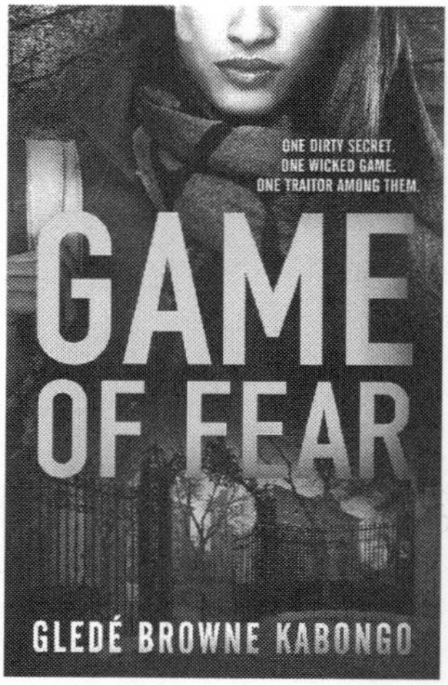

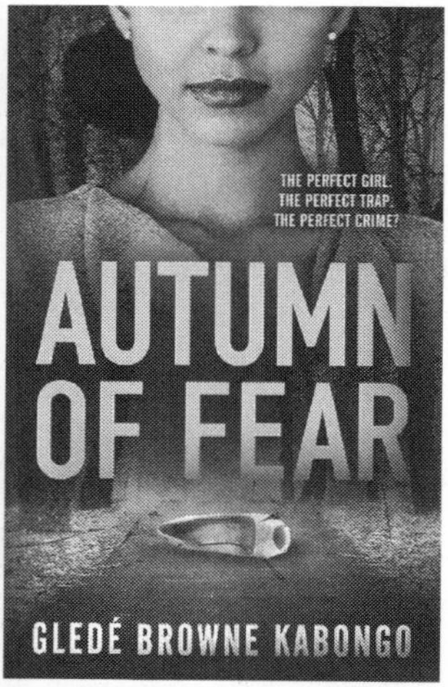

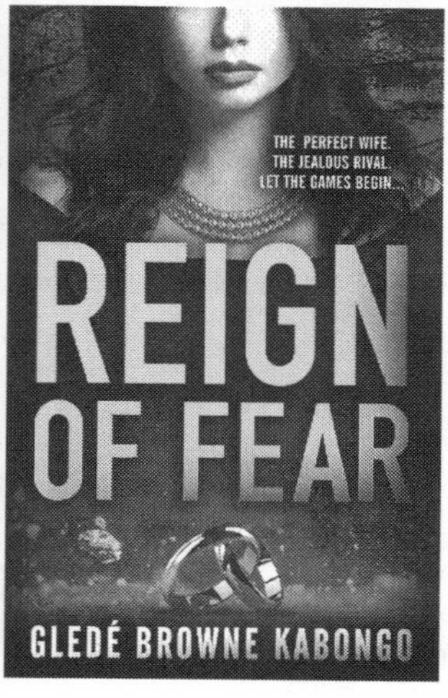

BOOK 1 - GAME OF FEAR

Abbie has her future all mapped out, the path to becoming one of the best surgeons in the country. She just needs to be admitted into Princeton, the Ivy League university of her dreams. But someone known only as The Avenger is threatening to expose her dark secret—the secret that could get Abbie expelled from her elite private school and ruin her chances of getting into Princeton.

Competition to get into the Ivy League is hyper-competitive and Abbie isn't about to let anyone shatter her dreams. So it's game on, and she will go to any lengths necessary to stop The Avenger—even if it means breaking every rule.

BOOK 2 - AUTUMN OF FEAR

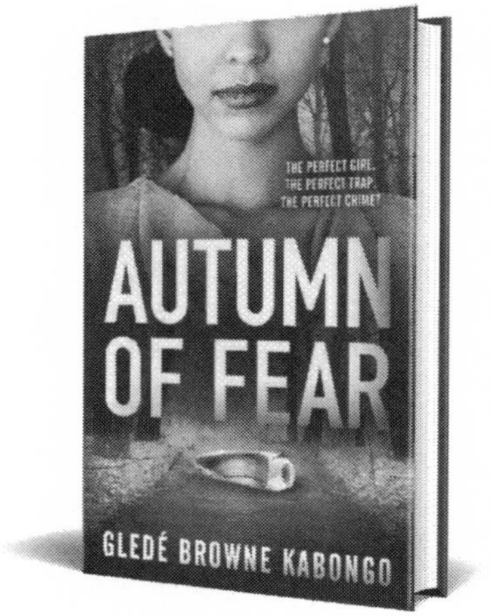

Abbie's dream of becoming a brilliant neurosurgeon is shattered when she wakes up in the hospital after a violent assault and no memory of the attack. As she grapples with the horrific aftermath, Abbie is determined to uncover the truth about what happened that night.

Who is the mysterious "Humble Admirer" who sent her expensive gifts and exotic roses? Why is charming senior, Spencer Rossdale, suddenly interested in Abbie and her connection to the wealthy and powerful Wheeler family? The deeper Abbie digs, the more she unravels a stunning web of lies that stretch back decades. Revealing them will change everything but the truth is the least of Abbie's problems. A vicious predator is watching her and he's willing to kill to protect his secret.

BOOK 3 - WINDS OF FEAR

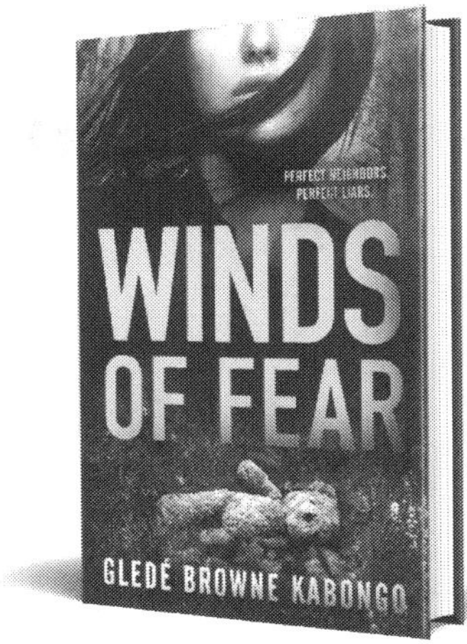

Abbie is now a stay-at-home mom who can barely balance it all. She's preparing her Ph.D. dissertation defense while raising three kids, and supporting her husband's career as a surgical resident. But when she meets the new couple next door, Abbie's already hectic life descends into chaos.

Why are the Paynes so fascinated by her oldest son and why do they ask so many questions about him? Soon Abbie begins to suspect that something is terribly wrong and the Paynes' choice of neighborhood was no accident.

Too many things about the couple don't add up, and when a stranger at a local café approaches Jenna Payne and calls her by a different name, Abbie can no longer ignore the danger lurking. The clock is ticking, and if she doesn't uncover what her neighbors are hiding, her son could pay a terrible price.

BOOK 4 - REIGN OF FEAR

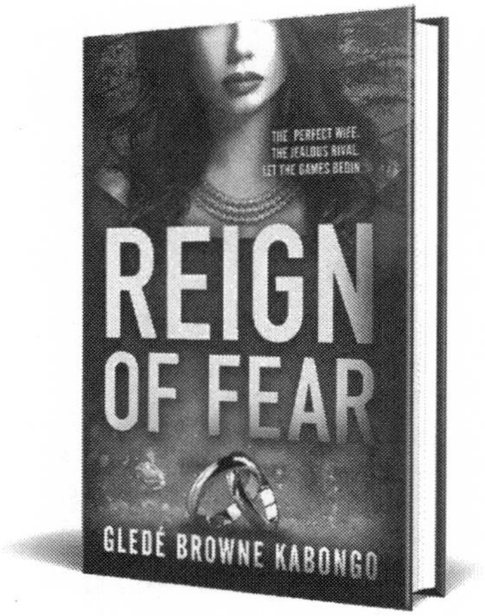

When Abbie runs into Kristina Hayward in the lobby of an upscale London hotel, her perfect life begins to unravel. It's been fifteen years since Kristina made a chilling promise after she spotted the glittering diamond engagement ring on Abbie's finger.

Abbie is now Dr. Cooper-Rambally, a well-respected neuropsychologist and Harvard instructor married to a prominent cardiothoracic surgeon—the man Kristina once deeply loved. Determined to claim the charmed life that should have been hers, Kristina sets a diabolical plan into motion.

But Kristina makes a costly mistake by underestimating her adversary. She's about to find out what Abbie is capable of, how far she's willing to go to protect her family and the devastating secret that must remain buried at all costs.

Don't miss the gripping and emotionally-charged conclusion to the multi award-winning Fearless Series.

GAME OF FEAR PREVIEW

PROLOGUE

I'LL NEVER TELL

Two years earlier

I'M OUT OF here. They're going to kick me out. That's what the meeting is about. The last piece of my lousy existence is about to crumple like a paper doll. Two weeks ago, Dad called a family meeting and announced his resignation as chief financial officer of Orphion—a multi-billion-dollar global technology company. He would have been CEO in a year.

The crisis is a greedy little monster that grows by the minute, destructive and never-ending, and the possibility that Mom could face life in prison are enough to make me want to crawl into a rabbit hole and never come out.

I pull my shoulders back, stick my chin out, and put on my game face. The door opens on the first knock. When I enter the office, my guidance counselor, Ms. Morris, and the school psychologist, Dr. Burns, are present. Our Headmaster, Dr. Stephen Kellogg, gestures for me to take the empty chair. He sits behind his desk, clears his throat, and adjusts his glasses. He spreads out a bunch of documents on the desk.

"None of us wants to see you in here," he begins. "You've been an exemplary student in every way, and we're all proud of your accomplishments."

I wait for the proverbial shoe to drop. Their solemn faces make my stomach heave.

"Dr. Kellogg is right," my guidance counselor says. "We understand you're facing difficult circumstances. It's our job to help you stay on track. This meeting is about your support system here at school."

"I appreciate the support, Ms. Morris, but I've already met with everyone in this room and the school chaplain."

Dr. Kellogg clears his throat again and picks up a piece of paper in front of him. "We're concerned about your academic performance as of late," he says, scanning the paper. "You're aware of our high standards here at St. Matthews. We've built our reputation on it. We think it's best to act now before it's too late."

I blink twice. "You mean before you have to expel me."

Dr. Burns stares straight ahead, and Ms. Morris opens her mouth to speak. No sound comes out.

"Goodness, no." Dr. Kellogg gives off a forced laugh and adjusts his tie. "We want to create a plan to get you through these tough times."

Dr. Burns speaks for the first time. "Processing your emotions and having the proper tools in place are critical. A parent incarcerated, awaiting trial for murder, and an uncertain future ahead are a lot for a young person to handle. We're here to help you cope successfully within the walls of Saint Matthews and beyond."

I sit ramrod straight in my chair. My muscles quiver. How dare they think my mother is guilty? I should set them straight right now. "My mother didn't kill that man; she's innocent. Someone framed her. We'll prove it. When we do, she'll come home where she belongs."

There's doubt in their eyes, a non-verbal challenge to my

statement. I can practically read their thoughts. *Poor, delusional kid.*

"Your teachers say you're unfocused and withdrawn," Ms. Morris continues. "They tell me you've given up. It's our responsibility to make certain you don't fall any further behind. You're one of our best students. We don't want to see you lose your edge. I'm sure your parents will agree."

I smooth out my skirt as I struggle to hold back the tears. They're right. I can't allow school to fall apart too, along with the rest of my life. If I don't get myself together, it will break Mom's heart. Dr. Kellogg hands me a box of tissue from his desk. I place it on my lap without using a single sheet.

"We can talk right now if you need to," Dr. Burns offers.

Dr. Kellogg and Ms. Morris take the hint and leave the room.

I turn to Dr. Burns. "May I have a few minutes alone, please? We'll chat. I promise."

After Burns disappears, I take a deep breath to rid myself of the humiliation threatening to overpower me. No more excuses. I must take drastic measures to solve the problem. I search my bag for the piece of paper I've carried around for weeks—the phone number of a classmate with a reputation as the guy who can make your troubles go away. I fish my phone from my bag and dial the number. He answers on the first ring.

"Need your help," I say.

"I'm surprised to hear from you. But I understand why you called."

"Good. I don't want to go to The Pit. Someone might see me."

"You won't have to. I can hook you up. How much?"

"As much as you can get."

"Whoa. Are you sure about that?"

"Yes. I've lost a lot of ground. It's time to make up for it."

"I can get you a discount, but it will still cost."

"Just do it," I insist.

"At your service."

"And one more thing."

"Yes?"

"This stays between us. Forever."

"I'll never tell."

CHAPTER 1

I ATTRACT trouble like a magnet, despite my best intentions.

It's because I attend Saint Matthews Academy, where the pressure is overwhelming, the secrets are dirty, and the games are wicked. But I don't let it get to me. I've already mapped out my path to becoming one of the world's top neurosurgeons: Princeton for college and then off to Harvard or Stanford for medical school. I'll complete my internship and residency at the Mayo Clinic and Massachusetts General Hospital respectively. My life is orderly, focused, and predictable, the way I like it. Yet some people have other ideas.

"What's up, Abbie?" he asks, making sexually suggestive motions with the lollipop in his mouth. I'm talking about Christian Wheeler, the resident bad boy.

Since school started in September, Christian appears at my locker every morning, asking me out like it's his new religion. I roll my eyes at him and turn my attention to swapping the books I need for my first-period class. The lollipop comes out of his mouth, and he pushes a blond lock of hair away from his eyes—a luminous shade of Spanish blue that's so hypnotic I've heard girls faint when they look at him too long. Whatever.

"You're so gross." Hostility rolls off me in waves. "Isn't there some poor girl at this school waiting for you to dump her? Oh, wait, there's no one left. You've hooked up with every girl at Saint Matthews. Man-whore." I glare at him.

"Since we never hooked up, does that mean you're not a girl?"

I flip him the bird, but it doesn't faze him. Christian makes obnoxious kissing noises with his lips.

"The ice princess thing you do is all an act, isn't it? I know you want me."

"No, thanks. I have standards, and an aversion to STDs."

"Ouch. Watch where you point that thing you call a tongue. Somebody could get hurt."

I snort in disgust and stuff a couple of books into my backpack. "Why are you all over me, Christian? I'm not interested in joining your fan club. Get lost."

"Come on. I'm an enlightened man these days."

Christian turned eighteen over the summer and thinks that makes him a man.

"You're still a boy. Don't get it twisted."

"I should get points for sticking my neck out. Every guy at this school is afraid to ask you out."

"I'm fresh out of brownie points. Besides, you don't want to date me."

"Why not?" He backs up a few steps. "If you stopped hiding your, um, considerable assets," he says, ogling me, "you'd be a total babe."

"That statement is deeply offensive." I want to to kick him in the shin until he howls in agony.

The corners of his mouth turn up into a smile, revealing perfectly even white teeth. I can't help it, so I grin too. I zip up my backpack and sling it over my shoulders. I'm about to close my locker, but my hand stops in mid-air.

Sidney Bailey Shepard saunters toward us, elbowing people

out of her way. Her eyes laser in on Christian like a lioness about to pounce on its prey. Sidney is a fellow senior, but that's where our similarities end. Sidney plants herself in front of Christian and tosses her hair back, the long auburn locks coming to rest in a perfect cascade past her shoulders. I've seen her do this a million times, her come-hither ritual.

Sidney hands Christian a brown paper bag. "You left this in my room. I know it's your favorite belt."

Christian's eyes bug out of his head. He doesn't take the bag, so Sidney shoves it into his hands.

"Oh, my bad. I didn't know we were keeping it a secret, us getting back together. You won't tell anyone, will you, Abbie?" She gives me a conspiring wink, but it appears as fake as her surgically enhanced nose.

I level a dirty stare at them both. Then Sidney melts into the crowd of kids on their way to first period, as if she didn't just stand here and stake claim to her territory. I'm so heated right now.

"Sidney's lying," Christian says. "It—"

"I don't care," I interject and return my focus to my locker. Something catches my attention. A glossy, ivory-colored paper sticks out of my psychology textbook at the far-right corner of the top shelf. I remove the paper, haphazardly place it in the side pocket of my bag, and then shut the locker.

Joining the crowded hallway of kids on the way to a meeting with my STEM—Science, Technology, Engineering, Math—advisor, my blood boils. How dare Christian think he can play me, especially since he's hooking up with Sidney? Gross!

Somebody crashes into me and makes a quick apology. My backpack almost slips from my shoulders, but I grab it in time. That's my cue to retrieve the paper before it falls out of the side pocket. Christian catches up to me.

"You don't have to keep showing up at my locker, pretending

to be interested. I don't even care what your motive is. Just stop it."

"I swear Sidney's lying. I would never do anything that shady to you, Abbie."

His lame attempt at honesty does nothing to calm me down. Instead of responding, I open the folded paper from my psychology textbook and read it. What I see written makes my blood run cold.

ABOUT THE AUTHOR

Gledé Browne Kabongo writes gripping, unputdownable psychological thrillers. She is the Eric Hoffer, Next Generation Indie, IPPY and National Indie Excellence Award-winning author of the Fearless Series, *Our Wicked Lies, Fool Me Twice,* and *Conspiracy of Silence.*

Gledé holds a master's degree in communications and has spoken at multiple industry events including the Boston Book Festival and New England Crime Bake (Sisters in Crime). She lives outside Boston with her husband and two sons. For more information, visit www.gledekabongo.com.

CONNECT ONLINE

www.gledekabongo.com

glede@gledekabongo.com

gledekabongoauthor

@authorgledekabongo

Made in the USA
Middletown, DE
28 September 2024

61462318R00194